FALL

Colin McAdam lives in Montreal. His first novel, *Some Great Thing*, was published in 2004.

ALSO BY COLIN MCADAM

Some Great Thing

COLIN McADAM

Fall

VINTAGE BOOKS
London

Published by Vintage 2010

2 4 6 8 10 9 7 5 3

Copyright © Colin McAdam 2009

Colin McAdam has asserted his right under the Copyright, Designs
and Patents Act 1988 to be identified as the author of this work

This book is a work of fiction

First published in Great Britain in 2009 by
Jonathan Cape

Vintage
Random House, 20 Vauxhall Bridge Road,
London SW1V 2SA

www.vintage-books.co.uk

Addresses for companies within The Random House Group Limited
can be found at:
www.randomhouse.co.uk/offices.htm

A CIP catalogue record for this book
is available from the British Library

ISBN 9780099535461

The Random House Group Limited supports The Forest
Stewardship Council (FSC), the leading international
forest certification organisation. All our titles that are
printed on Greenpeace approved FSC certified paper
carry the FSC logo. Our paper procurement policy can
be found at www.rbooks.co.uk/environment

Typeset by Palimpsest Book Production Limited,
Grangemouth, Stirlingshire

Printed and bound in Great Britain by
CPI Antony Rowe, Chippenham, Wiltshire

For Suzanne
and old friends lost

HALF AN HOUR of lips and silk in the front and back and her cheeks are like peaches like peaches like peaches.

I love your hands.

I love *your* hands.

I want to pull over. You're so beautiful I'm gonna pull over. Can we.

Now.

Can we.

Now.

I love that smile of yours you're blushing like a hot summer peach I say.

Yousupwiseme.

Mmm.

You surprise me.

Mmm.

She says she watches me. She says I'm shaped like a V. Your shoulders and your waist.

I can do an iron cross.

O god.

Can we. Please.

Now.

I don't know when you're joking or not, I love your smile so much. Can we.

Here.

I don't know, we could try back there I say and I run outside to open her door and It's so sweet and green around here she says.

Her voice always sounds like she's smiling and smart.

I kiss her up against the car and I feel like I'm William opening the back door for her.

Hurry up, Julius, it's cold she says. Do you like my bra.

Yes!

It's silk!

I take off my shirt and she helps and her fingers are feathers, look lick.

You're a woman I say.

Bingo she says.

But I mean it I can't explain it.

She smiles and shivers and says Keep me warm.

I want to ask if she's scared because I get scared no matter what, no matter how many times I've done it, fifteen, but I don't want to distract her.

I love the neighbourhood right now, we're hugging and I'm kissing her neck.

Look out the window she's saying. It's so green and black.

I'm afraid the whole thing is turning to talk, lipping words where kisses and mmms should be but she kisses my scar and bites my lips and unclasps her bra and says Clasps with her tongue and her teeth and a lisp.

I need to blow my nose.

I roll her on top and stare.

School on Monday she says.

Yeah I say.

You're shaking she says.

No.

You're frowning she says.

No.

Boys get very serious when girls have taken their shirts off she says.

I love your smile. Fffuck. I don't know what to say.

She unbuttons her jeans. She likes that since I said I liked it. Do you like these.

Yes!

They're silk!

She says she loves the back seat of the limo. I say we can roll around like we're in a field, a big leather field, and she says You're full of peaches and farms tonight.

I roll her underneath me and think I should undo my jeans like she did.

I'm not wearing silk tonight I say.

She makes me tell bad jokes.

I'm tired of being a stranger and telling bad jokes.

We should do everything right now I say, and then it would be over and we could do everything again, I mean it.

Mmm.

I've got the car from William, who doesn't like his belly, who says whenever I borrow it, This could cost me my job, and laughs because he doesn't want his job, the only thing he wants is girls and a place in the Indy 500, he told me. When William's behind the wheel he's in his own world, he says, and my dad's in the back seat in his own world, and I think about how two people in a quiet black car can be in two big worlds, driving along, where are we.

I want to be close to you I say.

I think I hear a car she says.

I want to do everything now.

I can't breathe like this.

No one can see in Dad's car. The windows are tinted I say. At a party I asked a marine to shoot at the windows but he wouldn't. You can't see in here or shoot us.

What she says. Wait, you're heavy. There.

You don't have to be scared I say.

I'm not scared she says. She's looking me in the eyes and smiles. I'm modest she says. She opens her arms to show me everything.

She's everyone's everything and she's here in the back seat.

I'm gonna calm down.

I sit back here with Dad sometimes, he's here in the back seat.

Don't move I say. I wanna see.

I've never looked so close. No one ever lets me look that close. Please.

Everyone I know.

Look through the window of this dark car.

You're not really scared, are you.

Do I need to be she says.

Noel

T HE DAYS THAT made me, that were supposed to change me, that didn't actually make me, are showing me now what I was. My days in the room with Julius. Years have provided some safety.

That was not a school with pipes and dons and tweeds.

It wasn't a place where people spoke like people don't speak.

It wasn't in the Highlands of Scotland or the hills of New England.

It was a place of traditions but the traditions weren't old.

Like most private schools it was part fantasy, part reality, and therefore all reality. A place where stories happened, not fables, where there was learning, not lessons, and no one came away with memories of neat moral episodes. I came away with memories.

There were too many contradictions for there to have been any sense, and my life has always been so. We were boys who wore suits, monkeys with manners. We didn't have parents but were treated like babies. We were left on our own but had hundreds of rules to abide by.

We were eighteen years old, as grown up as we could be.

My memories are twitching like morning in the city.

'Laundry day,' said Chuck. He was standing in the hall with Ant, looking into our bedroom, where Julius was lying with a cloth over his eyes.

'Laundry day,' said Ant, echoing Chuck, and he rushed into our room, swung his laundry-filled pillowcase and pounded Julius in the head.

Julius said, 'Fuck off, I mean it.'

I had to take a test to get into St Ebury. I was fourteen. My parents took me – just before they went away. The three of us sat across from the Head Master, who did all the interviews himself and I noticed that he never looked at me oddly.

'Noel will have to take a test,' he said. I looked for signs.

Money was all that mattered – that's what I'd heard about St Ebury. Money wasn't an issue. I looked for signs on his face to see if he was uncomfortable about my eye.

'It's an Intelligence test, essentially,' he said.

'We weren't told,' I said, speaking for my parents.

'There's no preparation,' the Head Master said. 'No need to study. All you need is this pencil.' I was sent to an empty classroom.

Julius had a hangover.

'He's hung,' said Chuck.

'Big night,' said Ant.

'Big hung,' said Chuck.

'He wishes,' said Ant.

'Better hung than you,' said Chuck, and Ant pounded him in the head with his laundry-filled pillowcase.

'Get the fuck out,' said Julius, his face in his pillow now.

It was Sunday and everyone had stories about the weekend.

'Ant found some of your barf on his shoes this morning,' Chuck said to Julius.

'I smelled it first,' said Ant. 'Then I found it. A bit of, like, potato, caught up in the laces.'

'Fffuh,' said Julius.

'And you're cleaning it,' said Ant.

'It's laundry day,' said Chuck. 'Clean away the weekend, man, wash it all away. I can *not* believe how Fuck In drunk I was last night, and there I am in the corner thinking I will *not* get any action tonight and I look over at you two, Jules over here, Mr Hurlius, hurling and heaving all over your shoes, and I think, man, I *will* get action tonight because I am *not* as ugly as those two chumps.'

'And the fact?' said Ant.

'The fact is,' said Chuck, 'that I did *not* get any action.'

'The sad truth,' said Ant.

'It is the sad truth, Antony, and the sadder truth is that you have barf on your sneakers, and sadder . . . the saddest truth of all is that Mr Hurlius here got action and we came back with nothing.'

'Sad,' said Ant.

'So,' said Chuck. 'Wake the fuck up, Julius, and tell us.'

'Cheeses, Choolius, tell us all about it.'

'Please get out,' said Julius. He rolled over to make it clear. 'Please, get out of my room,' he said, and buried his face again.

'Your room?' said Chuck. He leaned on the top bunk, looking at Julius on the bottom. He tapped on the empty top mattress.

'Your room?' said Ant, who looked towards the sink in the corner of the room.

'Come on, Jules. Wake up. Don't feel sorry for yourself. Wake up. It's two o'clock. It's sunny. It's laundry day. Three hours before Chapel. One load of whites. One load of darks. Two smokes. And Chapel is upon us.'

'Come on,' said Ant.

'Come on,' said Chuck.

'Come on,' said Ant.

'Come on,' said Chuck.

'Come on,' said Ant.

'Oh for fucks,' said Julius and he rolled out of bed, landing on the floor face upwards. He lifted up his shirt, exposing his nipples, looked at Chuck and Ant, and said: 'Suck 'em.'

Chuck opened the door to the closet and grabbed Julius's laundry-filled pillowcase from the closet floor.

'His nipples are brown,' said Ant of the nipples of Julius.

'Yum,' said Chuck.

'It's a tan,' said Julius.

Chuck threw the pillowcase at Julius. 'The man with the tan,' said Chuck. 'Now,' he said. 'Tell us. Tell us how this man with the weird brown nipples gets so fuckin lucky.'

They walked towards the door, one, two, three, and each raised his eyebrows at the sink in the corner.

I was standing by the sink and continued to brush my teeth.

*   *   *

St Ebury sat on a hill in the richest part of town, Sutton, where all the ambassadors lived. St Ebury turned 121 that year, making it one of the oldest schools in Canada. There were 114 boarders between grades 9 and 12. Only thirty of them were girls.

Usually Seniors could choose their room-mates. Julius had too many friends. He had so many friends that they all assumed he was spoken for. They all paired up and Julius was left alone. He didn't get the room-mate he wanted.

I had been at St Ebury since grade 8. Julius arrived from the States in grade 11. I was friends with no one.

Seniors had only one room-mate. When people arrived in grades 9 to 11 they got stuck with two or three other room-mates in big rooms with two sinks, two bunks and two closets.

Seniors lived in the rooms along the front of the school, looking over the main entrance and the avenue to the Head Master's house. The rooms were narrow, a bunk and a sink along one wall, and two desks with shelves along the other.

The Head Boy lived alone, and there was one other single room for one other Senior. Everyone thought Julius would be Head Boy but the story was that his father intervened and said it wouldn't look right.

Then once everyone realised he hadn't found a room-mate, it was assumed that Julius would get the other single room. Being alone was a privilege. It was quiet. You could have loud dreams or dreams where you would cry and nobody would know.

They gave the room to Chris, whose real name was Tim. Chris had acne all over his face and body. One day in grade 9 a boarder made him smell a dirty gym shoe. He put Chris in a headlock, held the shoe over his nose and mouth, and the struggle tore some of the acne scabs off his face so it looked like he was crying blood.

The grade 9s and 10s were mostly on the floor above. One of the Housemasters had an apartment up there, and two Prefects shared a big room at the other end of that hall.

Julius should have been a Prefect as well, but he decided that the extra duties would get in the way of things. The Prefects helped with monitoring Prep at night and making sure lights were out at bedtime. They were supposed to keep everyone in line, especially the Juniors, and every night between Prep and bed one of the Prefects would hold detention in room 21 – an hour for anyone who had misbehaved on the Flats.

Julius's and my room was right above the main entrance to the school. The entrance had a porch with large latticed beams that seemed designed for climbing. Most nights Julius would climb out the window to have a smoke in the park across the street from the school. Often enough he would only get as far as above the porch – stopping halfway across the beams, just outside the window, perched up high with his cigarette tip glowing and fading. Sometimes someone else would be out there with him. Our door would burst open at midnight and Chuck or Ant or both would kick the lower bunk, say 'Smoke!' and they would slide the window up and go out.

'Let's go to the park,' Julius might say, and 'Fuck that' might be Chuck's response. So they would perch out there just beyond the window and share a cigarette's length of talk.

Chuck: 'I hope we can still play rugby at McGill.'

Ant: 'I'll be too busy fucking.'

Chuck: 'Your aunt is going to McGill?'

Ant: 'Funny.'

Julius: 'I like the smell of the leaves.'

They had to leave the window open a crack so they could undo the latch to get back in. They would sit out there sometimes when it was cold saying jesus jesus jesus while the wind blew into the room. Later in the year Julius went away at night and never knew that the papers on his desk turned blue when the moon shone in.

The daily routine did not change much from year to year. The only thing that changed was curfew. Grades 9 and 10 had to be in their rooms at 9:30 with Lights Out at 10. Eleven had Lights Out at 10:45 and Seniors had to have lights off at 11:30. But things were more flexible the older you got, and everything depended on who was on duty.

When I arrived at St Ebury everyone said:

'Her father's an Italian count.'

'Fuck off.'

'They wear gloves when they eat dinner.'

'Her real name is Fallon.'

'Fallon Fitzgerald Destaad.'

'DeStindt.'

'She's cold.'

'She's funny.'

'She's a bitch.'

'She's not a real blonde.'

'She's smart.'

'She's the smartest in the school.'

'Her father's High Tech.'

'Rich.'

'Filthrich.'

'Started IncoTel.'

'*Is* IncoTel.'

'*Was* IncoTel, he ditched and made a stinkload.'

'King's ransom.'

'Mother took it all.'

'They're divorced.'

'I've seen them together.'

'They're always in the paper.'

'I've never seen them.'

'Lives in the High Tech Hills.'

'No one knows why she's a boarder.'

'Scholarship.'

'She's the smartest in the school.'

'She only looks Italian.'

'Born in the High Tech Hills.'

'Her hair is chestnut, pure chestnut, and natural and I think it's beautiful.'

'I want her to be my friend.'

'She is my friend.'

'She's everyone's friend.'

'I love her.'

I remember first seeing her in the downstairs common room floating across the school's eye.

One face could be my guide and salvation. It could be my comfort and the goal of superstition. It seems incredible that I can no longer picture her.

When I achieved a perfect mark on an essay, it presaged Fall's eventual love. When I scored a shot from the line in basketball, which I rarely did, it was because I would kiss Fall that week, that term, that year.

Whenever she was near, I knew it. At assemblies I always knew where she was sitting, almost without looking. If she was in a crowd at the end of a hallway, out of sight, I sensed that she was there, and I would come close, pass by.

I didn't need her to notice me right away. I knew that she would come to know me deeply. I felt like an explorer sailing past an uncharted piece of perfection. I knew where it was, I would land there one day and my race would grow.

And when Julius arrived and everyone, including Fall, was drawn to him, I somehow wasn't upset. I felt it was part of a plan. I saw them together in the halls and I liked his face, thought she deserved a guy like that for a while.

Certainly, I never wanted to hurt her.

Boarders had to arrive the Sunday night before term started. Parents drove up throughout that Sunday dropping off sons, daughters, suitcases. From the rooms along the front of the school you could watch it all happening.

The younger boarders usually came up to the Flats with wet noses from saying goodbye – the new ones especially. They wore clothes that they would probably never wear again – sweaters from home, jeans with holes, things that they either wouldn't be allowed to wear on the Flats or would learn to dislike once they saw what the experienced boarders wore.

If a room had two new boarders they would be friends right away. 'Should we wear anything in the shower tomorrow, like a bathing suit?' was usually the first question. One would have more answers than the other.

'There's no Prep tonight because it's the first night, but tomorrow it'll be at 7:30.'

'What's Prep?'

'Study.'

'What do we wear to Prep?'

'I don't know.'

'I'm thinking of showering early, just to beat the rush. Maybe I'll shower at night.'

'I'm not sure we can do that.'

They would unpack neatly, and would usually be careful about sharing space. 'Do you want this drawer?'

'No, you take it.'

'I've already got four.'

'So do I. You take it.'

'Sure?'

It was the last polite night of the year.

For the boarders who already knew each other it was all routine, and part of the routine was making sure the new kids knew they were more experienced. Chuck and Ant were lifers – they'd been there since grade 5 – and they sat around on those first Sunday nights like nothing was happening. New kids would bump into each other, be aware of everyone, look nervous or over-friendly; some of them would ask Chuck or Ant for directions. 'Umm, L Wing?' Chuck or Ant would raise a lazy arm and point, or Chuck or Ant would look at the kid's chin or ear, never in the eyes, and say, 'You're there.'

If they were curious, parents would come up to the Flats and look at where they were leaving their children. They always smiled and said 'Great, isn't this great' and whispered advice like 'You should take the desk near the window.' But it was usually just kids coming up on their own, dragging bits of their home with them – posters, stereos, favourite lamps.

The quiet, shy ones would be quiet and shy, announcing themselves more obviously than the ones who tried to make friends. They were doomed. Most of the bullying started in the lower grades.

There was a kid named Edward in grade 9 that year who was six foot five and skinny. He hunched his shoulders and leaned forward like he was afraid of being so tall. His dad came up to the Flats with him that Sunday and between them they carried a gigantic metal chest that attracted everyone's attention. The only difference between Edward and his dad was that his dad was smiling. They both ducked when they went through Edward's new doorway. His new room-mates were there, staring, and other people were curious about his chest.

Edward's dad kept smiling and said, 'I don't know what you've got in that chest, but I hope she's alive,' and he blew a laugh out his nose with a rope of clear snot which made him stop laughing abruptly. He looked around embarrassed and said, 'This is Edward.'

Edward's dad was serving in The Hague, and Edward had spent the summer in Holland. He was another diplomat's kid who would be at St Ebury as long as his parents were overseas.

Both of his new room-mates had arrived and unpacked and were quiet while Edward's dad was still around.

'Let's say one last goodbye to your mum,' said the dad.

While Edward followed his dad downstairs his two new room-mates moved towards that huge metal chest and started playing with the lock. A few other new grade 9 went in and they all started pulling on the lid and kicking the chest, gently at first.

When Edward came back up they moved away from the chest.

'You can't keep that there. It's too big. You'll get in trouble.'

'You'll get in trouble, Edward.'

'What's in it? You should just empty it.'

Edward had his pants pulled up high.

Edward's shirt was tucked deep into his pants.

Edward banged the toe of his big shoe on the corner of the bed when he moved towards the chest.

When he spoke and said, 'There's stuff in it, there's nothing,' his voice was a shaky version of his dad's.

When he opened his chest weeks later it was full of ugly treasure.

There was a dinner that Sunday for those who wanted it and nobody wanted it. Kids like Edward would pull out a book and lie on their bed. The quiet ones with pimples read science fiction or something about wizards.

That Sunday somehow always passed quickly, even though everyone was nervous about the first day of school or about their new home.

Julius arrived late that night and said 'hi' kind of nicely to me. It was dark and almost quiet. Someone upstairs was bouncing a basketball along the hallway and then there was a rush of foot-steps and an OWW and then quiet.

'I didn't know who I was going to room with,' Julius said. He had two big duffel bags which he threw into the closet. He unzipped one of them, took out his toothbrush and a pack of cigarettes and put both of them in his pocket. 'It's a nice night,' he said, and walked out again, closing the door quietly.

Everyone had to be awake by 7:15 every morning and the Prefects started banging on doors at 6:45.

There was one bathroom on every wing. Some had more showers than others but most of them had three in an open row. There would usually be about ten people waiting in each bathroom for one of the showers to be free. Most wore towels while they waited. Some wore slippers. A Chinese kid named Patrick Chu wore slippers, a shower cap and plastic gloves, and looked so weird that no one bothered to make fun of him. There were benches and radiators across from the showers which you could sit on while you waited, if you were early enough. In the winter the radiators were the best place to be.

The longer people lingered in the bathroom, the more senior they were, usually, and the more comfortable they were with being naked. At the start of the year there were always a few new guys who wore bathing suits while they showered. They waited their turn, got quickly into the shower, faced the wall so their backs were turned to everyone waiting, got out as quickly as they got in. After a week or two they would answer the question in different ways.

'Why do you wear a bathing suit in the shower?'

'It's warmer.'

'Why do you wear a bathing suit in the shower?'

'That's what I wear at home.'

And then they would start going naked.

Everyone's sleepy eyes wandered into the hot fog every morning. They found the radiator, they found the showers, they found the penises of everyone else on the wing. The sad wet mushroom belongs to Chris. The blue-white thing in the nest of red belongs to Archie the Scot. The half-hard penis from morning dreams, so big that it almost touches his neighbour's leg when he turns around, is the belonging of Carlos and if Chuck sees it half hard once more, he said, he's going to stomp on it and break its back so it never grows again.

You looked at everyone's, but when you were in the shower you never saw anyone looking.

Edward wore a bathing suit for his first shower. On their way back to their room Edward's new room-mates were trying to whip him with their wet towels. They were new to the technique so they were weakly hitting the air instead of snapping at Edward's skin. They were practising; and Edward was trying to figure out how to react. His towel was wrapped tightly around his waist, getting dyed blue by his wet new bathing suit and he was laughing like someone who has to choose laughing instead of fighting back.

Julius came out of our room in his towel, watched the young ones running down the hall, and wandered into the bathroom later than everyone. He timed it every morning so he never had to wait for the shower, and showered as long as he liked.

He was a chart of what the body should be.

We watched him in his towel.

At the end of the first full day of school after everyone's lights were out, Julius lay on the bottom bunk and said to me, 'I'm beat from practice, man, goodnight.'

He was a messy guy, but he tried to change. For the first few weeks he left his soccer clothes strewn around the room. Socks so wet with sweat that the carpet was damp when he eventually picked them up.

'This room smells like balls and an armpit,' said Chuck, and Ant said, 'Whose balls does it smell like?'

Julius would scoop up his clothes eventually, fill pillowcases with them and throw them in the closet for laundry day, but the smell lingered until someone came in and said it stank. Julius tried to be more tidy.

He could fill a room with his presence, but if you looked closely sometimes you could see he was somewhere else.

On the second night of school, after the lights went out, Julius looked up at the underside of the bunk above and said, 'I was talking to someone who said your dad's Ambassador to Australia or something.'

'Consul General.'

'OK.'

'Mmm.'

'I'm so fuckin tired, man, goodnight.'

Julius's father was the US Ambassador to Canada. His residence was in Sutton, a seven-minute walk from the school, but he insisted that Julius be a boarder. Julius could go home whenever he wanted, but theoretically the rules of the school said you couldn't go off campus during the week and could only leave on weekends if you had somewhere to sign out to. Julius went home most weekends, even though his father wanted him to integrate with the students at St Ebury as much as possible – to become part of the culture.

His father's time in Canada may be remembered for its curtailment. And he was unusual in some ways. A widower – a single ambassador in the days when the probity of being single no longer existed. He was outspoken, but as I look back through articles I kept he was also frequently misquoted and misrepresented. Perhaps I'm inclined to sympathise. I was a stranger to him, but was essentially responsible for his departure.

I am reading an article at the moment that says there are men listening to the noises of submarines. The men are in England, the submarines in the Arctic. The men are Canadian, the submarines Russian and American. I can see the men wearing earphones, straining their ears to hear muted signals; sounds bouncing off the ocean floor telling secrets they do not mean to tell.

I remember every night, every detail. The early days of love. There was a strange quiet on the third night. Prep was at 7:30 and there wasn't a noise for two hours except of pages turning and pens dropping on desks. Two hours later the lights stayed dim, and most boarders started getting ready for bed. All the new students were yearning for a routine, trying to keep the strangeness from growing. If they could be quiet, do homework, keep to themselves, go to bed, they wouldn't have to be so aware of how odd it was to be living with eighty-four friends and strangers – they could pretend they were on their own. One mood could settle on everyone.

Julius propped up his Algebra book first, stared at it like a possible enemy, let it rest again, open, copied some problems, worked for half an hour. He sighed. He stretched and yawned a silent roar. He closed the Algebra book, took down Philosophical Analysis from the shelf above his desk and opened it for the first time with a sort of delicate ceremony. He blew out his cheeks, turned a page, looked at me, closed the book. He took down Chaucer's *Canterbury Tales*, in the modern English version that he wasn't supposed to read.

When Prep was over he turned to me and said, 'Farts can be funny things to write stories about,' and then he farted.

He disappeared until it was time for bed, and then, back in the room in the dark, he said to the bunk above, 'Australia?'

'Yeah.'

'What's it like?'

'Bright.'

'But you're Canadian, right?'

'Yeah.'

'Diplomat's kid. Same here. American.'

'I know.'

'Were you there this summer?'

'Winter. It's upside down.'

Julius was quiet for a while, like he was figuring something out.

'So in Australia I'd be on the top bunk,' he said.

'That's right. And your pants would be over your arms.'

'Right.'

There were long silences in those rooms sometimes when one would wait to see if the other was falling asleep or was thinking of something to say.

'I saw a picture of Australia once,' said Julius. 'A beach. And sky. And a girl.'

There was another long silence.

Everyone was in their bunks, suspended on different planes in the dark, conversation going upwards, from the bottom bunk to the top, to the roof. Sometimes there would be understanding. Sometimes the one on the top would roll to the side, look down at the bottom and say, 'Really?' Sometimes we were corpses in drawers, dreaming up.

'Can a woman ever really be on top in Australia?'

'I know one who was,' I said to the roof.

★   ★   ★

I'd been working out for over a year. By that September I could bench-press 225 pounds. Julius later said that when the bar was halfway up, my eye would open and swell, open and swell, like something that kept trying to be born. He never shied away from it. He said 'shit' in a tone of admiration when I held 215 pounds above my head. The military press, weight pushed high, arms up straight in heavy victory. Once, he said, 'You should see yourself.'

In the first week I made a start on the *Iliad*, among other things. I read a lot during the week – after school, after dinner, during Prep. After Prep I went to the weight room. I liked going to bed with a mind full of someone else's words and my muscles full of blood. I don't think I really analysed it at the time – I simply got into that routine and liked it.

The sameness of each day somehow never gathered into a blur. The beginning of every year in boarding school holds a sense that something, this year, has to be different. I'm wandering the same halls, I'm restricted to the same things, but I'm older, bigger, smarter, and something has to change. A new knot in the tie, a conversation with someone you'd never talked to before – things like that would distinguish each day. The potential for anything to be truly different was so limited that tiny things would make a day stand out.

Julius was gone for the rest of that week. He hadn't left school, but he always disappeared after Prep and came back to the room after Lights Out. He said 'hey man' in the mornings when I was brushing my teeth. I kicked his soccer clothes to the side of the room, hoping he would notice that they bothered me.

Sometimes even though I exhausted myself with weights and was too tired to read I would still be awake after Lights Out. Usually at around midnight, once the Duty Master was settled in his own room, there would be a small storm of noises somewhere on the Flats. Pranks were one of the first signs that friendships were being made. You could hear footsteps thundering down the hall upstairs and you would know that at least two new room-mates were getting along well enough to disturb the sleep of someone in another room – usually someone who hadn't made any friends yet.

On the first Thursday I heard a huge bang, water splashing,

a shout, and at least four feet banging down the hall. Someone upstairs had been doused with water, and because I heard no more noise I knew that whoever had been doused did not retaliate.

When you sleep at home you normally don't expect to be awakened by strangers throwing buckets of cold water on you. The kid was probably in shock, had no idea what to do. When it happens the first time, you don't realise that you can retaliate; and he probably had no one in his room who was willing to help him get back at the others.

I was thinking of what it was like to sleep on a wet mattress when Julius came quietly through the door. When the Duty Master came around for Lights Out I had told him that Julius was in the bathroom, but I didn't know where he really was. A smell of cigarette smoke sneaked in behind him. I could tell he was trying to be quiet, and I couldn't decide whether to tell him I was awake or not.

I thought for a second that all the noise upstairs might have woken up the Duty Master, that he would come around inspecting rooms and find Julius there undressing and would know that he had been outside. I realised that if that happened I would probably get in trouble as well for covering for Julius. I remember thinking that I wouldn't mind getting in trouble with him.

But there was silence upstairs now and silence down the halls – just Julius taking his clothes off, the noise of the coins in his pockets. He sniffed, then sucked back the mucus in his throat and said 'sorry' very softly. He turned on the water to brush his teeth and said 'sorry' again after he finished, and said 'sorry' after he banged what was probably his knee on the bed below before crawling into it. I decided to whisper, 'It's OK, man, I'm awake.'

He said, 'Oh,' and then, again, 'sorry'.

In the morning I was dressed and sitting on the top bunk, reading. Julius was late and was frantically tying his tie, his wet hair dripping onto the silk and soaking his collar. He asked me if I was going to the party.

'What party?' I said.

'Tomorrow night at Brown's.'

Jeffrey Brown was the son of the Mayor of Sutton.

'No,' I said.

I was waiting for him to say 'why not'; maybe I was expecting him to invite me. I had my excuses lined up.

He didn't say anything more about it.

I hopped down from the bed because it was 8:29. Julius asked me if I was going to Chapel. I made a noise to suggest I had no choice in the matter. Julius said, 'Let's go,' and it was the first time we went down to Chapel together.

Susan
Harper
Jess
Mathilda
Julie
Sarah
Fall

Those were the girls who were in the mind of the entire wanting world. The bathrooms and beds were humming with them.

Some of them had boyfriends when the year first started, but every new year was full of hope for change.

For boarders there wasn't much opportunity for seeing someone who didn't go to St Ebury. The day boys had other chances with their evenings and weekends free. They had neighbours' daughters, friends of family, girls from other schools.

Even seeing someone from school was hard enough if you lived there. Most of the girls weren't boarders. The greatest luck you could have as a boarder was to have somewhere to sign out to on the weekend – a relative's place or some willing guardian's. There were a few boarders like Julius whose parents lived somewhere in the city. The luckiest were those who could sign out to a place where the guardian didn't actually know or care what you were doing. Julius's dad cared, but he was often out of town. Ant's aunt lived in Paris most of the year. As long as the school had a phone number, they rarely checked to see if you were actually being looked after.

If you could sign out on the weekend, you might at least have a chance to see day girls outside of school. Boarders could leave grounds on the weekend during the day, but they had to be back early and in bed by ten or eleven o'clock. The most a date could be was an afternoon movie and a coffee. The day students would get together on weekends for parties almost every week and girls from other schools would often go. Only a handful of boarders would ever get to be there.

The Flats got so quiet so soon. By five o'clock on a Friday even the boarders who hadn't signed out would be away somewhere until curfew, desperately breathing in the freedom of being off school grounds. The younger grades usually went to the Centrepiece Mall, where kids from downtown schools went – and there was always a story about someone from St Ebury who had forgotten to change out of his uniform and was beaten up for being a private-school fag. There were a few arcades, one music venue that let you in as long as you were over sixteen; and otherwise there was just the opportunity to hang out and look at other people. I got the sleeves ripped off my jacket once at the Centrepiece Mall but I was able to find a tailor in the mall who could fix it right away.

I stayed at school most Fridays. Sometimes I liked the change and the quiet. When I was younger I helped my parents at cock-tail parties, passing around hors d'oeuvres, asking people what they would like to drink. Sometimes the parties were huge and I got lost in them, overwhelmed – one question after another, a roomful of eyes, tiny false stars, staring at me with phoney curiosity as the son of the Consul General. I liked standing in the same room after the parties, thinking that a disease was cured, or poison purged, and the house was healthy again. On Friday nights at St Ebury I sometimes felt the same way, a comfort in knowing that week after week I could rely on time to kill everything that disturbed me.

In that hallway just outside my room at 3:45 p.m. there were three kids bouncing a tennis ball against the far wall. Two were waiting for a cab to take them downtown and one was waiting for his mother to take him away for the weekend. There was a window in the middle of the wall, and the kids were aiming the ball at the plaster below it. Every few throws the ball would hit the window and the noise would make them laugh. One of the kids was a lanky grade-niner from Pakistan. The other two were keeping the ball from him. He kept twisting and stretching and looking ridiculous, making whiny little grunts, and twice he said, 'My uncle's going to be here soon,' as though it didn't matter that he couldn't get the ball.

By four o'clock they were gone. I could stand in my doorway, look down the hall at the window and think that time and I had won again. There was a confidential feeling, like the window and I shared relief, like the hallway and I knew what each other was really like when no one else was around.

I could pretend I felt some sort of communion with that empty hallway, but it was just an empty space with creaks and draughts, a throat in the middle of a yawn.

It's 4:00 and what do you do? It's 4:08 and what do you do? I could do laundry, but the laundromat closes at six. I could go to a movie, but matinees on Saturday are cheaper and I only have twenty dollars to last me the week.

The carpet was green. Stucco covered the walls like a million senseless nipples. I made a fist and pushed it along the walls – a punch that lasted until the next doorway. If someone came out of his door, he would get a slow weak punch from my rubbed red knuckles; and no one came out of his door.

I can't read when I am completely alone. I never think of a book as something to keep me company; it's something to take company away. I can read in the middle of Prep and the book will take me away from all the burps, giggles and smells of a building full of boys. Six grade-niners could play ball hockey outside my door and my book would take me to Troy. But somehow reading on my own makes me more aware of the fact that I'm alone. I think of the effort of imagining myself into someone else's world, and all I want is my own. And I think about how small.

On Fridays you could still hear doors slamming, and laughing off in the distance.

I walked the length of the hallway with my fist along the wall and I went down the stairs at the end. Most of the classrooms were along the main corridor. The main building and Chapel were the oldest parts of the school, and the number of students was still small enough to fit most of the learning along that hallway. There were a few teachers and students at work or chatting. I had changed out of my uniform and drew a few stares.

From Friday at four until Sunday at six we were allowed to wear casual clothes, which we called 'Fridays'. Day students were never allowed to wear Fridays on school property, so they often stared if they saw a boarder in the main hall out of uniform. Fridays were supposed to be your true identity, but there were still rules. No holes in jeans, no shirts without collars, no running shoes, and if a boy had an earring (which he was never allowed to wear during the week) he had to cover it with a Band-Aid until he was off school property.

I think day students were jealous sometimes of boarders. I think they liked the idea of being casual at school, even of living at school. I think some of them thought it was all a big pyjama party.

I didn't know any of the students who were still around that day. I knew the teachers, but not to talk to. Mr Staples, who taught Algebra and Functions, nodded at me and said, 'Mr Reece.' His lips were tight and there was a look in his eyes that had developed a few years earlier whenever he saw me. Distrust or caution or just that squint of a half-formed opinion. I never liked him.

I headed to the end of the hall towards the main door. One of the secretaries from the front office pulled herself in from outside, soaking wet. 'Holy cow!' she said to me with a gigantic look of something. 'It is THROWing it DOWN out there!' I realised she was talking to no one. 'Just when I thought I could leave,' she said. 'HA HA HA!'

I went to the window beside the doors and saw hail falling like teeth. It calmed into rain every few seconds. The secretary came back with an umbrella in her hand and another big look of something more positive, saying, 'Let's try again ha ha.' I watched her outside still talking to no one and running down the front steps.

I wasn't sure I wanted to go out anyway. I settled into a numb state of indecision, a sort of mental slouch which got me through most weekends.

That foyer was what welcomed all visitors to the school. There were pictures of the last five graduating classes, and one old photo of the school during the First World War with all of the school's students – no more than twenty of them – dressed in military uniform with guns on their shoulders.

The office to the right was separated from the foyer by a counter and a sliding window. A receptionist usually sat there, with a few secretaries behind, and right at the back, hidden from view, was the Head Master's office.

The receptionist was still there but she was near the back searching through a file cabinet. Everyone said she was only twenty-one and that she liked young guys. Everyone called her Christine instead of using her surname because she was the one adult in the school whom you didn't have to respect. I saw her flirting with Julius once.

It was quiet now in the foyer. The sliding window through to the office was closed. I watched Christine at the file cabinet. She was bent over, opening drawers. She moved to the side, still bent over, and flipped through some files. Her hair fell over her face and she tucked it behind her ear, and every now and then she licked her finger to flip through pages in a file. I remembered seeing her once with an ankle bracelet.

She was moving slowly, as though she didn't mind being there, which was strange on a Friday at five. She might have been waiting for a ride. I wanted her to turn her back to me again and bend further forward. I tried to think of a question I could ask her, an excuse for being there near the window. She flipped her hair behind her ear again and saw me out of the corner of her eye. She stood up straight and looked at me and I didn't know what to do. I didn't know what the look on her face was. A bit of surprise. A bit of curiosity. A bit of 'can I help you'. I later thought there was a bit of sympathy or a sense of connection in her look. Definitely some fear.

I went upstairs to my room and looked at myself in the mirror. My eye was in a spasm.

In the sink there were toothpaste stains and whiskers. Julius had been the last to use it before he took off for the weekend. I washed it.

I had started weightlifting in Australia in December the previous year. It was summer there, and the best I'd ever had. We got long holidays at St Ebury so boarders could spend more time at home with their families. I had three full weeks of warmth in the middle of Canada's winter.

The house they gave my father in Sydney was huge. It was on a hill near the harbour and had a lighthouse on the property from earlier days when there were no houses between it and the water. I was proud of that house because it was bigger than anything my family had ever lived in – eight bedrooms for four of us, a great drawing room, all sorts of areas to escape to and be on my own. My favourite part of the house was a nook off the dining room. It had a big fireplace with a curved cushioned bench along the walls on either side. I sat there to read during the winters.

In the summer I sat by the pool. Our neighbours were closest at the back of the house, but one of my father's predecessors had nonetheless decided to wedge a pool back there right under their eyes. I wasn't keen on going out there until I learned how hot a Sydney summer could be. There were bush fires surrounding the city that year. Ash was blowing in the wind. It was cool in the house, but I wanted to be outside. I'd never known heat like that, and I felt like there was life in it.

The coolest place near the pool was a shady area directly under the window of our blonde neighbour's bedroom. She was too old to be interested in me, but she was often in my mind when I was out there. Every day I was one day older, thinking I might suddenly click into the right age and force her to come to the window and notice me. I ignored the fact that I had seen her once on Channel 10 as the wife of a rugby player. The shade was a place to hide from the sun, but not from thoughts of her. I never actually saw her near the window during the day – she was probably not even home – but I felt like she might somehow be watching and I couldn't relax there for long.

I focused sometimes on people who were most unlikely to notice me. Somehow it made Fall closer, part of a possible future.

I spent most of my time in the water or on the edge of the pool in the sun, with all my faith in sunblock and zinc. My skin would feel burned at the end of the day but there was usually no red or peeling. I often crouched low in the water, held my breath and let the water come up to below my eyes. Ash from the bush fires was falling like black feathers and when it landed on the water it dissolved into a film.

It was my time of evolution. The heat I had never breathed before, the ash and chlorine creating some sort of reaction, the thoughts of the blonde in the window a catalyst like constant lightning. I thought every day that I would emerge from the pool as something different.

One day I came out of the pool and saw myself reflected in our sliding door. I was a pale and skinny sixteen–year-old who had forgotten to put sunblock on one of his shoulders. My lazy eye was swollen shut, my face was ugly and drained, my shoulder was livid, and I was still unformed.

My brother joined us that December. He was in his third year at the University of Toronto and had decided to visit for Christmas. We weren't close, and I rarely bothered talking to him. He was an athlete. He wanted to play professional football. We were far apart in age and never really thought of each other.

I knew he had found a gym in Sydney because his only contribution at dinner one night was 'Coach says I've got to train hard over Christmas'. I knocked on his bedroom door later and asked if he had joined a gym.

'There's a police gym,' he said. 'Like a community centre.'

'Is it far?'

'No.'

'Can I join?'

'I don't know.'

I asked him if he would take me and he said, 'Once.' He would show me a few things but he needed to train on his own to concentrate.

It seemed like a slightly rough place. There were old rubber mats all over the floor, rusty equipment. It looked like a junkyard for weights. Some locals in tank tops were quietly bench-pressing a heavy-looking bar.

My brother said, 'This is a dump.' He walked around and implied that I should follow him.

'But all you need is one weight. One piece of resistance to define yourself against.' He sounded wise. 'Here,' he said, and started showing me exercises.

Do this ten times. Bring it further down. Wrong. Don't straighten your arms. You're cheating. Keep your back straight. Good. That's too heavy for you. Do it ten then eight then six then four. I tried to remember everything he showed me.

'I'll see you at home,' he said.

I started going every day. I took buses to get there, which had no air conditioning. At the gym there were just a few ceiling fans. I was soaked in sweat before I lifted anything. There were never many people around. The guy at the front desk was the caretaker. Every day he smiled at me when I signed in and said, 'Right, mate?' That was the only voice I heard for a while.

I did what my brother had shown me. I was very sore for the first few days. When there were other people in the gym I watched what they were doing, tried to figure out what muscles they were working. I wanted a bigger chest and shoulders. And arms and legs.

After a week I thought I'd figured it out. I felt less exhausted. I had gotten over my jet lag after ten days of being in Sydney. I was getting used to the heat. I was beginning to be in need of it. It calmed me.

From the upper storey of that house you could see most of Sydney Harbour. At night I often stared out my window, watching the Opera House, the lights on the bridge, the dark spaces between Mosman and Manly. I thought about how far I was from St Ebury. I thought about how much I would like to take someone down to the water. Sometimes I thought about asking my brother or my father whether they wanted to go out for a walk; but I realised I didn't really want their company.

There was an air conditioner in the window of my bedroom. The dust on the vents gathered itself into fragile brown lace. I liked to run my finger along the vent and destroy the dust's pattern. 'You're dirt,' I would say in my head. I tasted my finger once and felt stupid.

Four months earlier a girl with a ridiculous name had arrived at St Ebury, and her face and voice were my company whenever I imagined myself walking along the water. When the lamp was on near my window, all I could see when I looked out at night was my own reflection. I had a ritual of leaving it on, looking at my face, dragging my finger over the dust, turning off the lamp, looking past myself and over the water, thinking of being with that girl named Fall, she had more light and promise than anything out there.

At the gym I went up to strangers and asked them if they would spot me. One of them said, 'Sorry, mate, I'm working here.'

I vowed to be stronger than him some day. Others were friendly and gave me tips. 'The bar's going skew-wiff, keep it straight.'

I walked in one day and there was no one in the gym except a young guy with his back to me. He was wearing a tight black tank top and he was sitting at the machine I wanted.

His muscles were small but defined. He had his hair in a short ponytail.

I couldn't decide whether to ask him how long he was going to be on the machine. He was strong for someone small. The stronger guys were, the more I felt inclined to watch or be near them even though I knew they could get annoyed. There was a guy in that gym who could bench-press 305 pounds, and I noticed that everyone wanted to talk to him.

I found another exercise and waited for the guy with the ponytail to finish. I noticed that he shaved his legs. They were shiny and tanned. Then when he stood up and walked around I noticed that he was a girl.

She looked over and the sun through the window lit the gold of a thin necklace. I'd never seen a girl with muscles like that. When she wasn't exercising and her muscles weren't flexed, she looked feminine. I stared at her.

The day before I had been stronger. Now that there was a girl around I was all the more conscious of how weak I was. I took long rests between sets so I wouldn't get tired. The girl moved all over the gym as confidently as my brother had. I stared at her whenever she was exercising. She had a beautiful face. On every exercise she was twice as strong as I was. I watched her technique and thought that if she caught me staring I could say that I was trying to learn from her. I thought about going back home.

'Trade pozzies?' she said.

I had no idea.

'Sorry?' I said.

'Trade pozzies with you?' She was gesturing at the bench I had been resting on.

'Sorry. Sure.'

She added weight to what I had been lifting. I didn't know whether to watch her, try to spot her or leave her in peace. She didn't really have breasts, but the cut of her tank top drew my eyes towards the front of her. If I stood nearby she might catch me staring. She finished her set and reduced the weight for me. I still hadn't rested long enough but I went anyway. As soon as I finished she added weight again, hurriedly as though I was spoiling her rhythm. When she finished I wanted to delay.

'What was that word?' I said.

'What?'

'That word you said before. Pozzies?'

'Yeah.'

'What is it?'

'I don't know. Place.'

'I'm from Canada.'

'Position. It's short for position. You going again?'

'Go ahead,' I said.

She did her set. I moved closer to the bench but I didn't spot her.

'Pozzie,' she said when she finished. She was reflecting on it.

'I'm Canadian,' I said again.

'Right,' she said.

'It's quiet in here,' I said.

'Yep,' she said. She lay down and did another set and I felt like I should drift away.

I went at the same time the next day and she was there again. She was sweating and out of breath, wearing a white T-shirt that made her look more girlish – and younger. I realised she probably wasn't much older than I was.

I wanted to work on my shoulders. I went over to the upright bench and deliberately put a heavy weight on the bar. My brother had said that I was strong on the military press.

I also caught her eye. I wanted to say hi.

'G'day,' she said. I was always surprised when Aussies really said that.

We were the only ones in the gym again. I waited till she started her next set so she wouldn't notice how few reps I was doing. But it wasn't as hard as I thought it would be and I felt more confident. I put more weight on and watched her out of the corner of my eye. I thought about the muscles under her shirt that I had seen the day before.

'Would you mind spotting me?' I said. I had walked a little closer to her and waited till she finished her set.

Would she feel proud to be spotting me or would I seem laughable needing help from a girl? I put more weight on the bar. She stood above and behind me. I stared straight ahead, pressed the bar up high. I put the face of a guy named Shaughnessy in my mind – a guy who was a Senior that year at St Ebury. I saw his mocking smile. I pressed the bar again, and pressed it again, and I watched his smile diminish. Ten repetitions, and more weight than I had ever lifted.

'That's the way,' she said.

Later she said that her name was Meg. I got her to spot me one more time. She asked me what I was doing in Sydney if I was from Canada. When she stood close to me I realised that she wasn't as broad as she had seemed the day before. If I had seen her on the street I would have thought she was just a pretty girl in a baggy shirt.

Meg told me she was eighteen, but she winked when she said it. Anyone who worked out on their own at the gym had to be eighteen or older. I told her I was eighteen too. I asked her how long she had been working out and she said, 'I don't know.' I waited for her to calculate the time but she never did. She seemed really tough, which is why her smile sometimes surprised me.

There were more people in the gym over the next few days. Rugby types. Tans, freckles, square jaws, pale lips, big shoulders, short shorts showing off their legs. Meg was there and I expected to catch her admiring them. But she wasn't like that. I waved at her and she nodded and smiled.

Christmas was approaching and the gym was going to be closed for a few days. I asked Meg what her plans were for Christmas.

'Family,' she said.

I asked her if she had a big family and she said, 'Na.'

My parents hosted a lot of parties that Christmas. Sometimes I helped out. Usually I escaped. I piled food onto cocktail napkins and went up to my room. I tried to pile as much as I could onto each napkin so I wouldn't have to come down too often for more. I could usually avoid conversations by not looking anyone in the eye and moving with purpose towards the waiters with trays. Colleagues of my father's would generally choose to talk to my brother for token family interest. They were drawn to him more naturally. They talked about football with him and what he thought about Rugby League.

I ate a lot over Christmas. So did my brother. 'I should have made two turkeys,' my mother said. She said it two nights in a row with the same level of surprise.

The gym was open the day after Boxing Day and I spent four hours there. I went in the morning, took a break for lunch and came back in the afternoon.

Meg was there when I came back after lunch. I waved at her and walked closer. She looked down as I was walking towards her and then looked at me when I was next to her.

'Good Christmas?' I said.

'Yeah?' she said. I couldn't tell whether she was sure or not. 'You know?' she said. We looked into each other's eyes for the first time like we really saw something. She looked away and rested her hand on a barbell. She was wearing new running shoes.

'Christmas presents?' I said.

She smiled and jogged on the spot. Then she looked a little embarrassed and suggested with her eyes that I get out of her way and let her do a set.

I felt bigger after Christmas, and stronger. I had food in my stomach after lunch and I felt like I could go for hours. As I put my hands on a bar that day I looked at them and had one of those moments when I realised I was growing. My hands looked stronger and wiser. I worked out hard and burned my lunch.

'Would you like to get a bite to eat?' I asked her before letting myself think about it.

'Yeah?' she said.

We went to an Oporto for Portuguese chicken. I tried buying her meal but she shouldered me out of the way and looked at me like she was angry. We sat down outside and didn't say anything. There was still the smell of burnt wood in the air from bush fires. I thought about saying, 'Hot, isn't it?' but didn't.

Three nights later I told my mother I was going out with a friend.

'Who?' she said.

'A guy I met at the gym.'

Double Bay was halfway between my house and Meg's place in Kings Cross. We met at the beach after dinner in the dark.

We had worked out together a couple of times — I did her routine — and I wanted to ask her out. I had tried to imagine what she would want to do but all I could think of was going down to the water and looking at the harbour. I spotted her while she was bench-pressing and as soon as she had finished I said, 'I've never been down to the water and looked at the harbour.' I was staring at her legs. 'At night,' I added.

'You should do that,' she said.

The next day she told me after her workout that she had stolen a bottle of rum from a bottle shop. 'It was sitting in a carton near the door.' I didn't know how to react.

'Fancy meeting me tonight at the beach?' she said.

I felt sick and anxious for the rest of the day. I kept myself from thinking about my dreams of Meg. I felt guilty and disrespectful for having thought about her naked and told myself, to calm myself, that she was just a new friend I was meeting on the beach.

It was another hot night. I didn't want to wear shorts. I wanted to dress up a little, but not too much. I hadn't worn jeans in months because they weren't allowed that year at St Ebury and it had been too hot in Sydney. Our maid had ironed a pair and folded them neatly in a drawer at the end of my last holiday. They were crisp and thick and the buttons were hard to do up. I tucked a white shirt into them and I rolled up the sleeves to just above the elbow — a habit I'd developed according to the rules of St Ebury's Fridays. My mother said I looked nice.

'Bundy!' was the first thing Meg said when she came up to me on the beach. She was wearing a tank top and shorts, as always, but also lipstick. I didn't really like the look of her lipstick. She was holding a bottle in front of her. 'Bundaberg,' she said, with less of a smile, pointing at the label of the rum. She realised I didn't know what Bundy was.

'Did you bring Coke?' she said.

I didn't know I was supposed to. She had expected me to bring Coke and glasses.

There were sailboats moored near the beach and the water was mostly flat. Every now and then a set of waves from a distant ferry would come in and the boats would roll. Their masts made a dull ring and the waves washed ashore with a shhh! like they were telling the quiet to be quiet. Meg was mad and silent about the Coke for a long time. I said I could go buy some but she said, 'Stuff it, you couldn't buy glasses.' She took a swig from the bottle. She handed it to me and we sat down on the sand in a part of the beach where no one was likely to see us.

'I'm only seventeen,' she said.

I was going to tell her that I was only sixteen, but I didn't. I drank some rum from the bottle and coughed. I expected her to laugh but she looked out at the water like she was thinking of something else.

We sat a couple of feet apart. She passed me the bottle again and I braced myself for the burn. I passed it back and she screwed it into the sand between us. She hummed and mumbled a piece of a song that I didn't know and then she got up and stood near the edge of the water. I noticed for the first time that she hadn't been wearing shoes. In Canada you can't go out without shoes.

I didn't know whether I should stand and join her or not. I was too nervous to realise for a while that I was finally down at the water at night looking out at the harbour with a friend.

She walked back towards me, looking at me with a narrow grin. She leaned forward and took the bottle from the sand. She took a dramatic swig with the stars behind her head, and her tank top revealed half an inch of her belly. She pushed the bottle to me again.

'So?' she said.

'So?'

She sat down next to me, closer. 'I can't drink vodka,' she said. 'Sick as. Couple of years ago?' She forced the bottle on me again. I had never had rum before.

'You're quiet,' she said.

'So are you.'

She tried to do a headstand because she said she couldn't feel the rum. She fell and then I tried. I balanced myself and my face felt flushed with rum and blood. While I was upside down she yanked my shirt up out of my jeans and laughed when I fell over.

'It looks better that way,' she said.

I drank more rum and felt dizzy. I had only been drunk once

before at one of my parents' parties, and I think I was only pretending to be drunk because I only had a glass of wine.

'I threw up on wine once,' I told her. I don't know why I lied.

'I like wine,' she said. 'White wine. Nice and cold.'

I had some more rum and tried another headstand. So did she.

'I feel my upper body getting stronger,' I said after collapsing. 'I feel like my arms are stronger than my legs.'

'Gotta balance it out,' she said and drummed her palms on her thighs.

'I don't know whether you read much, Meg, but I've been reading about the Greek god Hephaestus.' I pointed upwards. 'He was lame. The other gods laughed at him because he walked in a funny manner. But he was strong in his arms and worked a mighty forge.'

Meg burst out laughing. She was upside down and her laughter made her fall over. She sat up and chuckled.

'Bit of a dag, aren't you?' she said.

I didn't know what a dag was.

She looked at me nicely then. 'What's wrong with your eye?' she said.

'Nothing.'

She kept looking at me. 'I bet I can do more push-ups than you can,' she said.

'I bet you can.'

'I bet I could do push-ups with you on my back.'

I didn't say anything for a second. I felt a little sick. Then I said, 'I'd crush you.'

'You reckon you could do them with me on your back?'

'Maybe. Most likely,' I said.

'Most likely,' she said, and before I knew it she had rolled me over and was lying face down on my back. 'Go on then.' She half whispered in my ear and I shivered. I pushed up and she wrapped her arms around my belly for support. She started laughing quietly and I could feel her shaking behind me. I did six push-ups and she said, 'That all?'

I was feeling weak with nerves. I'd never been drunk. I'd never been touched by a girl.

'My turn,' she said. 'Come on.' She wanted me to lie on her back.

I didn't want her to feel me.

'Come on.'

She was waiting for me on her stomach. I put my hands on either side of her, then my elbows. I was shaking and lowered my chest onto her back. I was glad I was taller than her; my middle was below hers. I didn't want her to feel how small I was. I tried keeping my weight off but she said, 'Don't treat me like a girl.' I felt calm for half a second thinking it was just a competition.

'I've gotta beat six,' she said. She seemed serious but then she started laughing. She pushed up and I almost fell off. She did it again and groaned a bit, and I liked the noise. Then she started laughing hysterically – maybe because she felt how small I was.

I got mad at her and rolled off and she was still lying face down in the sand, laughing. She looked over at me and I looked away. I turned my hips away and crossed my legs in case she could see.

'Look at him. He's won and he's gone all quiet. Don't think you won,' she said. 'You did not win.'

She got up and straddled me. She took off her tank top. She wasn't wearing a bra. Her breasts were smaller than I had thought breasts could be and were pale from not seeing the sun. It was a boy's chest with triangles of white from her bikini. I felt a little sick again. She leaned forward and pinned my arms on either side of my head and she kissed me. I didn't know what to do. I was trapped and sick and I wanted to bite her. Our teeth banged together. I pushed against her arms, tried to sit up and she fought against me.

She was still on top of me and started sucking on my neck. I sucked on hers and made her shout OUCH! because I sucked too hard, and I flipped her over. Her legs were wrapped together around me and I pushed against her then lifted her body up with mine and pounded her back against the sand. She said OUCH! again and it excited me so I pounded her again.

I have gone over this so many times.

I rolled onto my back and she kissed around my ears and her hand went under my shirt and started going lower. I didn't want her to feel me.

Her breath was in my ear and her hand was moving down. I wanted to grab her arm and either force it away or force it down fast. She kissed me and tried to undo my jeans. The material was so thick and unworn that she couldn't undo the buttons. I could feel her struggling and I didn't want to help her. She kept trying and kissing me and said 'come on' into my mouth, and with so much strength she forced her hand under the waistband. She touched me and I grabbed her arm, shouted and soaked her hand.

Three days before I went back to St Ebury, my mother said, 'I'll miss you when you go. I don't like seeing how much you're changing.' I felt like she could see all my secrets. 'I'm missing all your changes.' She smiled. I felt like crying and I frowned at her.

I spent several hours at the gym the next day, but Meg wasn't there. I couldn't stop thinking about how I wanted to meet her and do it right this time, be kinder or better with my hands. When I left her on the beach I don't think I scared her, but I wanted to make sure.

I checked in at the gym as often as I could. I wandered in every hour or so, got a smile or a 'mate!' from the caretaker. I had no other way to get in touch with her. It was the same the next three days – and then I had to fly back to Canada.

I decided to leave a letter for her at the gym. I wanted to give her my address. I thought of writing something brief, but I decided to go home and put some thought into it. I wrote it on my second-last night and left it with the caretaker.

Dear Meg,
   I have been thinking about you. I have been coming to the gym but haven't seen you. I hope you are all right and are not upset with me.
   I think about the first time I saw you. You were in your own world, working on yourself. You shape yourself like you are Pygmalion as well as his creation. You are so quiet and resolute. What is your world like?
   This summer has been the best of my life. This upside-down summer in the middle of winter. I can't tell you what I have to go back to.
   I think it is a miracle that we met. We are from such different places. We speak a different language. I find your Australianisms so exotic and funny and beautiful. I feel like we have connected despite our differences.
   This year I have been in love with someone else. I have

given her all my energy and thought. I know you do not want to hear this. But I am telling you because meeting you has banished her from my mind. I think only of you.

Meg, you are so strong and silent. I hope that I did not frighten you on the beach. I did not know how to say goodbye and I said some things I did not mean.

Perhaps this is too much for you. If you feel like writing to me, please do. It takes weeks for letters to get to Canada so I will be patient, but full of hope.

Noel

I left the address of St Ebury and never heard from her.

I think about that summer so often. It has changed when I have spoken about it, when I told Julius about it the following year. That summer is when I began to change and develop some strength.

I remember late one night during that next term I went to Shaughnessy's room. He was the Senior that year who didn't have a room-mate. It was two in the morning and I pushed open his door and stood by his bed. I stared at him for a long time. He woke up and was frightened. He didn't say anything for a moment and he never really bothered me again. I turned and walked towards his door.

'You're a fuckin freak, get out of here,' he said as I was leaving.

And now I somehow feel like I have become that presence at the edge of my own bed. For decades, the air in all my rooms has had the chill of things deliberately ignored.

Julius

MY HAIR LOOKS good.
 I ate too much salami.
I'm humming.
I'm humming a song I don't know.
No one knows this song I'm humming.
I'm gonna choose a song I know and I'll hum it.
I'll whistle it.
Why am I humming and whistling.
My hair looks good.
My teeth look good.
Scar on my lip.
From a zit.

She has a smile like, I don't know, something light and white and wide, but small and red and nothing anyone's ever seen, mouth-wise.

I'll tell you, my friend in my head: if you can look at her when she smiles and not smile your own smile, I will be honest and clean for the rest of my life.

Smile I say.
Why she says.
Just smile.
She's smiling.
See.

★   ★   ★

I'm gonna learn a lot this year and run faster and generally smell better. I'm gonna flick the switch, click, on the rest of my life and all the rooms will be new, click.

This blood is new and my father's house is huge.

I'll pack one bag, bring it to school, kiss my girl, maybe get a handjob standing up somewhere, maybe not. Empty the bag, come back later, pack and empty and I'll be busy and smart and practical.

I'll meet her again, tomorrow at ten.

Socks.

Cleats.

Pads.

Where's my pads.

Under the bed.

Under the bed.

Every old thing and new thing and lost thing and secret is under the beds of the world.

I'm smart.

I'm gonna look at those and jack off.

I'm gonna hide them somewhere better.

I'm gonna fart.

I'm farting.

Pads.

What else is under here.

Funny.

Ho.

Funny.

K.

Boxers.

These ones.

These ones.

These ones.

Those.

These.

Those.

Those.

These.

Those.

These.

No.

Shirts.

You can't plan. You can't say I'm definitely gonna wear this shirt in two months on a Wednesday.

I'm not gonna wear this shirt on any fuckin Wednesday it scratches like a cat.

White.

White.

Blue.

Blue.

In a year I won't need a suit.

I'll have a nap.

No.

Snack.

No.

Snack and a nap.

Yes.

I want some pepperoni.

Jules says Chuck.

Yes says I.

I've been calling for a week he says.

What a sweetheart I say.

So when are you going in.

Tomorrow I say. I'm packed.

Packed and ready he says.

You I say.

I'm here now he says. There. Let's meet he says.

I'm gonna have a snack and a nap and a dinner with Dad.

Oh he says. Anyways. I've had a look around and a think, and I believe I'm not getting laid this year.

That's too bad.

Yeah.

I saw Fall last night in the limo I say. William helped me out again.

Nice he says.

Fur coat.

Always the older woman in the fur coat with the bush on the hairy side whenever I jack off.

I'm sorry, Fall.
I'm sorry.
Warm hairy bush.
Gyah.
I'm sorry, Fall, I love you.

Dad's looking solid and good and I hope I don't grow all those chins.
Gotta cancel dinner, pal he says. I'm sorry.
It's OK.
On the weekend he says.
You bet.
Moving to school tomorrow.
You bet I say.
He chucks my shoulder.
I chuck his.
He holds my shoulders.
I hold his.
Smiles make noises.

Remember when you visited Vermont.
Yeah she says.
And you were wearing that green dress.
Yeah.
I remember your eyes in it. The green.
It was short she says.
I remember your legs I say.
She's smiling.
I gave it to my sister she says.
I dreamt about her mother's mouth around my cock.
I like sharing clothes she says. It feels like a hug. Like I'm wearing my sister she says.
Your sister's wearing you.
M.
I loved you in that dress I say.
I can get another one she says.
There's gum on the ground.
She stepped in it.
I should have warned her.

★   ★   ★

I'm taking Functions, Calculus and Algebra she says.

You're nuts I say.

She's smart I'm thinking.

I know she says.

I'm gonna buy my essays this year I say. And numbers. I'll buy all the numbers I'll need for Algebra. I'll hire someone, you know, to put the . . . put the numbers down the right way.

I'm gonna give up on that joke.

I think this'll be a fun year she says.

Yeah.

We'll both work hard.

Yeah. I'm gonna eat more fish I say. It makes you strong.

Your arms look good she says.

I love her.

We're walking.

Salmon. Stuff like that I say. Makes you smarter.

Good she says.

She's tall.

We're sitting.

Walk past us and say They're a couple.

She puts her head on my knee.

Sarah's gonna sneak into the kitchen and make brownies she says.

She's excited.

I'm smiling. I'm not excited.

How's she gonna work those big ovens I say.

I don't know she says.

We're hugging.

I totally forgot to ask who your room-mate is.

Wink I say.

Wink she says.

The one-eyed guy. Rince. Reece. You know. Noel Reece.

Really.

Yeah.

I guess that'll be quiet she says.

Yeah.

We're hugging.

I kiss her neck.

He's grown I say. Over the summer.

Everyone's bigger and wearing different colours I'm thinking.
I kiss her neck.

Hm she says.

She squirms and squeezes and I'm thinking about tits and cats
and baths and lips.

It still feels like summer she says.

Jules.

Hey.

Hey, Julius.

Hey.

How was your summer, man.

Short.

I hear ya.

Yours.

Shorter.

Ha.

Right on.

See you at practice.

I'm a green-and-white breath with a ball.

Check out this goal.

I had a dream she's saying. That I could fly.

I've had that dream.

I guess everyone's had that dream she says. Except my mom
was hanging underneath me, from like a rope. But she wasn't
pulling me down. There was no weight, right.

I see I say.

Chapel: Bong!

English: Argue.

Math: What?

Lunchtime: Eat.

Chuck says Big one Saturday at Brown's. I've signed out to
Ant's aunt's, Jules, so don't worry about putting me up.

There's mustard on his lips cause it's hot-dog Tuesday, they feed
us like kids when it's Tuesday.

My dad's home this weekend anyway I'm saying.

You don't have to be back early says Ant. Do you.

There's mustard on his lips.

No I say. If Chuck stayed with me I would. Do what you want, Dad says, Unless someone's with you. Then you do what I want. Did I tell you the vagina joke the President told my dad.

Yes.

Yeah.

The big vagina joke.

Yeah says Chuck.

I'm hungry and I'll have another dog.

Pass me the tray I say and I'm grabbing the last dog.

Bun.

I want to get some vodka for Saturday says Chuck. One of those litre bottles.

He's gonna sit in the corner and yawn his barf all over Brown's furniture says Ant.

I'm chuckling.

There's a little blue fire in me.

By the end of the year we will all be able to party legally I say.

I've said the same thing every hour this week.

I love repeating myself.

I'm the guy with opinons.

Chuck pours milk for me and I say Thanks chum because I like that word: chum.

Fall coming to Brown's says Chuck.

Yeah I say.

I'm hoping there'll be Lisgar girls. Glebe girls. Hundreds of girls from Lisgar and Glebe says Ant.

He's serious like he's on the news.

I'm serious he says. Chicks from other schools.

I like this feeling from dark old wood and friends being buddies, right now, and life from all the mouths, lap yap.

I burp.

Chuck burps.

Chuck farts.

We chuckle.

Chuck's ex-girlfriend Stephanie is plump and funny and smart. Is Stephanie going to Brown's I say.

Why do you think I want a litre of vodka he says.

They broke up because she was fat which was mean but understandable but Chuck is plumper than she was.

He looks into his world and gets sad.

Get over it says Ant.

You have never had a girlfriend for longer than a month I say to Ant.

Chuck nods. Exactly. You've never had sex for longer than nine seconds he says.

I get what I need says Ant.

I'm thinking I want to be alone with Fall. Uh-huh. I want to have a quiet night alone with Fall and be calm and she'll tell her jokes, and the look of her lips and teeth when she talks and kisses and hand on my thigh, yep, I'll hum sweet and quiet like that tuning fork of pretty Miss Klein's, St Patrick's Elementary grade 2. Bing.

I have a hard-on.

Half an hour left of lunch says Chuck. Let's go.

Wait I say. Let me finish this dog.

Hurry up says Chuck.

It's a sunny day says Ant.

Ant wants to work on his tan for the party.

Fuck, Chuckie, you're all sore. All I said was get over it. I like Stephanie. You're the one who dumped her says Ant.

What the fuck are you talking about. All I said is you wanted to get a tan.

I don't want a tan.

I was joking.

I know.

Right.

So fuck off.

My cock is down and I stand. I want a smoke I say, and I'm looking at Fall. Fingers to my lips the invisible smoke and she smiles. Shiny eyes says there's fun up ahead, and love and hands and kisses. She leans to Sarah and I see her lips say Smoke.

Chuck chucks my shoulder. Let's go.

We're out in the sun.

The girls coming says Ant.

I think so I say.
Should we wait for them says Chuck.
No I say.

I ate too many dogs I say.
A hot dog is the lips and ass of a pig says Ant. That's why Chuck loves hot dogs.
Sarah laughs and hangs her tongue from her mouth like she's being sick, and Fall giggles.
Except Julius is the one who ate too many dogs says Ant.
He's full of lips and ass says Sarah.
I've never liked her.
Smoke.
I look up at the trees and the leaves are as thick as they're ever gonna be. I'll tell you the difference I'm saying, between Vermont and this place. This time of year.
I'm thinking I don't know.
I'm blowing smoke.
I don't know I say.
They're looking at me like I'm cool or stupid, who knows, but I love these leaves and I want to party at Brown's or stay home with Fall or smoke an entire tree and rub and run and fuck, who knows.
I like this time of year I say.

Gym: Schloop! (Twelve baskets and two three-pointers.)
French: I don't care, You don't care, He/She does not care.
I'm touching her hip in the hallway, right . . . now . . . tip, two fingers on the bone of her righ . . . left hip.
I like you I say.
Come find me after practice she says.
My fingers tap tap on her hip.

I'm sick of wearing this tie she says.
You know I'm saying. Dad's got a picture of me when I was a baby and I'm on a little baby-bike, trike, thing. And there's a pair of legs behind me and they're my mom's. She's in a pair of blue pants. That blue from those days. And it's the same blue in that stripe.

Yeah don't get me wrong she's saying. I like the colour, I just don't like the tie.

I've always liked that blue I'm saying.

I love that blue she's saying. I bet your mom looked good in it.

I'm thinking my mom is my secret. I try to understand her.

There's a TREE and a SQUIRrel and a LIGHT and a ROAD and a HOUSE and a HOUSE and a DUDE and a GIRL no a GUY and a SQUIRrel and I'm TALL and a HOUSE and he's BALD and I'm NOT and I'm FAST no I'm STEADy keep STEADy keep STEADy it's WARM yep it's WARM and I'm HOT no I'm NOT I'm a DUDE and the ROAD and a HOUSE and I'll EAT yes I'll EAT what's the TIME fuckin A getting FAST fuckin OUCH watch the ROAD there's a GUY make him SMILE catch his EYE where's his EYE lookin DOWN fuckin GRUMP fuck his WIFE don't be MEAN.

Breathe Breathe Breathe Breathe Breathe Breathe Breathe.

I'm running way too fast.

So let's say you look at this car says William. You look at this car. Rubber on the tyres is touching the road. And the rubber has treads. There's a guy somewhere he says, maybe a girl who chews tobacco, who puts the treads on those tyres, Julius. Or runs the machine that puts the treads on the tyres. And there's a machine that makes the wheels, and people who run that machine, maybe a guy with no teeth and tiny fists. You follow. And what's his name. Why's he running that machine. He's got sparks in front of his eyes all day. And that's just the wheels and the tyres. There's this whole car here on the driveway. How many people with names and fingers touched the parts that make this car.

I wanna meet them I say.

Exactly, Julius. That's the spirit.

Except I also wanna borrow it, William.

I figured as much he says. It's not easy you know.

I know.

It's my living.

I know.

Well, you young and wealthy fellas know nothing about a

living. Let me tell you. I can guarantee you that you and I have a completely different idea of what an alarm clock is.

Maybe I say.

Maybe he says.

Maybe in a week or two I could borrow the car. Maybe.

Maybe he says. It's not easy.

I know.

I have to lie.

I'm sorry.

What's your girlfriend's name again.

Fall.

Fall he says.

Fallon I say. We call her Fall.

William is thoughtful and I really want this car.

I knew a woman named Paul once he says.

I'm waiting for a story.

We're on Dad's driveway and the sun's on William's watch.

I'm waiting for a story about Paul.

The other thing you probably don't know about is mortgages he says.

Pardon I say.

Mortgages. It's a kind of prison where you think there's freedom in prison.

Mortgages I say. I've heard of them.

See, when I let you take this car, I put my job at risk. And if I lose my job I'm not going to find another one that pays like this. I could start my own company, sure, but all I can make is hangovers. You come to a time in life, Julius, and you'll know this when you come to it. You come to a time in life where all you need to think is that I've come to a time in life. As soon as you think I've come to a time in life, as soon as you've had that thought, it's likely too late for anything. See.

Hmp I say.

I've got a lot of things coming at me he says. That's all. Banks. Banshees. Lisette. Outside those windows there's monsters with bills in their hands. You can't imagine what those monsters look like because no one's ever seen them. No one's had a strong and big enough mind to know what those goddamn monsters look like. But if I'm behind this wheel it means I can sleep in my apartment and the monsters knock on my neighbours' doors. I like that better.

You don't have to loan me the car I say.

It's true he says. It's true. In my day everything happened in cars that's why I love them. Maybe we can swing something when I know your dad doesn't need me. Maybe.

Maybe I say.

I like William.

How come there's wet on a match. When you burn it, there's like some water next to the flame.

It's moisture she says. There's moisture in the stick or the wood or whatever.

I really like her lips.

You shouldn't smoke so much she says.

I know.

I'm chuckling.

What's funny she says.

Ant was telling us about his mom. He said she smoked exactly forty-three cigarettes every day and her lips were puckered like an anus.

Gross.

It's funny.

Poor woman she says. There's something kind of gross about Ant she says.

Yeah I say. He's OK.

I guess she says.

I'm making smoke rings and I'm thinking about other people but now I'm thinking about what I'm thinking about and I forget what I was thinking about and now I'm thinking about other people. Ant, Chuck, Dad, Fall, blow jobs, Fall, Fall, Fall.

Are you cold I say.

I'm hot she says. I love these nights she says. No one else around.

I love other people I'm thinking.

I like other people I say. You know. I like the idea of meeting other people I'm saying.

Girls she says.

No I say. Just people.

Me too she says. Totally. I just meant it's nice that no one's around right now.

No I say. I know. I was just thinking another, like, thought.

Yeah.

Maybe we'll both have thousands of friends when we die. A friend for every mood, right. So, like, today I'm feeling thirsty, better call Bill. Right. Today I'm down because it's, like, raining. Better call my friend in the clown suit.

Fff she says.

We're never alone enough I say.

Chuck's bed is here and Ant's bed is there and I'm wondering why I'm eighteen years old and I'm sleeping in a bunk bed.

I'm thinking I don't always want to talk to friends and listen to problems and I have no fuckin clue what I'm gonna do next year.

You guys got lucky getting separate beds I say.

Yeah says Ant.

The further that guy is from me the better says Chuck.

What's it like rooming with Wink says Ant.

I don't know I'm thinking.

I don't know I'm saying. Quiet. We haven't talked a lot. No pyjama party yet I guess.

You say pyjomma like an American says Ant.

I am I say.

Chuck's wearing his robe. I'm gonna wear the Animal a lot this winter.

We're quiet and everyone's thinking about something and I wonder if my toes will get hairy.

This summer I fucked a girl with a really smelly ass says Ant.

Christ says Chuck.

I think you've gotta expect that of an ass I say.

Who was it says Chuck.

I didn't really fuck her says Ant. We made out in this night-club in Paris. I was kissing her and fingering her and I put my finger in her ass and she, like, melted.

Why do you always give us these details says Chuck. I have so many images of you that I just don't want.

I'm just telling you.

You had your finger in her ass in a nightclub in Paris I say. You're full of shit.

It's true. I couldn't get the smell off for eight or nine days. It was like woodstain.

You're lying.

I'm not he says.

What was her name I say.

I don't know.

Some guys tell lies and it's really fuckin weird.

We met in this dark nightclub he says.

What was her name I say.

I told you. I don't know. I picked her up.

What was her hair like I say.

I don't know. Long. Long and brown he says.

How old was she.

I don't know.

Was she twenty. Thirty.

Something like that.

Which.

I did make out with a girl in Paris but it wasn't this summer. It was the summer before.

You told us about her last year says Chuck.

Yeah. But I didn't tell you what her ass smelled like.

You're such a fuckin liar.

Why.

You looked like a twelve-year-old last summer says Chuck. That neat little hairdo you had and the moss on your lip.

So.

So what's a grown woman in a Paris nightclub doing with a twelve-year-old's finger in her ass says Chuck.

Melting I say.

Exactly says Ant.

You're such a fuckin liar I say.

He is says Chuck.

I'm not says Ant. I can describe the smell for you.

You'll just be describing your own says Chuck. Or your aunt's.

Anyways I say.

You know who else is a liar says Chuck.

Who.

Who.

Everyone he says. Everyone's a complete fuckin liar he says. I was reading this history of England, right. England in the early twentieth century. I read a couple of them because I am so much more intelligent and curious than Ant over there. And one of them says the collapse of the gold standard was the single most important event, right. The thing that affected everything from whatever to whatever. And then this other history says the gold standard meant nothing. It was the radio and train travel. Those were the things that affected everything. And then I read more because of my gigantic mind, and I find out that the two guys who wrote these books had been married to the same woman and they fuckin hated each other. And I'm thinking, this is history. These guys are trying to teach us what happened, and everything they say happened didn't happen, or happened in a different way because these guys hate each other. They're exaggerating and lying. Everybody lies he says.

I wasn't lying says Ant. Her ass smelled like a dead mouse.

Fuck says Chuck.

That's interesting Chuck I say.

I love Chuck he's interesting.

I should think more.

Everything's a little slower. It's all a little slower in this little world. I'm not as old as I should be. I should know it all better. Two years in a boarding school it's like a couple of months in the world.

This is me thinking.

Those are my shoes.

Your father doesn't need me to drive him on Friday night like I thought says William. I can give you the car for an hour at around seven.

Fuckin A I say.

And it's such a bad idea says William.

I'm excited.

Such a bad idea.

It's fine I say.

Drive that car quietly. Hear me. And safely. Wide corners. And don't drive it at all. Please. Keep it parked.

I plan to.

I don't want to hear about it he says.

It shakes when we fuck I'm thinking. It's hilarious.

It's my job he says. I WILL be fired if anybody hears about it.

I owe you, William.

And if you're late. One minute past seven. You won't get it. I have an awful lot of beer and forgetting to meet on Friday night.

I won't be late I say.

There goes Noel she says.

There he goes.

You should talk to him she says.

I will I say. I'm living with him.

It's weird she says. A school this small and there's people we haven't talked to.

Yeah. I'm just not seeing him so much. I haven't seen him much ever. He's not around much or something. Right.

I guess she says. Is he going to Brown's.

I don't know.

Anyways, I've decided to stay here tonight she says.

What I say.

I want to study she says.

What.

I just want to take it easy. I don't want to stay at home and tomorrow night we're going to Brown's.

But it's Friday night I say.

I know.

I'm getting the car.

I know.

I can't breathe.

I need to study she says.

I can't think.

Sex.

I only have the car for an hour anyway I say.

I know she says. Let's do the car some other time. Don't be mad she says.

I'm not mad I say, and I am, I'm mad and sad and mad.

You can't study on Friday nights I say. It's like trying to be happy on Sundays.

But I want to. Tomorrow's a big night. Let's walk she says.

We're walking.

So why do you want to stay here I say.

You're really having trouble with this aren't you she says.

It's lonely here.

It's lonely at home she says. I feel like taking it easy.

I hate coming here on Fridays I say.

You don't have to.

But you'll be here.

I'll be all right.

But I want to see you.

She's smiling.

We can spend some weekends apart sometimes she says.

I'm gonna try hard not to let that bother me. I've got to be quiet here for a minute.

. . .

The day's getting dark.

You should have told me before I say.

Why.

She's all grown up sometimes.

That why is a smart woman's why.

She's got it all figured out.

I don't know I say. I could have planned I say.

It's no big deal. I just want to study.

I thought you would study at home. And I could pick you up.

What difference does it make.

I don't know. I pictured you at home.

So you can picture me here.

I love her hands.

Picture me in my PJs she says.

Mmm. White socks.

Short white socks she says.

No pyjama bottoms.

You say pyjomma like a cutie.

White socks.

I'll be thinking of you she says.

Why don't you just come out. It'll be fun. It'll be a riot. A big pink hoot. We'll make out and I'll, you know, do things . . .

Stop.

What.

Just stop she says. I want to study.

I grab her hand and think it's gonna be limp but it's tight like a loving trap, and she's strong.

Maybe I should stay here tonight I say.

You should go out.

I could help you study.

You should go out.

Her hand's on my chest and it doesn't feel like pushing.

Let's go see a movie I say.

Fuckin A says Chuck.

Ball in the face.

Ow.

I look stupid.

But I'm good.

I'm a green–and–white breath with a ball.

Check out this goal, Mom.

Cheer up I'm saying to the people in my head.

Cheer up, sad teachers.

Cheer up, sad boys in your bunks.

There's a million mysteries and the ground's electric, I swear.

I've got fizz in my belly and a condom in my pocket. Who knows what's gonna happen tonight.

Mayhem.

Orgies.

Fights.

Police.

What a boring fuckin party says Ant.

It's just starting I say.

It's early says Fall.

Give it a chance I say.

I might do some knives in the kitchen I'm thinking.

Where's Chuck says Ant.

He's talking to that girl over there.

The ugly one he says.

She's not ugly says Fall.

Nyah says Ant.

Antony never looks at Fall she's told me. It's true. He won't look at her when she's talking.

I'm gonna go break it up says Ant.

He's walking to Chuck and the girl.

What an asshole says Fall.

I'm thinking about doing some knives in the kitchen I say.

I'm thinking about taking you upstairs she says.

I like her.

Bedroom one.

WE'RE IN HERE!

Bedroom two.

SOMEONE IN HERE!

I like the feel of her hand.

My body's in my cock.

Bedroom three.

Oops she says. Sorry.

Did you see someone.

I saw someone's butt she says.

Whose.

I don't know.

Nice. Boy or girl.

I don't know she says. Just a butt.

There's no more bedrooms I say.

She's smiling.

We're kissing.

Her tongue tastes like beer.

She's so fuckin pretty sometimes she makes me nervous.

Look what I'm wearing she says.

O god.

Hey.

Hi.

How are ya.

Good.

See ya.

Bye.

She was very cute.

Hey, Jules.

Where ya been, Chuckie.

Christ he says. I was talking to that girl. Very sweet, man. A truly lovely girl. And along comes Ant.

Yeah.

Every girl I talk to he's either trying to piss them off or he's hitting on them himself.

Yeah.

That girl there. We were connecting. Ant comes along and tells the big vagina joke.

The President's.

Yeah.

That's hilarious.

No says Chuck. No it isn't.

I'm barfing.

Are you OK says Fall.

Pwuh I say. Plah.

Are you OK.

I love you I say.

Plee.

Stay like this

OUR ROOM BECAME a refuge, a place where, for a while, I felt I could be myself more than anywhere else in the world. Julius created it. He dimmed the lights and closed the door to everyone else.

After Chapel on the second Sunday night I was reading in the room. I remember being annoyed that I hadn't washed my white shirt. On Sunday nights we had to wear Number One for Chapel – grey flannels, house tie, blue blazer and white shirt. We had to wear the same thing every Monday as well, and since I had only one white shirt I had to make sure I washed it every weekend. I remember I couldn't find it that weekend until just before Chapel, when I dug through a pile of Julius's clothes in the corner of the room and found it buried there. It was too late to wash it, and it would definitely smell by the end of Monday.

The door burst open while I was reading and Chuck stood there in the doorway, scanning the room but not looking at me. When he met my eye he said 'sorry' and closed the door again. Julius appeared around fifteen minutes later.

'Hey.'

He jumped up onto the top bunk and threw his blazer, which landed in the sink.

'Do you believe in God, Noel?'

'I believe in the maker of heaven and earth.'

'Of all that is known and unknown?'

'Seen and unseen.'

He laughed and I remember feeling cool. St Ebury was an

Anglican school, and in my years there I never knew anyone who was actually Anglican.

I stared at my book, pretending to read.

'You mind if I turn off the big light?' he said.

'No.'

He jumped down, turned off the overhead light, picked his blazer out of the sink, dropped it on the floor and hopped back onto the bunk. With just the reading lights on the room felt comfortable. For some reason I had always assumed that the overhead light had to be on.

I can't remember what book I was reading.

'I'm still hungover,' said Julius.

'Chuck came in here looking for you,' I said. 'Twenty-one minutes ago.'

Julius sighed.

'Maybe we should turn all the lights off,' he said.

'I can't read in the dark.'

'I forgot,' he said. 'It's so fuckin hard to be left alone in this place.'

'Yeah.'

'Chuckie. Someone's always banging through the door.'

I kept pretending to read. It might have been Hobbes. I remember reading *Leviathan* that year.

'Nobody bangs through the door at home,' he said.

I went through my usual list in my head.

Nobody showers with other guys at home.

Nobody wears uniforms at home.

Nobody lives with 113 people at home.

Nobody has twelve parents.

Nobody works, goes to church, eats every meal and plays mandatory basketball at home.

I put my book down and brushed my teeth at the sink. Julius jumped down and turned off his desk light and hopped back up. I turned off my own light and climbed into the lower bunk in the dark.

'I'm in your bed, aren't I?' he said.

'That's OK.'

'I'm not used to this room yet.'

'I fall off the top bunk anyway.' I fell during my first year and landed on my desk. I heard my room-mate calling me the one-eyed bird the next morning when he told everyone about it.

'I could keep the top bunk,' he said.

We were lying fully clothed in the dark and it was one of those shy moments, so full of potential, when people are about to get to know each other. I felt nervous, but I didn't think about the strangeness of it or worry about what Julius was thinking. It was two of us in the dark in our white shirts and formal trousers, a bright light and noise beyond the door.

'You have a good weekend, Noel?'

I said it was OK.

'You go out?'

'I stayed here.'

'All weekend?'

'Yes.'

I don't think he had ever spent a full weekend at school.

I wanted to ask him a question but I didn't know what. It was quiet for a while and I thought he might just want to sleep.

The door flew open and Chuck and Ant were standing in the light looking in.

'What the fuck?' said Chuck.

'Sleeping?' said Ant.

'Jules, man, Ant wanted to tell you that his cock hurts.'

'Kills.'

'He used some cream.'

'Exfoliating cream. My aunt's exfoliating cream.'

'To jack off.'

'Instead of lubricant.'

'He's not smart, Jules. Our friend Ant. He's dumb and his cock hurts. Are you asleep?'

'I guess he's asleep.'

'It's nine o'clock, Jules. You're, uh, no longer eight years old, man.'

'Jule.'

'Jules.'

'Joolie.'

'Jules.'

'He's asleep.'

'Little boy.'

'Sleepy.'

'Sleepy boy. So cute.'

'They're both so cute.'

They left, and left the door open to the light.

'Fuck's sakes,' said Julius. He got down from the bed and closed the door. When he stepped back up his foot landed on my hand, but I pulled it away before he would have to say sorry.

'Last night,' he said, 'Ant started crying because he thinks no girl will ever know him. "No one will ever *know* me," he kept saying. So drunk. We were drinking Jagermeister.'

I laughed and said, 'I got so drunk on that once. Well, it was more like rum.' I remember thinking I should find out what Jagermeister was.

It was quiet again. The bed moved and there was a thud, thud – Julius pushing his shoes off his feet and them landing on the floor. I could smell them.

'You stayed at home?' I asked him. I already knew the answer.

'I sign out to my dad's place every weekend. I don't always stay there. I got home last night at three in the morning and nobody cared. Except the marines.'

'Really?'

'And my dad. Everybody cared. We have marines all over and police at the gate of the place. Ever been over?'

'No.'

'It's this big place with a gate and marines and when I come home that late they get all excited. Then I have to walk through the house and not wake any of the staff. And usually Marie-Claude comes out in her robe and says "Du lait, Monsieur Jules," like I should pour milk over all the beer I've had and I say, "No, no, night-night." My dad always hears about it in the morning and shouts at me. You know, *You're an ambassador, too, goddamnit, I'm not letting you do this every weekend.*'

'He never does anything?'

'What could he do?'

'He could call the school. Tell them not to let you sign out.'

'True.'

'He could tell the marines not to let you out of the house.'

'Yeah. I'm glad you're not my dad.' The bed moved when he shifted. 'Dad's an Irish Caholic. He's strict, right, and his job makes him, you know, fuckin obsessed with the rules. But there's something about drinking. Staying out late with my buddies. He's kind of only pretending to care. He shouts at me for a while and nothing happens.' He stopped suddenly, and sighed, and said, 'Fuck, Noel, I feel so . . .'

'What?'

'I feel so weird today.'

He got out of bed again, and in the dark I watched him take off his clothes and brush his teeth.

Was he talking about his hangover?

I loved the darkness of that room.

He got back into bed.

He asked me if I ever got tired of friends.

I didn't say anything while I got undressed. I started sleeping in just my underwear that year, once I was working out regularly. It was liberating. We were supposed to wear pyjamas at St Ebury.

I got back into bed and said, 'Yes.'

'Me too, man.'

I asked him what was wrong.

'I don't know . . . Can you keep secrets down there, Noel?'

'I can keep secrets down here.'

'I don't know. I'm not tired of them. But I was at this party last night and it wasn't what I wanted it to be. Right? Not that it wasn't as fun as I wanted it to be. Just that I'm sick of other guys. You know.'

'I think so.'

'Not like I don't like my friends or other guys. But you think there's a connection. I was at this party and Ant kept moving in on girls. And Chuck kept getting pissed off. And I've been thinking about how guys do that. You think they're friends who care about what you want, and suddenly they're moving in on someone you love. The whole thing pissed me off, I guess. Because Chuck kept coming up to me and complaining, and I was looking around at this party and feeling like everyone's too close somehow. Or they're not close in the right way.'

'What's the right way?' I said.

'My girlfriend. Fall. You know her, right?'

I felt nervous, I remember, like I was going to have to reveal something or like he was going to make me confess something I wasn't ready to admit.

'Yes.'

'Those eyes. Right?'

I would have put more effort into describing them. I didn't know whether he wanted me to respond or not. Julius had been going out with Fallon since the middle of the previous year. I knew every skirt she owned and how she changed her hair. I knew how she had grown up over every year. She walked into a room and made it elegant and she was so disarming, stripping away all guile and fraudulence from anyone she spoke to.

'I dream about her ass,' he said. I remember feeling discomfort because I respected Julius. I didn't know what I wanted to hear him say about her.

'There were a lot of pretty girls at the party,' he said.

'There's a lot of beauty,' I suggested.

'There's a lot of beauty,' he said. He laughed. 'Why don't you go to parties, Noel?'

I looked for the right answer. 'I don't know,' I said. I didn't know whether he could really be ignorant of the fact that I was never invited to parties. That's what was so appealing about him. A strange obliviousness to the world, which somehow drew the world to him. 'I don't like not connecting with people,' I said.

'You're a smart guy, Noel.'

He said it after a pause, a warm dark pause that made it sincere and sympathetic. I feel like it was then that our bond really developed.

'I feel like I can talk to you,' he said.

I said, 'I'm your room-mate.' That's the way it was supposed to work. Find the right room-mate and he could be your confidant. Your wife. I wanted to say that I felt like I could talk to him.

'I feel so weird today, man. I love my girlfriend.'

I caught myself saying, 'She's beautiful.'

'I'm lucky. I feel really lucky. About everything.'

I didn't know what to say.

'But I feel like things aren't working somehow. This space. I'm not usually anxious, you know. Fall. What's going to happen? How do we get close?'

'I know.'

'Because, you've seen her *ass*.'

'I know.'

'I think I feel scared,' he said.

Over our time together, I wanted him to think. I wanted him to slow down and reason. I wanted him to consider things from the bunk below. Look at things another way.

I thought about him up there above me, scared, and I found more comfort. I liked the idea of him being scared, admitting it to me. No one else in the school would see him scared. And I loved possessing his secrets. I didn't realise that night that they might be useful to me. I simply thought that I was lucky to know him like this.

'Everything will work out for you,' I said.

I had seen the way she would flirt with other guys. I didn't know whether it was just her manner, her openness, or whether she was willing to be with other guys besides Julius. Everyone respected him. It was hard to imagine that anyone would deliberately try to steal Fall from him or even respond to an invitation from her. But if she truly invited, if she saw a bigger world.

He was quiet. I spent a long time considering what little I knew of his life. What was it like to have this girl who was everything, and still be uneasy? How much was he actually thinking? I wondered whether Julius's life was just a series of reactions. Put him in a room and watch people come to him, watch how he reacts. Is there any thought behind each reaction? There must be. He was up there thinking now. I wanted to help but found myself speechless. I imagined that it *would* be difficult to be in his situation. He clearly loved Fall, but what should one do, so full of love, when a beautiful girl comes into the room, into the bar, into the party and seduces one? Should love be negated for the sake of love? What if Fall did indeed find one of Julius's friends superior to him? I think we all started wondering more profoundly about the future that year.

I felt the bed shaking a little and realised he was crying. I felt terrible. I wondered whether I imagined the shaking, and thought he might have fallen asleep. He sighed and I realised he was still feeling bad.

'Sometimes people surprise you,' was all I could offer. I didn't even know what I meant, wondered if it was one of those platitudes, borrowed from someone else, that appear on the tongue at awkward moments. I was trying to remain essentially quiet, to let things happen at a calm pace, but being privy to his secrets, being there in that private space with him and feeling a potential friendship bloom, I felt like I should offer something of myself.

'It's just a lazy eye,' I said. 'I think people think it's something more serious. It's just a muscle problem. I can't control the eye.'

'OK.'

'And the eye and eyelid go into spasms. I know it makes people uncomfortable.'

I felt like I had stepped off a cliff. Why did I talk about my eye out of the blue? I cast about in my mind for some way to change the subject, for a joke to tell, some way to bring the talk back around to Julius. But all I remember saying was 'I find it hard'.

There was silence again and I found myself retreating. Shutting everything down and thinking this year is only a year and I will get through it quietly and on my own terms.

Julius said, 'I think it's cool. I think you're a handsome guy.'

It was still noisy and bright out in the hall. I was still wide awake.

I was warmer than I'd ever been in those strange beds.

'Goodnight,' I said.

'Goodnight.'

I had seen Fall that weekend. I saw her come out of the front door of the Girls' Flats on Saturday during the day. She had a book in her hand and I wanted to see what it was, but couldn't. I had never spoken to her.

I saw her that Friday night, too, in the TV room. It was the one place on the Flats (between the Girls' and Boys') where both sexes were allowed to mingle. People often wore their pyjamas there on the weekend. Someone would rent a movie or two and usually whoever was staying on the Flats would gather in the dark on the old couches and watch movies until a Master would come around and call lights out.

I often found it an annoying scene, people in their pyjamas getting cuddly. Occasionally a boyfriend and girlfriend, or several of them, would be in there and often enough they would be making out, their hands busy under blankets, and I found it all repellent. Everyone seemed to settle into a phoney vulnerability, as though wearing pyjamas and slippers revealed their soft nature, as though they were all the same. People made sure they laughed in the right places, groaned in the right places, the girls always cried when a movie was sad. A group of flannel-clad, insincere emotions.

I would walk through the TV room most Saturday nights to see if there was a movie I was interested in. I rented Fellini's *Satyricon* once, but only a handful of boys stayed to the end in hope of more nudity. I was generally not interested in their movies, and the sight of them all irked me, but Fall was there that Friday and I stopped for a while.

I sat at the back of the room and the couch she sat on was to the side. She angled her head towards the screen and I saw her in three-quarter profile. There was little danger of her noticing that I was staring at her.

There was such a hungry curiosity in her look, regardless of what banality was on the screen. I stared at the light flickering over her eyes and thought of some lost white sheet blowing in the night and settling into dark water. I wanted her to look at me and I wanted to be absorbed, transformed in her mind into something calm. I wanted her to help me. I had wanted that for years but I had never articulated it, and I was shocked to realise it. I felt weak. I realised that the only way to be helped by someone was to surrender, to be honest and say this is me, I'm yours, please fix whatever's wrong with me. I discovered that night that it was more than just desire I felt, it was that higher level of need and an acknowledgement that she could own me – maybe owned me already.

I stood up and attracted attention. I know she looked at me, but I kept my eyes on the screen as I walked past it and out of the room.

Some people don't know their words and some writers deliberately lie. I believe in the effort of words chasing thoughts: the spectacle of it, the truth of that alone. Words chasing thoughts are like greyhounds chasing the mechanical bunny. What's interesting is not the bunny, but the dogs: the hunger, the sinew, the energy and movement. I know my words. I write policy papers and memos. The right words are the dogs in front, one sniff behind the truth. There is never disappointment.

Never the disappointment I feel when I don't have the opportunity to write. When I awake and find nothing but the apartments all around me.

I am drawn to giving details.

IS THAT YOU, sir.
  It's me it's me, cough cough.
  Step into the light please, sir.
  I want my bed.
  Step forwards. Thank you, sir, goodnight.

Ah, Monsieur Jool, du lait du lait du lait.
  I want my bed.

Oh when Dad shouts I smell his breath. When will that breath
happen to me. How many bad things do I have to do before that
breath happens to me.
  I am
  Never
  Ever
  Drinking
  A single
  Shot
  Of
  Ja
  Ger
  Meister
  For the rest of my blond-haired life.
  Dad said I was lucky to be young. When you're young you
don't get hangovers. This is a hangover. I want juice. This is a

hangover on the sun's brightest . . . When is he gonna finish. I
need to leave. I need my bed at school.

Why am I in this room.
    Why am I dreaming about canoes.
    There's that French girl on the banks I can smell her.
    Laundry day!
    Ow, motherfuckers.
    Fuck off I mean it.
    Ow.
    Laundry day says Ant. Christ he annoys me. What is Wink
doing over there.
    Let me sleep, let me sleep, let me sleep.

Give me a smoke I say.
    Chuckie can be relied on. How many times are we going to
walk down this hill for laundry.
    I don't know says Ant.
    About thirty says Chuck.
    The cigarette's helping and I blow some smoke into Ant's face,
he's pissing me off today.
    Ant, man, do you remember the bullshit in your mouth last
night.
    I don't want to talk about it. You were the drunk one,
Mr, Mr I was the Drunk One, fuck. You were hurling
everywhere.
    I won't push it.
    No one's ever gonna know me says Chuck.
    I'll let Chuck push it.
    Do you remember saying that, Antony. About eighty-six times.
We were all a little drunk. Right. So, Jules, man: tell. A little Fall
action. Barfing.
    Barfing I say. None of your business.
    You had your hand down her pants by the bathroom says Ant.
Everyone went to the bathroom.
    I'm thinking about blowing more smoke in his face.
    Nobody saw it says Chuck.
    I can't believe you barfed on my shoes says Ant.

★   ★   ★

76

I just want peace and quiet. I just want to be alone. I just want to be alone with Fall and hold her beautiful hand. There's peace there in her palm and we won't have to talk.

Chapel: Bong!
La la la la la, England, Jesus, Canada, Jesus, Jesus. I'm gonna leave this chapel and Niles is gonna point to my hair and say cut it. Someone is gonna fart on a pew, someone will joke P.U., and we'll sing out of tune cause we're jokers. I'm so fuckin tired and bored and I wish I was back at Dad's tonight.
I just need to sleep.
La la la la la, Canada, Jesus, Jesus.
Julius says Niles. Cut that please by next weekend.

Wink's here.
Hey I say.
Hey.
Hot. Bright. It's too bright in here. He's a quiet guy.
I just want to sleep.
Mind if I turn off the big light I say.
No he says.
I'm tired. Big run. Why do I have to be on the top bunk, it's hard work, oof, wait. Is this my bed.
Chuck came in here looking for you he says.
Leave me alone. Please, leave me alone.
What is this fuckin feeling I'm like a bruise and a scared old man, bitch bitch.
Ah, he's turned off the lights.
Nice.
I'll ask him about his weekend.
He stayed here all weekend. Fuck that.
Noel down there's a lonely guy. He's a quiet guy.
In comes fuckin Chuckie with a bang. Chuck and Ant and a joke about cocks, and I'm so, very, tired, of, them. I just want to relax. I just don't want to think. I just wish.
Now I've got to close the door.
Ow.
Nice and quiet in here. That was nice of Noel.
Should I jack off or ask him a question.

So you stayed here all weekend I say.

Fall took my smokes. Does Noel know Fall. He must. Why don't I know this guy.

Does he know my dad. My dad's the guy who says that Canada is weak. That's how they know him. Funny.

Funny funny funny.

You been to my dad's place, Noel.

No.

You should try sneaking into it, man. Try it at three in the morning I say.

My dad's my friend I'm thinking.

I love my dad.

What's this feeling it's like guilt and I wanna tell everyone I love them.

It's hot. I've got to sleep.

I need to talk.

Can you keep secrets down there, Noel.

I love Fall so much it makes me ache and want to cry. I feel like I'm gonna cry in front of Wink, come on.

Don't don't don't.

She has eyes that are so sad and smiling. I stand above her and she looks at me and it's like she's asking me but she's my answer.

I want to give her everything, take all of her and pour those eyes, those legs, that Fall all down my dusty throat.

You know Fall I say. Those eyes, right.

Everybody knows Fall. Everybody loves her.

I dream about her eyes I say.

I feel like I can talk to Noel.

These fuckin guys I say. I don't know. We were at this party and Ant's hitting on everyone Chuck's hitting on and Chuck's always complaining about small spaces and the party seemed like a small space I say.

Only three bedrooms I'm thinking and this was the fuckin Mayor's place.

Maybe it was too crowded.

Why am I angry about a party.

Lots of pretty chicks there I say.

There's a lot of beauty he says.

Is that what he said. What does that mean. There *is* a lot of beauty.

There's a lot of beauty I say.

Try saying that at a party.

Why don't you go to parties, man.

Why's it so quiet in here.

I don't like not connecting with people he says.

I could have done more with Fall. I should have.

Who wants to kiss my barfy lips.

I could grow up. I should grow up.

I should stop calling Noel down there Wink.

You're a smart guy I say.

He is.

I feel weird today, man. Hungover. I love my girlfriend.

Why did I just say that.

I know he says.

How does he know.

Because you've seen her eyes I say.

I know he says.

I feel sort of scared I say and I don't know what I mean or why I said it.

I'm scared of Monday, the world opening its grumpy eyes all wide.

I wish I'd seen Fall before bed. I wish she'd given me one of those hugs and pressed against my heart right here. She could walk into this room and climb up here, she'd giggle and I'd help her up. Nice warm smile and I kiss her quiet laugh. Long body up here beside me and her hand all sly, and it does what it wants and it wants to tickle touch wander and slide below the magic line. Yes please.

Fuck, I am aching.

I'll have a quick one.

He's falling asleep.

I'll just quickly . . .

Woman in fur. Where's my woman in fur and the big round tits.

Sometimes people surprise you he says.

Shit, he felt it. These beds. I should have stayed on the bottom bunk, you feel the top move but you don't feel the bottom, not so much.

We all jack off who cares.

What did he say.

It's just a lazy eye he says.

What.

I think people think it's something more serious. It's just a muscle problem he's saying. I can't control the eye.

OK I say.

And the eye and eyelid go into spasms. I know it makes people uncomfortable he says.

His voice is shaky.

I find it hard he says.

That's the saddest thing I ever heard I'm thinking.

Why am I still holding my cock.

Why did I call him Wink.

He's a sad and handsome guy.

I think it's cool I say. I don't know what to say. I think you're a really handsome guy I say, cause he is.

He is.

Goodnight he says.

I've got to end this day.

Fuckin A it's Monday and I'll eat French toast.

I was talking with Sarah last night says Fall. Up late. She was crying.

Why.

She's looking for love. She's not in love. She doesn't want the year to end. She doesn't want to lose me as a friend. She feels dumb in class.

Is that all I say.

She misses her parents.

Yeah. Everybody needs a holiday I say.

It's only the second week she says.

A ND SUCH A friendship developed. From that Monday onwards we were room-mates, secret sharers, a united front against the troubles of the world. Something made me get up late with him – I slept in, happily, for the first time ever at that school – and we showered together after everyone else. Julius stood under one shower facing outwards, I stood two showers over facing the wall. We finished at the same time and he tossed me my towel. He beat me back to the sink to brush his teeth in the room, but I didn't mind. I dried my hair behind him, both of us looking in the mirror, and that became our routine. Every morning. I stood in such a way that when I looked at us in the mirror my bad eye would be hidden by Julius's head in front of it. There we were in the reflection: friends.

Nothing much happened that week and I spent the weekend alone.

The contents of Edward's chest were discovered to be the largest collection of pornographic magazines anyone had ever seen. He had brought them from Amsterdam. They were disseminated.

I thought of filthy Amsterdam.

My summer with Meg taught me how different two countries can be, even those that purport to be so similar as Australia and Canada. I realise now as an adult that the globe's concept of nationhood is a simple recognition that every person is a country and there are private customs we should all respect. There are certain people who can never be together.

★   ★   ★

The more friendly Julius and I got in our room, the more I wondered how it would transform our interaction downstairs, during the day, when classes were on and the school was full. We were in Algebra, English and Philosophy together. It was a small school, so it was hard not to see everyone several times a day. I generally kept my head down when I was walking between classes – not down, exactly: I looked forward to a space beyond the halls. And I have to admit that when I heard many conversations as I passed I felt contempt, no interest in joining. I had trained myself to be oblivious to possible greetings.

Things didn't really change for a while. Lining up for the Dining Hall once, I felt a hand on my shoulder and Julius smiled and walked by.

I spent another weekend alone.

Julius was sometimes unaware of what belonged to him and what belonged to me. He used my comb occasionally, for example.

On the weekends when he was away, I, in the same spirit, wore his clothes. Usually just in the room. When it was quiet on the Flats I would close the door and enjoy having the time to look through his clothes and possessions. His jackets weren't especially fine or expensive.

I wore the shirts that smelled like Fall. It was somewhat unsettling at first to see myself in the mirror, perhaps the same disappointment one feels when seeing a new actor step into a role that another had long embodied. But I grew used to it. I think that children of diplomats become good mimics, having spent so many days adapting to other cultures.

I could do a good Julius.

I couldn't sleep so I wandered the halls. Everyone was in his own bed, in his own box, with no idea that I was outside. The EXIT signs hummed in the halls. Edward was in his room alone that weekend. I held my hand an inch from his door. I could have done anything. I stared at my arm and realised how much it had grown.

WHEN I'M HAPPY I run.
When it's sunny I run.

When the leaves are on the street I run.

When there's everything to think about, or nothing and I'm bored, I jack off, or I run.

When it's five o'clock, one hour and thirty-five minutes before we line up in the hall in front of the Hall for a meal of slop or sometimes good potatoes, I'll probably go for a run.

When Coach says run, I run.

I'm thinking about the dark red belly of the world and how I want to know it. I'm thinking about the future and its mouth and it drives me crazy that there's nowhere anywhere to settle for a cuddle with Fall.

My room.

Her room.

Dad's place.

Common rooms.

Her mom's high place in the High Tech Hills.

I get the car from William and the back seat feels like a place for fast fingers, I love it, but where's the warmth for a cuddle.

We should rent a hotel sometime I say.

Yeah.

With red rooms.

OK.

Or curtains. Red curtains. I don't know.

And big white towels she says.

You bet.

You're on.

I'm serious. We'll find a red hotel and lie there getting to know each other.

Mmm she says.

I love your mmms.

It's a serious issue. Parents don't understand. The school doesn't understand. A young, attractive couple needs room to lie down. Nothing dirty or filthy, just some space to understand each other.

We need to understand each other. We can't keep moving or we'll slip away. If she's over there and I'm over here, we can love each other but we won't understand.

How can we be close here.

It's a pretty serious issue.

You look good I say, hands out at each other because we both want more.

I believe we should skip Algebra and smoke some American tobacco I say.

I believe you may be right she says. But I like Algebra.

I'm all for Algebra I say. But when was the last time we skipped a class together.

Last year.

Too long.

Maybe.

We're like an old couple. Last year. Who talks about last year. We should have kids.

How would we do that she says.

I'll show you.

After Algebra.

We should talk sometime.

I want to talk she says.

I want to get that hotel room.

And talk.

And then some.

Our anniversary's in December she says. It's only a couple of months away.

No way I say.

One year she says.

So we've gotta get a hotel room.

Let's go to Algebra she says.

K.

She's wearing her red leather belt.

She looks good in everything except that sweater with the pompoms she looks like a poodle.

I have a hard-on.

I love cuddling with you she says.

Me too I say.

I want my cock to go down.

Sort of.

This toolshed is sovereign American property I say.

Yeah she says.

Did you see the marines watching us come in here.

No she says.

They did I say. We can't stay long.

We've gotta be back anyway, J.

Yeah.

Bed she says.

I have such a hard-on.

I will think about complicated things.

I will be smart.

A gentleman.

A human with no cock.

How do you turn a cow into a red leather belt.

What are you thinking about she says.

I don't know I say. Agriculture.

Are you she says.

She's looking at me.

We're sitting in the gardener's shed I'm thinking. I'm looking at that bag of dirt and I'm thinking about the bag of dirt and she's looking at me like I'm interesting which is funny.

She's touching my face.

Agriculture she says.

I don't know. Vermont I say. It's funny thinking about home you know. Growing up in Vermont. I had fun there.

Yeah she says.

She knows all my stories.

But it was small I say. Right. I was thinking when Dad said he was going to Canada that it would be this big open place. I mean. Dad took me to Montreal when I was ten and all I remember was getting an electric shock, right. On an escalator. I knew Canada wasn't just a big open place. Right. But I also knew it would be bigger than Vermont. I was pretty excited about coming here.

Look at her.

I am excited about being here I say.

Kiss.

Bang.

On the lips.

But look at where we are I say. Right. I was excited about trying out boarding school even. You know. I thought it would all be this big new world. And it totally is. I mean. I didn't know you, I didn't know Canada. But we're on the floor of the toolshed.

I know she says. It's weird.

It's weird I say. It's this feeling like I came here because I thought it would be cool to see a bigger world and we're actually in this tiny space, and this space is supposed to be America and Canada's out there and we can't go out there together because we actually live in a little school. I can't get my little head around it. Right.

I know she says. But we're here she says.

Yeah.

We're here together she says.

Yeah.

We're hugging.

My mind's too fast to think what I'm thinking.

I might put my hand down her pants.

Stay like this for a while she says.

Pink and blue

JULIUS TOLD ME that when he and Fall first got together she wouldn't let him kiss her. They pressed foreheads together and whenever their lips came near she made a quick mhn mhn sound . . . no . . . no . . . and he said it drove him crazy. But they held on to each other, kept their foreheads together and looked in each other's eyes, so close that Fall's two eyes looked like one. And Julius said that you'd think it was a tease, you'd think a girl who wouldn't kiss would take a lifetime to go further once you kissed her. But it wasn't a tease. Kisses were important to her. He said it never annoyed him. They walked around school grounds and stopped, got close, walked again, and stopped. He said he had never paid much attention to kisses before, just to where they were heading. But when he kissed Fall that night it wasn't just a signal or a relief, it was a loss of bones and a jump that wouldn't land.

I remember starting to picture their kisses from her point of view, enjoying a new perspective.

He rarely said anything in class. He would respond if a teacher asked him something directly, but otherwise he was quiet. I was often impressed by his responses. People occasionally thought Julius was vaguely stupid because his answers were brief and oblique, but I knew how perceptive he was.

I can't think of examples offhand.

'We're going to Dad's for lunch. Wanna come?'

We technically weren't supposed to leave school grounds

during the day – everyone was supposed to eat in the Dining Hall.

I didn't hesitate. We left through the door beside the gym. Chuck ran and caught up with us. 'It's lamb stew today,' said Julius, referring to the menu at school. 'Chuck here found a Band-Aid in his stew once.' Whenever lamb stew was on the menu Julius and Chuck had a pact to eat somewhere else, usually Julius's place.

The walk to his father's residence was beautiful. Sutton had the grandest houses in the city, and many of them, like Julius's, had been turned into ambassadors' residences. I felt a little anxious about being off school grounds, but I dismissed it. 'I'm eighteen years old' was a refrain I kept repeating through that year.

Chuck gave Julius a cigarette, put his pack in his pocket and then remembered he hadn't offered me one.

'No thanks,' I said. I don't think I said much more until we got to the residence. I had only heard about it, and when I finally saw it I was amazed at the size of the house, and its grounds. I asked Julius how large the property was and he said he didn't know. I caught a look from Chuck that suggested there was nothing interesting about the size of houses.

The property was surrounded by a stone-and-iron fence, with cameras pointing everywhere. We walked through the main gate and Julius gestured to the RCMP.

Chuck said, 'I want steak and fries.' He apparently always told the police what he wanted for his meal.

I saw a marine stationed near the front door.

We went in through the staff entrance and into the kitchen. The chef was a French-Canadian woman named Marie-Claude. When she met me I noticed that she felt no need to hide her curiosity about my eye. I in turn was impressed by her moustache. Julius said 'this is Noel' and 'you know Chuckie'. She had a nice smile and said, 'Trois steak et frites, avec un Band-Aid.' I could tell that she loved Julius.

We stayed in the kitchen. I saw no more of the house. I was trying to settle into how casual the event was. Julius inviting me out of the blue. Chuck not showing any obvious curiosity or disapproval of my company. The steak wasn't as good as I thought it would be. Marie-Claude turned her attention to us as we were eating and said, 'OK?' She stared at my eye as I ate. It usually goes into spasms when I chew.

I wondered whether Marie-Claude was the kind of woman who liked to be asked for second helpings. Julius asked me if I wanted more.

'Please.'

'Noel is beefing up,' he said.

Chuck looked at my shoulders.

'You play rugby?' he asked.

'Not really.'

'There's a game this Saturday. We play pickup with local teams. You could play prop.'

'Ant plays our prop,' said Julius.

'And he sucks,' said Chuck.

'He doesn't suck. He just wins by filth. Pure dirt. He puts his fingers in eyes and assholes.'

'Beware Ant's finger,' said Chuck.

'You could be a backup prop for when Ant gets his head knocked off by whoever he gooses.'

'I've never really played,' I said.

Chuck gave me a suit-yourself shrug. I wanted to push the table across the room. I liked the idea of rugby, of running at someone's shoulders. 'I'll play,' I said.

Neither of them said 'good' or 'great' because that's not what they were like. Marie-Claude gave us three more steaks with less friendliness and we walked back to school.

A strange suspense lingered through the rest of the day. Was this a new world, and how should I prepare for it?

'You can borrow my cleats,' said Julius, 'I'll wear my soccer ones.'

I was nervous and didn't say much. The game was on school grounds and the opponents were the Ottawa Irish – mostly middle-aged men.

'These guys like violence,' Julius said when we got to the pitch. 'They're bald and full of resentment.'

They were all solid, and I remember thinking that the hair on their legs looked unashamedly pubic.

I had no idea how to play rugby. I had spent the rest of that week doing research. Invented at Rugby School. *Tom Brown's*

Schooldays. Game of ruffians played by gentlemen. I had never liked watching it in Australia, but that was Rugby League, a vulgar version. We were going to play Rugby Union, and my role as prop was to anchor the scrum. 'Stay low and push' was the advice I got from everyone. Julius told me to tape my ears and put Vaseline on my face and I thought he was joking.

I had expected to be nervous throughout but once the game started I felt absorbed and hungry. I focused on Ant, who was playing my position. I thought I could at least mimic his movements.

We learned about the strength of older men, the power of fat and disappointment. Speed was the crucial element in those games for us. Get the ball out to the wing, to Julius, who could run like the goal of upright evolution. Every time he got the ball it moved to surprising places. But if we couldn't get the ball to him there was a swamp of pain around the scrum. The men would push our team back, stomp us into the ground.

I realised that Ant wasn't very good. I noted that his legs in shorts were not as big as mine. He laughed whenever the scrum fell down, the laugh of someone pretending not to be embarrassed. And I saw how he cheated. It was hard to spot, but the aftermath was obvious. One of the old men would shout *who the fuck was that* and push a few of the St Ebury boys. It happened a couple of times in the first half. Ant would always be at the back of the fallen scrum, having wriggled out, smirking and pretending to be innocent.

The more we fell, the more I felt from the sidelines a gathering sense of injustice. We were young and should have been strong. I felt the comfort of being mad, of the soft green frame of that field that allowed us to be honest and infuriated. I never got to play that day. In the second half, one of the forwards from the Irish emerged from the scrum holding Ant by the collar and punched him in the face with a fist as fat as a butcher's. Everyone from both teams ran towards the fight. All of us from the sidelines. I had never punched a face before. I never forgot the feeling of how a nose gives way.

'You should hear the songs sometimes,' Ant told me. 'Everyone singing.' His forehead was swollen above the eye socket and all of us were drunk by 5 p.m.

I had almost missed the party. I walked off the pitch alone, before everything had settled, and was back up in the Flats, showering. I wondered if the blood on my hand was my own, but when it was clean all I saw was a bruising knuckle.

In the room I found Julius wearing his rugby shirt with jeans. He hadn't showered. 'You coming?' he said.

The ritual was to gather at the Earl of Sussex pub which was a cab ride from St Ebury. The pubs required us to be nineteen, but the Earl would serve anyone who seemed convincingly mature.

Normally both teams would gather, but since that game was called off after the fight it was only St Ebury boys who met. Actually only four of us.

'The songs are fuckin hilarious,' Ant said. He started to sing a rugby song but nobody joined him. Chuck stared at him and asked if he had washed his fingers. 'What's wrong with you?' Chuck said.

'They're animals. Those old guys just want to hurt us. So I humiliated one of them. A few of them.'

I couldn't help laughing. Not because I found Ant amusing. I was simply confused. Five pints of beer in me on a Saturday afternoon, sitting there with Julius and his friends, a game I never played but learned to love. There was a sense of new momentum, of pistons urging me forward.

'Noel here got a piece of one of them,' Ant said. 'You guys see that?'

Chuck said yes and Julius shook his head, and I was holding the table, I remember.

'Boom,' said Ant.

'It was an ugly game,' said Julius.

Ant said Julius always said that when he didn't get the ball. 'It was a battle,' he said.

'I do want to know why you stick your finger up their asses,' Chuck said. 'Can you confide in me, as a friend?'

'It unsettles them,' I suggested.

'Exactly,' Ant said.

Chuck and Julius stared at us.

I started to feel my head spinning and when I closed my eyes I saw that man's head snap back after I smashed his nose. I looked at Chuck's sideburns and found them annoying. They looked affected. I wanted to tell him he was only pretending to be a man.

Out of the blue he announced that he wanted to be a journalist.

Ant said, 'That's fucked.'

And Chuck said, 'Why?'

Ant said, 'I don't know.'

I kept being frightened that I was only eighteen, that the waiter would eventually turn to me and say, 'You're too young.' And then I felt angry. I wanted to declare that I was a man.

Ant started touching my earlobes and said, 'You've got thick earlobes. They're soft but they're thick, eh?'

Julius had a streak of mud under one side of his jawbone. When he turned one way he looked gaunt. Haunted. He was my friend and I wanted to know what was wrong, but it was only mud.

'Leave the man's ears alone,' he said.

I kept to myself that evening.

YOU WEREN'T HERE in grade 9 says Chuckie. You never saw that thing with him and Will Anderson.

Right I say. I'm hungry.

You didn't know Will Anderson he says.

Right.

He was only here for half a year. Him and Noel were roommates. And a couple of other guys. He was annoying, Anderson, you know, kind of . . . he looked older than he was and he tried to be all fuckin tough. Dad owns Anderson Ford.

Right I say. I don't know what Anderson Ford is.

And he was . . . you know, except for me and Ant, he kind of thought he was better and bigger than anyone in grade 9. He bumped into me once outside the library or the gym and he, you know, squared himself up and I started laughing. And he smiles like he wasn't squaring himself up and he's, like, slapping my back without slapping my back. There's a word for that. When I'm a journalist I'm gonna use it. Pfff he says.

There's tobacco on his lips cause he's smoking a rollie.

So he was the guy who first called Wink Wink.

OK.

Always. Wink this, Wink that.

It's a mean name.

Yeah.

And funny.

It is he says. And Noel, he was always quiet about it. Didn't complain. You know that way, he looks sort of past everything, right.

So you couldn't tell whether it bothered him or not, and Anderson kept at it, kept pushing it in a really obvious way. And in gym class, you know, he would fire a basketball at Noel's head and say Wink blinked. That sort of shit.

Mm.

And I don't know whether Anderson would have lasted or not. One of these fuckin losers who's proud of being at St Ebury. Dad with his car dealership. And it's pretty obvious that he's never gonna fit in. What they call an arriviste, if you did your homework.

You're a genius.

So one day. Pfff. One of those weird witches' days when everything's happening on the Flats, me and Ant are tossing the Frisbee down the hall. Fling, fling, and out comes everyone from different rooms. And zitty Chris, you know, Tim, he's walking innocently down the hall and out comes Anderson. He takes off his stinking gym shoe and shoves it in Chris's face. He puts Chris in a headlock and makes him smell his shoe, you know, and Chris is struggling and all the zits in his face are popping and bleeding.

Nice.

So whatever. Another dumb day. Anderson's laughing like a moron and a couple of others are smiling and Chris is bleeding and away he walks and I toss Ant the Frisbee. Anderson's walking around looking for mischief. And there's Noel down the hall, looking on in his weird way. And Anderson starts walking towards him saying Wink this Wink that. You know, Hey, Wink, what *aren't* you looking at. He walks up to him and does the old shoulder push. And, fuck, have you noticed how much Wink has built up.

Yeah. I told you.

Yeah. Beef! Eh. He was *nothing* like that in grade 9. He was a little guy. So Anderson walks up to him, does the shoulder push, and Noel falls back a mile, like a comedy fall, you know, like he's falling and falling and it's funny, and finally he falls and it's, you know, pretty sad. And Anderson's laughing his *ass* off when Noel falls. Crack goes the tail bone and Anderson's in hysterics. And he's standing over Wink and laughing. He tries to get up and Anderson holds him down. And Wink shuffles back and gets up, Anderson does the shoulder push, then Noel does the shoulder push and we all think, here we go, and next thing you know

Anderson is popping him in the eye. In his *bad* eye, you know. Pop, pop, and Wink is just kind of taking it. Ducking a little, you know, flinching, but not knowing what to do. And Anderson's getting a taste for it, you know, he's popping Noel harder, always going for the eye. It made you want to cringe, you know. I remember squeezing the Frisbee and thinking, what the fuck. Should we step in. And a Prefect comes by, what's his . . . Haffey. He comes by and shouts hey! And those two, you know, Anderson barely looks over, gives Reece another, both of them in their own world, right, and Noel, skinny Noel, he grabs Anderson's arm . . .

Hm . . .

I'm not finished. He grabs Anderson's arm after the punch, and he fuckin chomps. He takes the arm, right, holds it and he bites right into Anderson. And this is not a bite, Julius. This is fuckin *feeding*. Haffey runs over and I swear to Christ, Wink is attached to Anderson's *fore*arm and Anderson is screaming like a fuckin seagull or something. Screaming. Because Noel Reece has bitten like a coin's worth of flesh from Anderson's forearm.

Fuck.

Yes. Flesh. We're all looking, and there's your room-mate with this swelling, crazy fuckin eye and a mouthful of Anderson's, you know: body. And Haffey the Prefect's screaming *that's enough!* And everyone finally rushes in. And it was a pleasure seeing Anderson all pale, sort of shocked into reality, you know. But I'm telling you, J. Ever since that day. You know, it all blew over. There was talk about kicking out Anderson, kicking out Wink, and Anderson's dad was gonna sue the school, supposedly, and try to press charges. Because, you can't repair that, right. A piece of his arm's missing forever. A small piece, but it's not like it would grow back. But everyone saw it was Anderson's fault, seeing him pound at Noel's eye. You don't do that, right. So I guess it blew over and Anderson left at Christmas.

OK.

But the point is, ever since that day, there's something about Noel. You know, man.

Noel is cool I say. He's a nice sad guy.

There's something I don't trust, J. You had to see it. I mean, fuck, I was, whatever, fourteen, fifteen, and I'd never seen someone take a bite of someone. It was pretty fuckin spooky. But it wasn't just that. And it wasn't the look on his face. Look at your forearm, man. It's tough, right. Imagine how hard it would be to bite a piece off that. Right.

OK.

But it's not even that. It's just, right away, you know, Noel is completely back to normal. As normal as he is. Quiet as usual. Calm. Eh. In class he was, you know, he's sitting there the next few days with his eye all pink and blue like a baboon's ass, and he's answering questions as calm and fuckin smart as ever.

He's smart.

Yeah. But it's like it was all normal for him. Like he just forgot about it.

Or like he's just sad I'm saying. The guy was beating him up because of his eye. He's a nice guy, Chuckie. He's smart and fine and sad.

Mm.

It's true. He's one of those mysteries. You should get to know him.

I don't trust him.

Fff.

And he's gotta be on roids or something. Horse balls. Look at the size of him, man. Check him out in the shower.

I know.

Pow. Small cock though, eh.

Is it.

Tiny. He always hides it. I don't trust him.

He should play rugby.

Maybe.

Replace Ant.

You think.

Yeah.

Maybe.

HE SAID SHE helped him with Math.
He said, 'She looks, like, elegant.'

He said she cried easily and saw things he didn't see.

He said one night while we ate pizza in the room that she didn't like pizza, didn't eat much at all except chocolate and small delicious things, 'you know, like, I don't know: goat's cheese'.

He told me her room at school and room at home were neat and I remember wondering how he saw her room at school.

He said, 'If life is short I fuckin love her, and if it's long, who knows.'

And I got annoyed sometimes, wondering what he could possibly know about love, when love was what I felt for her.

He said he had a girlfriend once who had a problem with her jaw but with Fall the blow jobs were amazing.

I could feel close to both of them sometimes, enter both their lives when he described certain scenes, but some of his crass intimacies I could never bear, never quite believe. I could feel happy for both of them, stand outside and watch with pure and honest pleasure. I could think these are two beautiful people, and knowing about their lives is a privilege. Her mother had a dog that lay on Julius's shoes whenever he took them off. He liked standing in her mother's gigantic kitchen, drinking ginger ale and looking out at acres of distance while the dog was near the door keeping his shoes warm. Every night a new glimpse of his green good luck and I felt so involved with him and their world; but sometimes he spoke of her in a way that could have nothing to do with Fall's real self. Pictures of her that I knew she never could have intended to project. Fall the girl he had sex with in his father's limousine was not the Fall I wanted or the Fall she wanted to be. I had faith in that.

I watched Julius play soccer sometimes. My toes got cold. I remember the smell of the leaves. I remember black mud, black-limbed trees, darkening autumn days, and Julius a relentless force on the field, finding a way like water around stones. I remember thinking that the way to reach a goal was by finding fissures between people that no one else could see.

Fall stood on the sidelines with friends. I watched her smile from the corner of my eye. I started to time my arrival at the games so that I could stand near her group. I stood with Ant one day, five metres away from Fall who was with her friend Sarah. Ant was sizing up the opposing team and remarked that their goalie was fat. He said it loudly enough for Fall and Sarah to hear. I said to Ant that having a fat goalie was like having an oversized glove in baseball. A few minutes later Ant turned to the girls and said, 'That fat fuckin goalie's like an oversized glove, in baseball.'

Julius scored two goals that game. Ant was to my right, Sarah to his, and Fall was furthest from me. When Julius scored, Ant and Sarah hooted and danced. I smiled. Fall smiled. I caught her looking over at me and it was the first time our eyes ever met.

I said out of the blue, loudly to everyone, that there was no chance that Julius would score again. Fall looked at me with half a smile and half a frown.

'That's not very nice,' she said.

'It's just a feeling,' I said.

'He's right,' Ant said. 'There's no fuckin chance.'

Fall gave him a mock-angry slap on the shoulder and looked over at me flirtatiously.

'If he scores,' I said, 'I'll pick up his laundry for the rest of the year.'

I liked reminding her that I lived in Julius's room. I figured she might eventually want to know what it was like to live with him. He and I had a routine of cleaning each other's backs before bed with a cotton ball soaked in rubbing alcohol. We both had a problem with pimples on our shoulders. I knew that Fall must have shared all sorts of secrets with Julius, but there was much she didn't know: that space which he and I shared, that yellow light and the darkness in the corners while we cleaned each other's back. I knew for a fact that they had never spent an entire night together, that she didn't know what it was like to feel his feet land by her bed in the morning.

'I'll tell him what you said,' she said.

I smiled like he would.

Julius didn't score again.

It was my first conversation with Fall.

Julius left his sweaty soccer clothes on the foot of my bed that evening. They were so wet that they soaked through the blanket and sheets. I knew he wasn't thinking, that it hadn't been intentional. Later that night while he was out I filled a mug with water and poured it over the foot of his bed. He didn't say anything when he went to sleep.

I often looked at the particle board underneath his bunk while I lay in bed. I thought of dragging my teeth along it somehow, of what it might feel like to get splinters in my gums.

I enjoy the privacy of pain; the knowledge that in this world of sameness and institutionalised experience, there can be a sensation which no one else will ever exactly understand.

After talking to her for the first time I felt somewhat emboldened, more at ease with showing her who I was. I tried to be spontaneously amusing. It was a while before I spent time alone with her. When she and Julius were talking I would sometimes join them. We never talked about anything substantial.

Other, minor things rush back to me.

I approached them one afternoon, seeing them laugh together. It seemed like a moment when I wouldn't be intruding.

'Hey, guys.'

'Hey,' she said.

Julius looked hard at me. 'I'll talk to you later in the room,' he said. 'OK?'

I felt quite stung.

There was no perceivable change to her face, so as I walked

away I did wonder whether he really had been rude or whether it was something I should simply brush off.

On another occasion I stole his lighter. I never smoked, but I wanted to take it. He mentioned its absence later. I was curious to see what he would do when something he liked was lost. I suggested that someone had stolen it. He didn't seem to mind at all. 'I've got lots of them,' he said. From then on I was careful to keep it in my left front trouser pocket, where I held it as I walked.

I remember also on another day I waited on the sideline until after a game, hoping to share a moment with Fall nearby. Julius had scored, as usual, and enjoyed the customary praise of his friends. Someone said 'You must be tired' and he said 'I'm OK'. It occurred to me suddenly that this might be an opportunity to beat him in a race. 'How about I race you to the end of the field,' I said.

We ran and were even for a while. I was in my suit, of course. He started laughing and pulling ahead. I was trying so hard that I could barely stay on my feet. He was still laughing when I reached him at the end of the field, and I pretended to share his amusement. I suppose everyone else saw him laughing.

Things began to relax for a time. I think of a man easing into a chair, loosening his belt, dozing off for a few moments. Dreams that disappear as quickly as they come and leave no trace but relaxation. The middle of the term was very peaceful.

I would be lying if I said that I told Julius a lot about myself. I tended to be quiet and wait for him to start a conversation. I occasionally mentioned things that I was reading, passages I found interesting.

Various people would come in and out of the room. I liked it when Julius and I were considered a corporate entity, when people would say, 'I went by your room, but Julius wasn't there.'

I was able to settle into the TV room, even, as long as Julius was there. I grew more comfortable hearing that Fall was about to arrive. I usually left them alone.

Ant wrote on me with toothpaste one night while I slept and I spent the next two days with the word ANUS faintly burned into my forehead.

Julius told me it was Ant who did it. Ant said Julius did it. Julius said he wouldn't have known how to spell anus. That made me wonder whether Ant really could have done it. I asked Ant to spell anus for me and he looked away from my forehead and said, 'C-H-U-C-K.'

That prompted Chuck to say, 'It was Ant, he did it at three in the morning after we smoked a joint and he laughed about it for the next eight hours.'

'It's how it happened,' said Julius.

Ant was smirking.

I thought it was funny. I felt welcomed somehow. I was at the oven of anger for a second, just when I washed off the tooth-paste and the letters were at their reddest. But I knew there was friendliness in the joke. I had a dream that Fall was sitting at a table across from me with no expression at all on her face and I saw myself, my eye in a spasm and red like the letters on my forehead, and in the dream I cried but Julius woke me up saying, 'You were laughing in your sleep, you fuckin nut,' and I spent the next waking moments wondering why Fall's face was impassive in the dream.

In the past I never contemplated public retaliation, but some-thing had changed. It was partly that I knew Ant was a friend.

I snuck into Chuck and Ant's room with a bowl of lukewarm water and tried to dip Ant's fingers into it while he slept. I'd heard that would make someone urinate in his sleep. I couldn't get the bowl near his fingers.

The next night I lay my head on my pillow and found that my pillowcase had been filled with shaving cream. I stayed awake for a long time and dreamt about cutting a poem into Ant's face with a razor.

We smirked at each other for weeks, wondering what would happen next.

Julius told me that he felt a sweet sadness with Fall sometimes and a feeling of completeness and comfort and yearning like his body held a family dreaming at midnight. I can't always remember his nonsense verbatim. As close as we sometimes felt, I occasion-ally thought I was losing him, or like there was something that would always keep us apart.

He was planning an anniversary evening with Fall. I felt

breathless when he told me they had been together for a year. Time was running away from me.

One night in November Ant taped down the nozzle of a can of aerosol deodorant and threw it into the room while Julius and I slept. We took our revenge together.

My brother and I used to play together, before our minds latched onto the interests that pull children apart. We had friends in common and played a game called Ditch, where someone would shout, for example, 'Ditch Noel!', and everyone would run away from me. I would have to catch them all, one by one, as they hid in various places. It was like hide-and-seek, but with a greater sense of abandonment. I didn't mind being ditched, but I preferred running and hiding.

That giddy feeling of mischief and suspense was predominantly what I felt when we retaliated against Ant. I was excited and nervous, and felt a pure, childish anticipation.

'A flood,' is what Julius proposed. 'So he forgets what life is like on dry land.'

We wanted to get him while he slept. In every room there was a large plastic garbage can with a handle for lifting. If you took out the garbage bag, the can could be used as a large bucket, holding about ten litres of water. Julius borrowed garbage cans from other people's rooms so that altogether we had four of them.

Ant slept on the bottom bunk. The idea was for me to sneak in and tie a sheet around his arms as quickly as I could while he slept. It didn't matter if I failed because we would soak him anyway, but we thought it would be better torture if we restrained his arms.

Julius told Chuck our plan in advance to prevent him from shouting out if he woke up when we came in to get Ant. Julius also bought ten litres of Coke to put in one of the buckets instead of water.

We carried the full buckets to various points in the hallway and left one outside Ant's room. I got a sheet and opened the door. I could tell they were both asleep. Julius stood close behind me with a bucket of water which made quiet plips and slapped the carpet when it spilled. I felt like giggling. I remember looking at Ant and holding a rolled sheet and the closer I got the more a sort of angry smile stretched across my mind. I leaned over his body and pressed the sheet firmly over his chest and arms. He didn't wake up and I thought about how stupid he looked with his mouth slightly open. In one quick movement I lifted his torso and tied the sheet together sharply behind his back. The honesty of his scream was unexpected. He was upright and, as he was saying 'what the fu—', Julius dumped his bucket of water on him.

Ant was soaked and the water made the knot tighter behind his back. He squirmed out of his bunk to chase Julius out of the room. I came up behind him as he ran and soaked him with the bucket I'd left outside his door. He turned on me shouting 'untie this fuckin sheet' and I ran around the corner. Julius turned around and ran behind Ant and poured the bucket of Coke over him.

I was gone around the corner and didn't see what happened next. One of the House Masters had woken up and caught Julius with an empty bucket in his hand next to a sticky brown Ant. They said the first thing he said was 'Are you two not eighteen?'

I had torn a muscle in one of Ant's shoulders when I tied the sheet and it took weeks to heal.

When love is missing there is no longer blood in thoughts or words, there is nothing that flirts and says *come here*. There's a glint in the eye of a world with love, and even if the eye is false, the owner untrue, there's a necessary charm, an illusion that's impossible to bear the absence of. When Fall went missing, love went missing, and life no longer smiled its invitation at any of us.

Julius's mother had killed herself when he was seven. He said she had been sad since he was born. He didn't remember much about her except that she cried a lot and that his father loved and cheated on her. Julius said he remembered walking into their big house on a Sunday, and he probably only imagines it was a Sunday, and the house took him in like he was a breath before a sob, he said. And his father taught him to respect it, even after her sadness took her away. He said his dad was funny and full of life but that there was a sadness in the middle of everything and he taught you to know it.

I remember thinking when I was older that the things I'd learned about Julius's father seemed at odds with his public persona. Apparently his wife's suicide won him affection when he ran for

Governor of his state. I remember wondering why a man who seemed to embrace sadness and fun would become famous for hard-line policies, for a public obsession with defence. That obsession with unexpected evil, even in the minds of balanced people.

Of course, what I did that year would no doubt have confirmed his belief in self-protection.

Julius said, 'Fall has a bit of the sadness.'

Apples

I LIKE APPLES.

I don't know what the simplest thing in the world is but I love it and I know I can taste it. The simplest thing in the world is something you can eat or maybe eat while you're fucking but that's complicated.

I fuckin love spaghetti with butter and a Coke.

Fall's hand will pick up the simplest thing in the world, her thumb and perfect pointer, and plop the simplest thing in the world, pip, right in my mouth at the back of my tongue because simple is breathing not eating.

Fall's mom's picking us up and she's late again so Fall's gonna say She's late again.

There's a darker light in Fall when her mom's around and maybe this whole parking lot's darker on a dark Fall day. It's Julius and Fall, October afternoon, I'm saying, and someone's dimmed the brightness on our TV.

I'm a little high.

She smiles and things brighten up and I kiss her and kiss her again with one of my better kisses.

Our anniversary's in six weeks or something she says. What are we gonna do.

Lots I say.

Let's think of something.

Here she comes she says and she pulls away from me like we shouldn't be close around her mom. I have a hard-on but I'm holding it in my pocket like a roll of quarters but bigger, ho ho, yes. Thicker.

I hope she makes spaghetti, I'm fuckin starving I say.

You know she won't she says.

I sit in the front because I'm the male of this car and Fall's mom gives me the soft, weird, nice, hot, mean and kind of creepy Hi, and it's the same for Fall but there's that thing between them I will never understand. I don't want to figure them out tonight I want to eat a lot and kiss Fall's neck and fuck her for forty-five seconds while her mom's out of the room, Hello.

I feel sick when she reverses and now I'm panicking from the weed and I'm wondering if Fall's panicking too and now we're moving forwards and I'm not panicking.

You both look so nice in your uniforms.

I look down at it and I look back at Fall and I'm FALLING would everyone PLEASE look at that fuckin BEAUTIFUL face.

Face!

I'm not smart, ma'am.

You look smart. When I was on TV I knew nothing about what I was saying, did I, Fall, but I looked like I did.

I wasn't born when you were on TV says Fall.

Mean.

But I saw the tapes and you were beautiful.

She turns the wheel slowly and I like her hands, they're like Fall's hands but drier, and Fall's compliment's hanging in the air so I breathe in through my nose because the car smells sweet and private.

Thank you, darling.

It's a long highway drive to the High Tech Hills and I'm thinking about beef and soccer.

I hope you brought your appetite, Julius.

I was just thinking about my appetite I say and Fall says That's all he thinks about.

I laugh because she knows that's not all I think about and I look at Fall's mom who's smiling.

What else do I think about.

When were you on TV I say.

I'm thinking about clothes and whether anyone was truly hot a long time ago.

She's beautiful.

The highway's grey.

I used to think everything was predictable she says. When I was on TV. I didn't know what outfit they would put me in or exactly how make-up would do my hair.

She's driving really close to that car.

But I knew my blocking, I knew my cues, and I told everyone what was going to happen tomorrow. Such pretty clothes. Always skirts. Right, Fall.

I want her to change lanes.

I wasn't much older than Fall.

You were beautiful says Fall.

And then modelling.

She's moving her hand.

Love. Daughters. Age. No day is predictable. People are in a house one day and the next they aren't. You can't stand still looking pretty and expect nothing to change.

I'm thinking she'll say more.

She's looking at me and smiling and I'm thinking she's flirting and now I'm thinking that's not a smile I don't know what that is and she's gonna hit that fuckin car.

Her palm's on the back of my hand and it's weird. And nice.

She slips away and cooks.

Let's go upstairs says Fall.

I want some ginger ale I say.

Later.

There's Ronnie lying on my shoes already with his floppy ears and smiling tip of tongue, Hey, Ronnie.

I'm in a house.

I love the smell of your room I say.

It loves you she says.

When our hips are together I think she's the same height but she isn't so why are our hips together.

I'm gonna get out of my uniform she says. Wait outside.

Fuck that.

OK.

I love you in your uniform.

I love you in your bra.

I love your feet and toes, look at those toes, come here.

Wait.

Come here.

We should go downstairs because if we're gone long and I'm in different clothes.

OK.

We'll just say hi to her OK.

Let's say more, I like your mom.

Why she says.

Ronnie blows a bored sigh of love out his nose and I say Hey, Ronnie.

Fall's mom's pouring a ginger ale because she knows I like ginger ale.

Thanks I say.

I love staring out this window, all those trees and everything finished but growing and I don't know. This is a house I'm thinking.

They're talking about fennel and lemon and I wish there was a guy around with jokes.

It's good I say.

Good she says. I'll get you more she says.

I look at her ass when she's walking away and I smile at Fall and we're quiet.

I'm chewing.

She's walking back and she's frowning.

I'm looking at cupboards and couches.

Why's she frowning.

You have a way of not engaging that feels really familiar.

Mom.

It's the way he moves his eyes around she says.

He's eating, Mom, leave him alone.

I'm talking, Fall. The three of us are grown up and I'm making an observation. Julius doesn't mind.

You're making him uncomfortable.

There's a potato in my throat.

You are both at the age when habits start to form. Habits of interaction.

I saw a counsellor once I'm thinking.

I keep thinking that you can both set yourselves perfectly onto the right path she's saying. Develop ways of behaving with each other that will mean you get the most out of every situation. If you look around, stare at this, stare at that, not engage, you won't take life in. But maybe I'm wrong.

Her eyes and fingers remind me of a bird or something mean on a diet.

Fall's father didn't engage, Julius.

Mom.

OK I say.

I'm telling Julius because I think he would be interested.

Sure.

He's not.

He never took me in she says. Right from the beginning. If you don't engage, you don't understand, and if you don't understand, you can never love.

OK.

You have to take life in to love.

Fall picks up plates and salt shaker and sighs.

OK I say.

She's smiling and saying But maybe there's a time for looking and a time for thinking.

I think that's right I say. It sounds right to me.

I'm trying to think of a joke.

She gets up and goes to the kitchen and says something to Fall and Fall's walking away and going upstairs and I'm not enjoying myself.

I'll take this plate to the kitchen.

She takes the plate and smiles.

Thanks I say.

I'm gonna go upstairs

I touch the side of Ronnie's mouth where it looks like meat.

Good boy I say.

Fall shows me pictures.

Fall tells me a story about when she was eleven and I'm not listening.

Fall cries.

She says her mom just told her in the kitchen that we won't last.

I say that's a fuckin mean thing to say.

She keeps crying.

She shows me more pictures.

What did she mean we won't last.

Forget it she says. She turns away.

She cries for a long time.

Where's the fun in having a girlfriend I'm wondering and wondering and working it out.

It's OK I say.

She snots a lot when she cries.

Your mom's a little kooky I say.

She gets up and stands by the window.

I look at the line of her.

I want something.

I want some attention.

I want to go.

I have everything she's ever written she says.

Your mom.

Yeah.

All her cards and letters.

That's nice I say.

She sits.

She shows me pictures of her sister in a poncho and sombrero.

I don't know what to think.

Our legs are touching.

I'm thinking about taking my cock out and maybe she'd do something with it, who knows.

She goes to her closet.

I sigh.

We should go downstairs soon she says.

I say we should go.

I love you she says.

There's horses in my blood.

I want to be alone with you so bad I say.

She gets a box from her closet and puts it on the bed.

It's full of cards and paper and envelopes and coins and I'm thinking about paper cuts.

She gave me this letter in a card for my birthday she says. When I was thirteen. She made me think of it at dinner.

She's reading.

Dear Fall. I watched you dance over the mat today, my darling, and I realised that you are my only friend. I need you more than I needed your father and certainly more than your father needed me. I saw a maturity in you today, darling, and felt it was a grace that can only come from understanding, and that I could rely on your understanding as we both get old together.

She clears her throat.

You were such a beautiful little baby. There have been so many times in your little life when I have not wanted you to grow. Everyone said such fine features. And often when people complimented you they were really complimenting me, and I love the beauty we shared. I wanted to hold you forever on that pillow while I fed you and see that look in your eyes. Your sister grew away from me and I didn't want that to happen with you. She and your father never understood how hard it was to do on my own. They assumed that a mother's love should be enough for everything, but a mother needs to be loved. There were times when I held you in your little bath and was frightened by how easy it could be to let you slip.

She clears her throat.

We have come through so much together and now I can tell you everything. Thirteen years old and such a beautiful woman already. So strong. So graceful. You are my friend, and I wanted to tell you that. To let you know that I need you, and if there is anything you want to tell me I will be here for you. I'm so proud of you for winning your medal. Happy birthday, darling.

Her mouth sounds dry from reading.

I expect her to be crying.

She's somewhere between me and herself.

I don't know what to say so I say Fuck.

I think about my mom sometimes I say. Sometimes I talk to her. When I was younger I did that a lot I'm saying.

I'm sorry, J. I don't mean to be complaining about my mom.

I know. That's not what I'm saying. I'm just talking. You know I'm not sad about it.

I know she says.

I tell her jokes. She, you know, appreciates it when I score a goal. I don't wonder about her any more. I did that a lot when I was twelve, and mad at her and . . . I don't know. There's just a nice lady in my head who doesn't really look like anything and is probably nothing like my real mom. It's kind of nice.

You look sad she says.

I'm not though. Seriously. She's nice. She thinks I'm a riot.

I don't know why we come here she says. I'm sorry, J.

I like it here. Right. I don't see your mom like you do.

I'm sorry.

Sometimes her mom's in the fur coat with the hairy bush I'm thinking.

What do you want to do she says.

You know I'm saying.

I DESCRIBE MYSELF variously as a lawyer, a policy adviser, a researcher. If someone presses me further I will say I work at the Canadian Radio and Television Commission. I watch the light diminish in their eyes. I have played various roles there over the years. Assessing content, determining suitability, granting and revoking licences. I have some rising to do. I expect I will never be made a Commissioner.

I could properly say that it's an affliction of approaching middle age to know that I am so much more than what I appear to be. My colleagues come to me with legal questions, policy questions. We nestle in a web of minutiae and unstick ourselves in the evening.

Even though I spend most of my life, now, with this identity, it is never what I see in the mirror. I won't pretend that I have not spent a great deal of time restraining myself.

I nonetheless believe that my job is important. Determining what should be heard and seen. My life has taught me that the promise of others is illusory and it is sometimes necessary to define oneself against them. I believe in demarcation, in the refinement, articulation and protection of different cultures.

I want to believe in predictability and patterns – perhaps the subtler the better. I don't believe that there is a straight line to any human behaviour, but there is a line, and I believe in tracing it.

And if my life has been a process of concealment, I am not surprised by how quickly revelations come. It is as though the myth were true that water always melts more quickly than it freezes.

I assume that my colleagues hide themselves in one way or another, that perhaps their secrets are less grave but nonetheless define them. I sometimes think of Julius in those terms. There were injuries on his body which I was never able to see. I don't know how he was affected by them. I don't know where or how his life has progressed. A paradox occurs to me that he hid himself like he hid that damage, and was consequently himself, and happy. But we were different.

His father, a public figure, was easier to follow. I know they moved back to Vermont. He made some disparaging comments about the 'unpreparedness' of Canada. I know there was a later move to Boston. I have pictured Julius on a generic university campus for an almost laughable number of years. Some days he is smiling and the campus is rich with green. He is always young. Some days I am in his body and looking at the campus and no one and nothing is living.

OCTOBER 13

Party tonight at Brown's

October 20
Party tonight at Brown's

October 27
Party tonight at Brown's

Noel has a calendar that says Literary Figures of England and I ask him what the red letters are and he says Saints' Days and I say what's wrong with a calendar with tits and oil and tyres and neither of us finds it funny.

Hum.

Dad said call so I call and it's Harry, Residence Secretary, and I'm waiting for his United States blah blah get through your sentence I want to talk to Dad.

It's Julius Harry is Dad around.

One moment Julius I'll put you through.

And that's the loudest fuckin piano.

Hey, pal.

Hey, Dad. Why's the piano music so fuckin loud.

I've got the night off, pal. How about a run.

Sure.

Will you walk over.

I'll run.

Dad rubs Vaseline on his balls and armpits and pulls his shorts up high and puts trackpants on over them now and says I gained eight pounds last month and all I ever eat is hors d'oeuvres.

He has a bit of a gut and that's not gonna happen to me it's impossible. His back's big when we walk out of the bedroom and we're going down the stairs a pair of joggers.

Harry says Do you want security and Dad says I've got it, pat pat on my back, we're the same height but I always feel shorter.

I'm not taking a bullet for you I say.

Let's do three miles around the neighbourhood he says. All around the world he calls it.

It's dark already and it's only five o'clock and Dad straps his headlight around his head and I've pretended for a couple of years not to be embarrassed by it.

The marines salute.

It's funny.

RCMP follow in the car.

It's funny and fuckin dumb.

We jog.

Let's go slow for my knees he says.

I used to feel grown up when I ran with him and now we're buddies and I want him to understand everything in my heart.

I had drinks with the Mexicans last night and I told them I go running with my son. Let's run by the residence and wave OK.

His light's jogging ahead of us and swiping at trees and houses.

I'm telling you. Sometimes I can remember to limit my calories. But sometimes all these cocktail parties.

He's smiling like he's being watched.

When I ran for Governor the President gave me one piece of advice. Put lots of soda in your whiskey.

A pebble jumped into my shoe.

And this ambassador thing is even more unhealthy. The drinking. The hors d'oeuvres.

He looks at me and his light's in my eyes and The hors d'oeuvres he says again.

Now there's a green circle in my eyes from his light and a green circle of nothing in the middle of everything and I'm trying to blink it away.

I've been to over four hundred cocktail parties this year and the year's not over. How's your math.

I figure that's more than one a day I say and I'm looking at him from the side and his smile's not so phoney.

There's Benicio's place he says and his light jiggles on the stone of the Mexican Ambassador's place and we wave and smile in the dark.

I was at the Swedish Ambassador's place two nights ago.

He nods his light across the street and it check-marks the Swedish place and I'm thinking of a blonde in the window in her bed and a light shines in and she's thinking Cat Burglar but it's the US Ambassador and I want to be with Fall she's prettier than Swedish blondes but I haven't met many.

Harvard man he says. So's Benicio. I'm telling you. Being American has kick-started a lot of good relations with these guys.

. . .

. . .

We're jogging.

. . .

. . .

Sarbjit over there. MIT man. Sikh too. We're inking a wonderful software agreement between India, Canada and the US. Don't get Sarbjit started on software it's like talking to someone from Liechtenstein about false teeth.

What.

He knows everything.

It's getting cold I say.

Ottawa's the snowiest capital in the world he says.

We're jogging.

I'm thinking all the cocktail parties make Dad a bag of facts. I'm thinking of rooms of guys smiling and nodding and facting.

I'm thinking girls get bored by facts and facts are holding Sweden and Mexico and everyone together in these places with hors d'oeuvres and I wish I could get the thoughts out in time and talk about something true.

Fall asked When did you lose your virginity, and it was an

exciting talk, and I said I think about it a lot I was honest and said When I was fourteen this girl Sue she was older and I was inside her for two seconds and Sue asks What does it feel like and I was so fuckin turned on by her asking that so I lost it in two seconds. And I couldn't describe that feeling to Sue. I couldn't get my feeling across, not in time, and I called Sue the next day and said it feels like a glove of tongues.

Dad I say.

Yeah.

I feel happy.

You're happy.

Yeah.

Good, Julius.

I'm thinking I feel happier than I've ever felt so I said that and now I feel embarrassed and I always feel younger around him.

This is a great time of life for you he says. I was thinking about it last Thursday. I was invited by the Chancellor of Ottawa University to watch a hockey game. Those young guys. I thought about you . . . I've got to slow down a bit here . . . These young guys were incredible. A couple of them could have played professionally. Probably will. I said so to Norman and he appreciated it. He invited me there to show me the potential of these young Canadian men, with their French names, their Engineering degrees, their tremendous sporting ability . . . You have to absorb as much as you can, Julius. And the thing that . . . blew me away . . . You can be smart enough . . . old enough . . . to know so much . . . and you still aren't afraid. Fear isn't defining your life like it does . . . when you're older . . . because these young guys don't know yet what it is they should be afraid of. All the things that can happen.

They're hitting each other.

Absolutely. They're taking big hits and I bet it hurts like hell. But I'm telling you . . . There's a kind of pain you're just not aware of . . . at your age. A bodily pain *and* a mental pain . . . And not being aware of it allows you to do anything. I need to walk he says. My knees.

He's out of breath from talking.

I'm not totally into hockey I say.

His hands are on his hips.

I'm not tired.

There's a woman and a dog and we smile and Dad says Good evening and his light catches the eyes of the dog. I'm thinking about devils and animals and the dog's really friendly.

Hey, buddy.

Dad starts running again maybe to show off to the woman.

Most of the houses are stone and grey and hiding.

She looked familiar he says.

We jog.

It's a very small community he says.

Are your knees OK.

Sure. I meet so many of the same people at so many different places. National Gallery. Places. We get to know each other.

He waves at someone I can't see.

It's an important part of the job. Diplomacy is about many things . . . Trade . . . Security . . . Hoo . . . But it's about getting to know each other . . . I know so much more about Canada than I ever could have imagined. Going to a diamond mine up north . . . That landscape . . . Meeting the workers . . . And Switzerland over there.

He jiggles his light with his hand and it scratches the stone and the flag.

It's more than watches and chocolates and banks. Not a lot more, but these are people, Julius. And it's wonderful . . . to get to know them.

. . .

. . .

Damn he shouts.

He stops.

My goddamn knees.

I clear my throat.

It's all this goddamn extra weight.

It's OK let's walk.

When I'm thinner my knees don't hurt. Goddamnit.

We stop.

. . .

. . .

Sorry, J, it makes me mad.

It's OK.

I had a dream he says after the last time we were running that I was eating something with shaved Parmesan and the Parmesan shavings were actually slices of bone from my knees. It's a sharp pain he says.

That's fucked I say.

I'm feeling happier now like now we're getting to the heart and he's himself.

My room-mate talks in his sleep I say.

Does he.

And laughs sometimes.

He's shining his light right on me.

You're shining your light right on me.

Sorry.

I think I'm dreaming sometimes but I realise I'm awake listening to him dreaming I say.

You get to know people in a different way he's saying when you're sleeping in the same room with them. I remember that from college.

You get to know everything I say.

Maybe. I can't remember his name.

Noel.

I should meet Noel he says.

His dad's a diplomat.

It's a very small community.

Dad's quieter now and softer and we're walking and his light's nodding calmly on the road and trees and signs.

They say avocados are good for the knees but the last thing I want to do is eat more.

Yeah.

You eating OK at school.

No.

You know you can come home whenever you want.

I do.

I have to fly to Toronto on Thursday to speak to the Empire Club and I'm staying till Saturday. That means Friday I won't be here. Will you stay at school.

Maybe.

. . .

I'm excited and I'm trying not to be. Control it. I'm trying not to think of sneaking Fall in that night and lying there in the solarium in the dark there's a view of the river and lights blinking across the city in worlds I want to see, she'll love it. And every step I'm taking is touching some new space, there's so much space outside of school.

All these embassies I say. People work in some of them right.

In the residences. Some of them. Most of them don't have the separate Chancery like we do.

K.

They have offices he says. The Most Reverend Papal Nuncio there. That's the largest residence in Sutton. He has lots of officials and apartments there.

I'm quiet.

I'm thinking I don't know much.

It's colder now that we're walking.

A lot of interesting people he says. And we're all protecting our interests. That's what you have to remember, Julius. We're learning about each other and getting along but it's all about looking out for ourselves. And for the United States it's even more important because if we don't look out for ourselves then nobody is free.

I figure we're not connecting. I want him to tell a joke or maybe I could make him proud somehow. I want him to ask about Fall.

It's cold he says. Come on.

We're jogging.

You can be curious about other people, and you should be. But you should know yourself he says.

His light makes circles and questions.

I want to spit.

I spit.

How *is* your math he says like he wants to know seriously.

OK.

Work on your math he says. Math is the language of the future. All this English Spanish French is going to look pretty silly in a hundred years. We will all be speaking in ones and zeros.

100 I'm thinking.

I spit.

Stop spitting he says.

In a hundred years we'll be dead I say. Two zeros.

The future is to be prepared against he says.

It's Fall who's good at math I say.

Fall.

Yeah.

Good for her. She's a catch he says.

He doesn't know her. I want him to know her. Fall says Your dad scares me.

We're jogging.

I want to ask if he ever wanted to breathe in the life of life because I know there's always life and the breathing's so much fun I want to eat something.

I want to ask if he ever feels stupid, who cares.

I want to ask if he knows what we looked like when I held his hand and he bought me the bat in Boston. I can see him and maybe he can see me but I can't see myself and that's why memory's not true. And I want to say so and I want to know sometimes why it's hard to talk.

And I run faster and he keeps up and it's a quiet competition and the air's getting clean in my head, I'm smarter. And his face is hard to see. And when you shine your light on someone you can look and not be seen. And I think about a foreign house with another country's light shining through the window.

I think of watching with one bright eye.

I don't think the world is small.

I can't he says.

We stop and he rubs his knees.

SHE CAME UP to the Flats and stood in the doorway of our room, an unimaginable thing. Girls were simply not allowed to be at the door of a boy's room.

Julius was gated – confined to the school – for three weeks for soaking Ant. The Coke and the water had damaged the carpet, Ant was injured, so the school took it seriously and Julius never said I was involved.

Fall was smiling, at ease, joking about the fact that Julius was gated. He lay on the bunk above, I imagine with his hands on his head, bemoaning his punishment, while I sat up, below, my head leaning forward, joking along with Fall and more nervous and excited than I had ever thought possible. I was vibrating.

Julius said, 'I need to piss,' and Fall said, 'Nice.' She looked at me like she was apologising for her vulgar friend. He left the room, and somehow I controlled my nerves enough to say, 'I fell off the top bunk once in my sleep.' It was somewhat out of the blue, but I wanted her to know me and she seemed perfectly comfortable.

'Ouch,' she said.

'I'd been dreaming I was in the circus and I think I did a hand-stand on the bed, and I woke up when my spine came down on the corner of the desk.'

She said 'ouch' again with genuine concern.

And I laughed.

'Hey, Noel,' she said. 'Since J is stuck here for three weeks, I wanted to get him something for the room. Like a present.' She asked if there was anything he particularly needed, and I remember for a moment thinking, with jealousy in my heart, that it was I who needed. Julius needed nothing.

'I don't know,' I said.

'Maybe you could help,' she said. She suggested that I go shopping with her.

'Tomorrow? After school?'

I felt like it was the moment that had brightened every dark night, the moment I had ritually re-fantasised for years while in bed to give myself hope. Somehow, through all that ritual and replaying, I had implicitly acknowledged that it would never actually happen, but now there she was inviting me to go out with her alone.

'Sure,' I said.

Julius walked back into the room saying, 'Sure what?'

'I asked Noel if he would help Sarah with Shakespeare,' Fall said.

He looked at me with his sly smiling face, suggesting I might have an opportunity for something with Sarah.

I looked at Fall with silent complicity and had my first real taste of the thrill of betrayal, the joy of setting out down the wrong dark path. I looked at Julius again and genuinely admired his face. He always had such humour and purity in his eyes. And I thought about how he would clean my back before bed and say, 'Your back's getting big.' He was kind.

My bones felt fluorescent. Friendship, love, betrayal, promise. The energy of that room becoming something bright inside me.

Fall said, 'Sarah can meet you in the library, tomorrow at four o'clock.'

I undid the top button of my shirt and loosened my tie. I also untucked my shirt a little. But I wore a coat and scarf which covered my shirt and tie.

Fall was waiting outside the library and said we should take a bus to the Centrepiece Mall. I had resolved to be more silent than talkative, in case of later regret. We walked across the playing fields to catch the bus and all I said over that long stretch of grass was: 'It's cold.' I couldn't look at her, even when we were sitting across the aisle of the bus from each other. It seemed to me that we were fifty of the chosen, being driven to our heaven. I looked at no one, simply assumed that for inscrutable reasons everyone was gathered on that bus to be taken where everything was given.

I followed her off the bus.

She asked if I went to the mall much and I thought about saying it was a disgusting carnival of vanity and artificial need. I said, 'Not much.'

'I hate it,' she said. 'If we do this quick, maybe we can get a coffee.' She asked me if I knew Café Wim. I said I didn't, and she said, 'It's like Whim with a W but no H and and it's called Wim like Vim with a V.'

I said I understood.

We were in the mall and I was always conscious of how far apart our shoulders were.

'I was thinking about buying J a cardigan,' she said.

I tried to picture it.

'I'm joking,' she said.

I said I had been thinking that I would like to buy Julius something too. Something about feeling slightly guilty about going shopping with Fall had augmented my sense of friendship with Julius, had brought out a keener realisation of how much more I wanted to be his friend.

'Julius is great,' I said. She looked at me. After our long walk across the fields I realised she was generally quiet. We shared a look now that said we both admired Julius. We liked each other for admiring Julius. She felt closer to me for my admiration of Julius, and admired me, and her curiosity about me was heightened because I said that Julius was great. It was all there in her eyes.

'So maybe there's something both of you can use in the room,' she said.

I never had quite as much money as everyone else in the school, certainly less than Julius and Fall. My father's salary as a diplomat was modest — he lived well abroad and I was at St Ebury all because the government paid for everything. If he hadn't been overseas we would have lived in a middling house somewhere and I would have attended a middling school.

'I don't want to buy anything too big,' I said. 'I don't think he's that great.'

She got distracted by a store she liked and looked in for a moment. She paused at the door and looked concerned, then smiled and kept walking. 'Sometimes I'm bad at shopping for other people. I see stuff I want to buy for myself and then I remember what I'm supposed to be doing and I feel, like: guilty?'

She occasionally struck me as younger than she looked. But there was suddenly a charge to our outing, some sort of quickening, as though we were both now alive to the fact that we were out of the school and that there was some sort of potential for ourselves, not just for Julius. Even though we were in another building with forced air and bright lights, there was suddenly some sort of greater possibility than we ever had at school. This was the world. Clothing, couches, jewellery, magazines, food, music, movies.

We wandered without saying much at all but our wandering itself was eloquent. It seemed we each knew where the other was drawn and we were always respectful of space. I thought it would have been risky to get any closer. She said at one point that she couldn't believe how big I had become over the past year. 'I brought you here for ideas, Noel, come on!'

'I think I was surprised to discover how nice Julius is,' I said.

She was quiet for a while and then said, 'He's fantastic.'

I thought it was good that she said that.

I thought about how wonderful it was that two strangers were shopping for someone else, both involved in something bigger than or beyond themselves, as though Julius was our religion. He brought us together and the three of us would thrive in the name of his benefit.

And I ached for something.

'What should we buy?'

'I'm not sure yet.'

I ached for something with throat-felt force, with innocence and purity, as though my motivating heart could ignore the complications of friendship, the obstacles of bone and convention and contradictory limbs. Somewhere within was a desire that knew nothing but itself. I ached like the sky aches for blue.

'Something you could both use,' she said.

We were in a shop selling kitchenware. I separated myself from her and looked around. I realized the utility of getting something that Julius could enjoy in the room; something that I could enjoy with him so we could have each other's company; something that would keep him in the room, because keeping him in the room, whether I was with him or not, meant keeping him away from Fall.

I suggested a coffee pot and she said, 'I'll buy the Bodum, you buy a kettle.'

I found an inexpensive black kettle and Fall found a very expensive Bodum.

She said she *loved* having coffee with Julius. 'He's like a kid with cake. He gets all excited then he crashes. And you'll have to deal with that,' she said.

She used a credit card, I paid with cash.

My father, after many years of 'shame', told me what it was like to grow old with an ugly past: how life ensured that sometimes one could forget, but that regret would surprise and harass the mind like Banquo's ghost.

He was a terrible snob, my father, so concerned with what other people thought. I remember writing him letters from St Ebury and receiving such absurd bourgeois advice from his replies. 'It's more correct to say napkin than serviette. Read Waugh and Mitford.' And when I told him about Julius he emphasised the privilege of rooming with the American Ambassador's son. He told me to foster that connection. He really knew nothing about me.

I remember feeling grown up, shopping for that kettle.

We went to a magazine store where she bought a *Vogue* for her mother. 'It's something she expects,' she said. 'I don't know if we have time for coffee,' she said. I said I thought we did.

Café Wim was a block away from the mall. It was full of young people in black.

It was a common experience to feel older than other students because we wore suits and ties, but there were times, like that evening at Café Wim, when the uniforms had the opposite effect. I felt unsophisticated and part of a club or a team that I did not want to belong to. Fall seemed to fit in immediately.

She was still quite quiet and it was making me more nervous.

I wanted to talk about everything that had never been talked about.

I tried to keep my eye under control. Sometimes looking down and then up can make the eyelid do its rhythmic spasm.

The *Vogue* she'd bought her mother was on the table and she was resting her forearms across it. There was the faintest mole on her wrist. I thought about how Julius must know that mole. Then I thought that he possibly didn't, that there were probably a hundred aspects of her beauty that he wouldn't notice because his eyes were not as open as mine. I even thought that she probably didn't know his body as well as I knew it, and also that loved ones could identify bodies by marks like her mole, no matter how disfigured the body may be by death.

I had actually not drunk much coffee at that point in my life and remember thinking it was bitter. I was finding her silence difficult. She was looking at me in a pleasant way, but I found it hard to look her in the eye. I wondered whether she was simply as eager as I was to avoid small talk or whether she was somehow uncomfortable. I barely dared to think she might be shy around me.

'Mom has read every issue of *Vogue* as long as I have lived,' she said. 'I started buying it for her when I was thirteen. Like a bonding thing. Now she expects it.'

She had a way of smiling while she talked.

'Ever read it?'

'No.'

'There's actually nothing to read. It's like: Countess, you know, von Something had a party last year and this is what everyone was wearing. Otherwise it's just pictures.'

'Right.'

It's hard to convey her manner. After she spoke there were such long silences. She would keep looking at me, but there was no indication that she wanted me to say anything, no real sign of self-consciousness on her part. She wasn't aloof, she didn't seem vain or overconfident. I never got the impression that she didn't care about what I had to say. I think she simply expected nothing from me. We could communicate or not. I've tried so often to see the world through her eyes. I know that café looked different to her than it did to me.

'That's what I like about this place. People are stylish, right, but they're not *Vogue* readers. There's style, and then there's caring a lot about what other people think. If you want to know who wore what at the Countess's party, it's because you care a lot about what other people think, right? Usually people here aren't looking around caring what other people are thinking. Definitely not the girls.'

I looked around. She was by far the most beautiful girl in that room.

'The women in here all seem really cool. No pretending, you know? I think girls pretend less than guys do anyway. Even if we don't always stay friends, I think girls are honest,' she said.

I looked her in the eye. Then I looked away. 'All the guys are looking at you,' I said.

It took courage for me to say that. Her silence felt all the more fraught. It was nonetheless true. While she stared at me or at her coffee or at her mother in her mind's eye, I glanced around and caught several other guys staring at her. I think I only confirmed what she must have known. I think I was trying to make a point, too: trying to question whether anyone could be oblivious to what other people thought. But more than anything I felt that I had declared that everyone, including me, wanted her beauty.

'I never got into *Vogue*,' she said. 'I don't think you can have a true relationship with anybody if you care what they think. My mom never got over my dad leaving her. Dad doesn't know me, so, whatever. I don't need someone to know me. I think you either love or you don't, right? My mom never got over expecting something back.'

I tried so hard to look at her. She picked up the magazine, saying, 'So I buy Mom *Vogue*.' And she smiled.

We had to hurry to get the bus back to school for dinner.

It was so dark and cold. Everyone on the bus was huddling into themselves.

I was so overwhelmed by having been alone with Fall that I still wasn't able to respond properly to anything she said. There was no time for analysis. I never trusted myself in moments like that.

We stood next to each other on the bus. I thought about how she had acknowledged my size.

We decided to give Julius his presents that night. She said they had a regular rendezvous at ten o'clock and that this time I should show up.

I only wanted her to know me. Maybe she truly expected nothing from people she loved, but I expected everything. I knew she could be my everything. I only wanted to take her hand when we got off that bus and to hold it tightly when we looked at the field between ourselves and school.

I never felt so keenly the entrapment of St Ebury, the enforced infantilisation. We could have stayed sitting at the café and shared intimate thoughts; instead I had to sit at an assigned place in the Dining Hall with grade 9 and people I did not want to talk to.

I can picture us walking towards the school. Her coat was red. She was small next to me. We both looked small in the dark.

William

THE BOY WROTE to me today and said he just turned thirty and I thought Jesus Christ Fat William you have twelve more years of cheese in your veins it's no wonder the belt feels tighter.

Little Julius has made the age of thirty. I wrote to him last year and said all I can do these days is shrug. I don't know, is all my body can say. Here at the wheel. Is that lady going to cross the street? I don't know. Is she a nutcase? I don't know. Does it matter? I don't know.

It's how you stay healthy, I told him. Shrug the shoulders.

Jim Shank got the cancer. Am I going to get the cancer? I don't know.

Bring on the cancer, I say. Sometimes I say sit me down and pour me a nightful of cancer. Mugs of it.

Jim Shank's a skeleton, the poor fucker.

Bring on the cancer.

And some days. Eh. How many up and down days in the endless life of William? Some days it all looks like a beautiful gift, all wrapped up for me, and my memories are mine, and somewhere in beer number three everything looks beautiful.

When you see enough that's ugly you lower your standard there on beauty. I saw a pigeon pecking on a plastic bag last night for half an hour in the parking lot and I found it pretty beautiful.

Sometimes I wish the boy Julius could ride with me here in the bus, but he's thirty. Like in the limo days. He says he'll come up and visit one day. I don't know what he would think about seeing me. Casino de Hull on my shirt and I'm waiting in a parking lot for gamblers to come out of the lives they're not living and I shuttle them to the casino and I drive back and forth along the same line, some days, some nights. That's what he would see. But he knows me.

He knows life.

He's together.

Every year his letters get me thinking.

Last night I'm watching the pigeon peck at a crumb it sees in the plastic bag. It was a quiet night last night. And the guy in the leather jacket gets on, pretty friendly. Lucky night coming, he says. Most of them don't talk about the gambling unless they're in groups. But this guy, we talk, we fill each other's ears and he gets off at the casino. A few hours later, sky's as dark as tomorrow, I pick him up at the casino and take him back to the parking lot.

Sure enough, like the rest of them, he goes to the back of the bus and stares out the window and he's too down and shy to talk to me. Except this guy, just when he's getting off, he says, what's the secret?

He wants some sort of answer to how he's going to make it through whatever's left.

I liked him for asking me.

But all I could do was shrug. I don't know, I said.

Except I did kind of know. Driving back and forth all night, so there's time to think. Wondering what I liked about the pigeon. I could have told the guy. There was a crumb in the plastic bag I could have said. And the secret is you've either gotta really want that crumb or you've gotta like the feel of plastic banging against your face.

And I guessed that wouldn't have cheered him up.

Now, this is a true story here. I tell this story.

I knew a guy with just the one arm. He called himself Johnny Five on account of what was left. He woke up one morning with a sore throat and next time he woke up he had just the one arm. It was the flesh-eating disease. I tell this story at Hurley's.

He lost the arm and he always said, you don't know how fond you are of your arm until you lose it. And you don't know how worthless your arm is until you lose your eyes. Because he lost his eyes a little later.

This was way back when I was driving cab and Johnny was

working dispatch. I was on the radio and complaining about one of the other drivers, and at the end of the day Johnny took me aside and told me this story.

He lost his arm and hated the world and one day he decided not to hate the world. There. He cheered up and started doing things and he took up refereeing kids' hockey. Little boys. Loved the mischief of them, he says. They always liked getting the one-armed referee cause there were some calls he couldn't make and they could make fun of his skating and everything else. And one day he's checking the nets before a game and the kids are warming up and two little fellas think it'll be funny to fire the puck at him. And this beautiful miracle occurred where puck number one and puck number two fly at him when he's looking up and hit him at precisely the same time in each eye.

He doesn't remember anything except waking up and being blind. What the hell are the chances of that I enquired and Johnny shrugs and says, I don't know.

But he was a really cheerful guy. And I asked him, how do you stay cheerful? I'd want to die. And he said, all I do is remember what it was like to throw a ball. He said he used to love throwing the ball, almost became a pitcher. And the memory of it was right there in the ghost in his sleeve and for some reason it was just a simple thing there that kept him cheerful.

I drove home that day thinking about Johnny Five and I thought, Christ, William, he should be a lesson to you. And I felt guilty about complaining and all the rest of it. I thought about his story a lot, whenever I heard him over the radio, and I visited him in the office sometimes. I watched him doing everything easily, one-armed and blind, and I said to him one day, you must have had trouble getting used to doing everything left-handed. And Johnny said, no, I was always left-handed.

So I was surprised. I thought about his story a little and I said, so you always threw a ball with that arm, and he says, that's right, and I was confused.

So I said, what about your story, the ghost in your sleeve and all that?

And he says, I made that up. I was trying to get you out of your little head, he said. It turned out he'd lost his eyes and arm making a bomb for the Hell's Angels.

You know, William, he said. I'm not a good man and I don't like other people's rules. But the one rule I give myself is never complain to someone else. Cheer people up or shut your fuckin mouth.

There's nothing else

I MET FALL and Julius that night and we presented him with the coffee pot and kettle. I was able to see where they had their regular rendezvous, near a large maple tree standing leafless at the edge of school property.

Julius was surprised to see me there and I said I wouldn't stay.

He said he loved the gifts. He was talking in a silly way and kept saying 'stay, stay, stay' but I didn't want to get in the way. I said goodnight to them. I walked away wondering what they were thinking as they watched me grow smaller towards the school. I heard Julius laugh – the same laugh he had when he beat me in the race.

I turned the light out before he came back and pretended to be asleep while I listened to him undress.

Once Julius's gating was under way he had to get a sheet signed every hour by a Master, every day right up until bedtime. This was to ensure that he didn't leave school grounds.

'It's not the days that get to me,' he said. 'We're stuck in fuckin school anyway. But the nights. Right? And every Master who asks me: what did you do, why are you gated? I've got to admit that I threw a bucket of Coke on someone. How fuckin dumb is that?'

I was cautious around him, getting out of his way, making delicate suggestions. It was he who first suggested that I talk to Fall on his behalf.

It was at each Duty Master's discretion to punish Julius further or not. That is, some might make him do more each hour than simply get his sheet signed. I began to get a sense of new modes of confinement and began to feel relatively free myself.

On the first day after school one of the Masters made Julius vacuum and clean his apartment on the Flats. He was going to be kept at it until dinner time and had no way of seeing Fall until then. He asked if I would find her and tell her that he wouldn't see her until dinner.

It was the beginning of discovering Fall's routine, of learning who she was. She had no routine. I asked Julius where she was likely to be, and he said, 'She'll be in her room for sure.' He was never right about where she was.

Her room was on the ground floor of the Girls' Flats. I rang the bell at the main door feeling very nervous – mostly because I was about to see Fall, but partly because I had never rung the bell at the door of the Girls' Flats. The Duty Mistress came to the door and said, 'I'm not in the business of knocking on people's doors for them. If you want to know if Fall is in, find your own way of knowing.'

She turned around, leaving the door open, and walked down the hall. It seemed she meant that I could go into the dorm and knock on Fall's door while she turned a blind eye. I was deeply curious about what it was like inside that building, and as full as I was of anxiety about breaking a rule, the idea of knocking on Fall's door felt appealingly grown-up. I nonetheless walked away.

Would it matter if I didn't deliver Julius's message? They would see each other at dinner anyway.

By chance, I found Fall in the library, which was small but had a surprising number of corners and dark spaces where one could feel alone. She was sitting on her own, which struck me as unusual.

'I have a message for you.' I told her Julius had to clean the Duty Master's apartment and she laughed. She thanked me. I walked away.

I started seeing more of Ant during those weeks. It was getting too cold for rugby and the proper season wasn't until spring, so he was usually at a loose end. We would work out together some-times, although his injured shoulder meant that he usually just watched me. I began exploring the late-night freedom that Julius had usually enjoyed. Ant and I would wander the halls and intimidate anyone who was awake. It was quite fun.

'I had such a great night with Fall last weekend,' Julius said. 'It was so fuckin beautiful.'

I couldn't bear to hear it. 'I'm meeting Ant,' I said, and I left him in the dark.

Ant and I went into Edward's room and I tied a long sock tightly over his eyes before he woke up. He didn't see us. His room-mates were afraid of us. We knocked all his books off the bookshelves and tipped over a wardrobe. It wasn't especially funny – I wondered why we did it – but I liked all the noise.

It meant there was a crackdown on late-night misbehaviour. A Duty Master would patrol the halls later than usual. It meant that Julius wasn't able to escape at all after Lights Out.

He gave me notes and I became a go-between. He would send me to the library and she would be in her room. I would spend an hour tracking her down. I found myself asking everyone in the school, 'Have you seen Fall?'

She gave me notes in return sometimes, in an embarrassed, apologetic way. I knew she was reluctant to use me as a messenger. I had the moral resolve not to read the notes at first.

I was able to spend more time with her. People saw us together in various parts of the school. I even met her by the bare maple one night. She was expecting Julius but I appeared instead. She seemed a little shocked to see me – I suppose she had been prepared for intimacy. I simply went to tell her that Julius had been putting his coat on and was seen by the Duty Master and was told to stay put. I didn't say much more to her on that occasion.

God I remember a look in her eyes though. A look that said: I'm vulnerable to surprise; I wanted company and now I'm lonely. A look that without a doubt showed more curiosity about me.

And surely that is what has died in me. I am curious about nothing. I am enthusiastic about nothing.

I've forgotten the joy of seeing things for the first time. Or never mind the joy. I don't even feel the motivational fear. I'm afraid of nothing, so I am interested in nothing, and tomorrow is always Wednesday.

I saw my first coyote that year, when Julius was gated and we found ourselves in the room together. One of the Masters had reported seeing a coyote on campus. We were told to be careful. The Head Master's terrier went missing. I imagined an indiscriminate carnivore and was eager to see it. I read about coyotes in the library and learned how their territory had expanded across all of North America. The decline of wolves, I read, meant the clever coyote could thrive.

I clearly remember their appeal. It had nothing to do with a boyish love of beasties. It was a fascination with adaptability and a realisation that human boundaries didn't have to be respected. Here was an animal that would eat anything from a berry to a dog in order to survive. It loped across important borders and was finding a feeding ground in a space we thought was a campus.

When I walked outside I not only imagined the coyote watching me, I imagined everything I saw as a habitat instead of a neighbourhood.

Perhaps that was a death in itself, looking at this world uncoloured by certain illusions. But I certainly didn't feel at the time like anything had died; I felt energised.

'There's a coyote outside,' I said, one night in the dark. I didn't know whether Julius was awake or not.

I imagined it every night before I slept.

And one quiet Saturday morning I was sitting at my desk while Julius lay on his bunk. 'There it is,' he said above me, and I turned and he was pointing out the window. The coyote was on the front lawn.

I stood by the window and wondered why Julius remained in bed. I supposed he had a good view.

I had imagined some sort of noble predator or at least a crafty scavenger, and all I saw was a smallish dog. Its tail was the only unusual feature, but I found myself saying things like 'it looks pretty strong' and 'it's really well camouflaged' – searching for remarkable traits because I knew it was supposed to be extraordinary. I had wanted to be awed.

Julius said nothing. I assumed he had seen coyotes in the past. Would we ever have the same reactions?

The coyote pranced away, ragged and light, and I remember wishing for some sort of noise to mark the passage of experience. 'It's gone,' I said, and I wondered why I had learned about that timid little thing.

I passed more notes back and forth. I felt less and less invisible. Fall became jocular about it — still apologetic and respectful, but more light-hearted.

I remained fairly quiet around her but I seemed to dream about her and Julius a lot, and it felt like communication. Julius and I were both active sleepers. I found him standing by my bed sometimes; once he touched my arm affectionately and said, 'I love you.' I couldn't believe that I didn't reach out. When he awoke he was mortified and said he had been dreaming about Fall.

I encouraged Julius to write more notes. 'I really don't mind,' I said. Sometimes she would open them in front of me, sometimes she would wait.

I know that they were able to see each other occasionally because Julius would mention it. I nonetheless passed notes between them at least once a day.

The three of us were together outside the Dining Hall once and Fall asked Julius a question. He didn't answer orally, he wrote a note and passed it to me laughing. Fall had a look that shared amusement with Julius and pity with me.

Things began to grow sour after that. Even though I wanted an excuse to see her, I was less eager to be their Pandarus.

I learned that minimised contact was the strongest fuel of forbidden love. Knowing that I would have less opportunity to see her, I thought of her all the more and when I did see her I could feel my want at the roots of my teeth — that pure desire for desire which I had felt around her before.

I made excuses for a few days to Julius, pretending for various reasons that I couldn't deliver notes. Then I found myself missing my involvement in their lives so much and thinking about them more than ever. Julius got stuck with cleaning another Master's apartment and I told him I would be happy to swing by Fall's place after school to let her know it.

He wrote a note and I brought it to the Girls' Flats. Another girl was leaving as I arrived and I instinctively put my foot in the door. I went into the hallway. There was a bulletin board and a bag of sheets beneath it, and things seemed just as untidy as the Boys' Flats. It was the last note I delivered for him.

A few years ago I was walking through the market and passed a convenience store. I was about to go in to buy some wine gums – I have a weakness for wine gums – and as I held the handle I looked through the glass of the door. Behind the cash register stood Fall's room-mate Sarah. I recognised her but couldn't place her; I retreated from the door instinctively because I never like to meet anyone I know in uncontrolled circumstances. She was a large woman, and I wondered whether she had perhaps been one of the cleaning staff in my apartment building or possibly a waitress at some sort of diner I might have been to once. But as I discreetly looked through the store window I gradually realised it was Sarah.

Unimaginable disappointments had filled her body like water from a hose, and there she was looking swollen and red behind the register of a store selling cigarettes and unnecessary treats. I must admit that blowing over the surface of my shock was the slightest breeze of a smile. I toyed with the idea of going in and talking to her. I liked the idea that simply by standing on the other side of the counter I could confirm my superiority to her. But I didn't like being reminded so vividly that we can never ultimately avoid the pugilism of life, the dumb constant blows of unpredictable moment that – fat, thin, one-eyed or beautiful – make us all, ultimately, revolting to strangers passing our windows. They don't see us getting hit, they only see the aftermath. I didn't want the slightest knowledge of what put Sarah in that state.

Julius's gating ended. I felt such a fear of things reverting to what they were.

All that week, all Julius could talk about was their upcoming anniversary. My breathlessness became simple impatience. I trained myself not to listen to any of his plans, and I never really learned what they did.

I missed the daily contact. I suppose I wondered why she wouldn't come and find me any more. I suppose I was somewhat hurt. She was friendly enough to me in the halls between classes.

Julius signed out that weekend. Their anniversary was on the Saturday.

There was a letter on our floor which I picked up and read that Friday night. Fall must have slipped it under our door. It was in an envelope, more elaborately presented than her usual notes; her J on the outside. It was a letter of such simplicity, vanity, vacuity and obscenity. I never could have imagined those things being said by one real person to another.

She talked of meeting by the tree on Sunday before dinner. By then, she said, they would have had their anniversary. She loved the idea of looking ahead, she said. And she would have a little present.

I assumed, quite rightly I believe, that everyone was different depending on the company they kept, and if she were with me she would be a little less simplistic. Everything gathered that weekend to make me realise that now was my time to have her. I had to play a greater role in their lives; he had been enough of a prelude.

I spent Saturday and Sunday planning. I determined that I would keep her note hidden from Julius and meet her myself by the tree on Sunday evening. I was going to declare myself to her.

I smelled shirts that Julius had worn while with her. I trimmed my hair and immersed myself in the idea of love. *So are you to my thoughts as food to life*. I tried to think of my own words to say, and I smelled her enough that I loved the idea of her smell and could pay no attention to the fact that our bodies ever existed. I wandered the halls forming phrases and coercions, with the one consistent premise that the world did not have to be as it was. And in the shower on Sunday afternoon I cleaned and chastened myself so my formal shirt would be white on white and my skin was alive to beginning.

I took one of Julius's coats and avoided the room until five o'clock when she was expecting him. I hoped that nothing had changed during their night together, that no other arrangements had been made since she left the note on Friday. In his coat I would appear like him and possibly ease the transition. I looked better in it than he did.

It was dark, and snowflakes landed in my eyes as I looked for her. She was there by the tree in her black coat, not red, and leaning on a pair of crutches. Her smile changed when she realised it was me.

'What happened?' I said.

'Where's Julius?'

'Did you hurt yourself?'

'I twisted my ankle on the dance floor.'

I thought about her dancing and felt a little sick.

'Where's Julius?'

Plans were changing slightly in my head because I hadn't expected the force of my nervousness.

'He sent me,' I said.

I wanted to be alone with her and the lights of the school behind me were insisting that I couldn't. I just wanted to walk with her so I could have the time to figure out exactly what I wanted to say.

'He said we should meet him by the river. He bought us presents.'

'Presents?'

'I don't know,' I said.

'Where is he?'

'I don't know. He just took off in my coat a little while ago. He told me to meet you by the tree and take you to the river.'

'Weird.'

'He meant *go with her* not *take her*.'

'Weird. I can't get all the way there on crutches.'

'It's not too far.'

I tried to say it casually. It was a twenty-minute walk in the best conditions. It was the only place I could think of where we could feel properly alone, and I knew that I would do anything to achieve that. I would get angry if I couldn't.

'I can help you,' I said. 'It's not that far.'

'I guess,' she said.

We started walking, and I was resolved not to do it in silence.

'Julius and I hang out by the river sometimes,' I said.

'Do you?'

'There's a great sheltered sort of a grove down there. We got high there a couple of times.'

'He never told me,' she said.

'It's where he wants to meet.'

I didn't want to fill the time with lies. I watched her crutches make targets in the snow.

People in the neighbourhood were warming in their private lights and as we moved along slowly I had one of my first true feelings of bone-coloured bleakness. I felt that I needed to find our own golden living room, somewhere down the road.

'I hope it's not too hard,' I said. 'Walking.'

'It's OK,' she said.

'Pretty thoughtless of Julius,' I said.

'He didn't know. I didn't have crutches when I saw him this morning.'

I didn't want to hear about their night.

'Still, he must have known you were hurting. I'll give him hell when we see him.'

The houses and lights were thinning. I thought of her hands on the crutches – her weight on the crosspieces I somehow felt in my gums.

'I had a girlfriend in Australia,' I said. 'A girl named Meg. She wasn't very thoughtful.'

'I didn't know you had a girlfriend. That's nice.'

'It was a while ago,' I said.

The more the school and neighbourhood receded, the more I felt like I could be myself. There was a trail through woods which we would have to find and travel, and a steep descent to the river where I had sometimes secluded myself over the years.

'I used to go to that grove to think,' I said. 'I was the one who showed it to Julius.'

'He's never told me,' she said.

'Do you want to know what I thought about?'

'So what ever happened to Meg?' she said.

I moved a little closer to her, solicitously. 'Are you managing?'

'I'm good.'

'Your perfume is lovely. I've smelled it on Julius's shirts.'

She smiled.

'This is so freakin weird,' she said. 'You're kidding me, right? Julius is waiting for us.'

'Of course he is. It is weird. I bet it will be worth it. Something funny. He's such a funny guy. Meg was beautiful,' I said. 'Not as beautiful as you are, but I really loved her.'

'Good,' she said.

'Long, brown hair, slightly dyed by the sun.'

'OK.'

'She was unique, in some ways. Not extraordinary. She used to make fun of my words.'

'Your words are pretty long,' she said.

'She was cruel to me,' I said. 'I've really hated her for a while.'

'Why do you hate her?'

'You know how it is,' I said. 'She just never really had nice things to say about me. You're probably nice to all the guys you break up with. You're so nice to Julius. Meg just didn't have those silken kindnesses, and I hated the way she chewed.'

'I hope Julius plans to carry me back,' she said. 'We're gonna be late for dinner.'

'I think the perfect person exists,' I said. 'Meg wasn't the perfect person. It makes me mad sometimes, imagining what she thought of me. I'd say you know me better than she does.'

I was finally going to have her.

'Where's my stupid boyfriend?' she said.

'It's not too far,' I said. 'I can carry you.'

'No thanks.'

'It's down a little hill. Just over there.'

'Where are his footprints?'

'I don't think we'd see footprints. Anyway, he might not be there. I guess he might come after. I was just thinking of how you and Julius have to sneak around to be close. Meg and I kind of had to do the same. We had a special night on the beach once. She admired my body.'

'We don't sneak around.'

'Do you want me to run ahead?'

'No. OK. Maybe you should.'

'Do you want me to?'

'Yeah. You should.'

She held up her crutches to show me it was the obviously chivalrous thing to do.

'I'll go see what he's up to.'

We had come quite far. I jogged ahead down the trail through the trees, knowing I had to keep planning but feeling an inexorable momentum which made plans seem irrelevant.

I knew it would be warmer in the grove and that she would be comfortable down there. 'The chill from the water seems distant,' I told her later.

I stayed away long enough to pretend to have seen Julius. When I found her again she had retreated out of the woods.

'Where is he?'

I laughed.

'It's hilarious. He's down there, but I can't give it away. He's done something really funny.'

'Why can't he come up?'

'I told him. I said she's on crutches. He was sorry, but you'll see when you're down there. I didn't get it at first but he said it was an anniversary thing.'

'Like what?'

'I can't say.'

'Is he fourteen? I'm on crutches.'

'I can carry you.'

'No.'

'It's not far.'

I was getting nervous now. I would have to explain myself soon. When she said no to my offer to carry her, I wanted to carry her all the more.

'I'm gonna go back,' she said.

'Why? We're so close.'

'You guys are tricking me or something. It's cold.'

'It would be so easy to carry you. Seriously. It would take one minute. Leave your crutches. I'll carry you down. I'll come back up and get your crutches.'

'I'm not going without my crutches.'

'I'll carry them with you then.'

She hopped a little, turned around, and I thought she was turning again to go back to school but she handed me her crutches. I realised this was finally my chance to hold her.

I was conscious of shaking. I wanted to seem as strong and reliable as possible. When I picked her up I held her as tightly as I could to keep my shaking under control. I wanted to be affectionate with her but I thought I could save that for later.

'It's cold,' I said.

'It's freezing,' she said.

I was holding her crutches underneath her like a bed and I wondered for the first time what on earth I was intending to do. I tried to keep my face away.

When I close my eyes I imagine her looking up at me. My grip is looser.

'Sometimes my mind races far away from itself,' I said. 'I can't slow its movement. As soon as I wake up in the morning it surges through these odd, poisonous labyrinths. I catch myself sometimes thinking I can't believe I just thought that.'

'Put me down, Noel.'

'It's OK. I'm just saying that I need some calm. I need something to make me calm.'

'I can walk. We're coming, J.'

She shouted it.

'We're coming, J.'

I shouted too. 'We're coming, Julius.'

The hill down to the river was steep. I hadn't realised on my own how narrow the trail was but now that I was carrying a girl and crutches crosswise, I was surprised.

'Slow down,' she said.

She clung to me and I loved it. I felt like laughing the way Julius did when he was keeping the ball from someone.

I hit her foot against a tree and it twisted her injured ankle. The crutch caught against my arm and I almost fell.

I hadn't realised how much I had hurt her until we were down by the river and noticed she was crying.

She was strangely heavy when I asked her what was wrong. It was terrible to see her like that. I was down on one knee and holding her and saying, 'It's OK, it's OK, what's wrong?' and I kissed her cheek. Her limpness, I discovered, was the coil before the spring.

She flailed away from me in a panic and I didn't understand. She was crouching and looking around. I didn't understand what pain she must have been in with her ankle. Possibly I broke it.

'I'm so sorry,' I said. 'I didn't mean to hurt you.'

'Where is he?'

'He's coming.'

'You said he was here.'

'It's part of the game.'

'What game?'

'The surprise. He told me to pretend. He's coming.'

I really didn't know her.

When she was crying like that, in her honest teenage frenzy, I really didn't know her. We both needed to be calm but I didn't know what to do. 'Julius is coming. Don't worry.'

It looked like she didn't know where to turn. The river was near at her back. She was standing on one foot. I was holding her crutches.

'It's warmer over here,' I said. 'The chill from the water seems distant.'

I was trying to figure out what to say. My pity for her was somehow making my desire more acute and I felt I could articulate none of it. I just wanted her to touch me. Carrying her down the hill felt like a missed opportunity.

'Can I please have my crutches?' she said.

I went towards her and I felt like I couldn't stop. I dropped the crutches and pressed myself against her. I felt I could convince her.

She said 'stop' and I held her arms and I was a concert of 'please', an octopus of 'please'. Wake up in a field of poppies and weeds: my please was all around her. I didn't want to stop.

She kept turning her face away from my mouth and all I wanted to do was convince her.

I was pushing her backwards – forwards in my mind – and she tried to get around me.

Our feet were in the water and the cold was slightly sobering. My fingers were sore from holding on to her coat.

I told her that nobody owned her like I did, that he couldn't be hers any more. She kept saying 'don't' and 'Julius'. I thought that maybe she was resisting because she was afraid he would see us together. 'Please,' I said.

I wanted her to be quiet. I wanted to calm us both. When I ran away later I remembered reading somewhere that shock or just the right blow could make someone choke on her tongue. I wanted silence, the right new start.

'He's not coming, is he?'

'He's coming.'

'I'm going to tell him,' she said. She pushed and said, 'Get off me.'

I couldn't stop pressing.

'I don't like you.'

I never understood.

I remember raging and not knowing why. The why never stops the rage. I was picking up gravel and frantic in the cold, punching at nothing, and knowing I had to change everything. 'I'm sure he'll come and find you,' I said.

I threw her crutches into the river and ran up the hill to change things.

This shirt looks good on me.
 I've eaten beef and milk.
I'll light a candle in the sunroom.
I don't know where they are.
Marie-Claude.
Jool.
I need a candle.
For what.
For a candle.
I get you dat. What collar.
Red. White. I don't know.
I love her. There's nothing but love in her fat.
I'm excited more than nervous and I feel like barfing.
I give you tree.
Three's great.
Her fingers are fat.
A friend's coming over I say.
Bon she says.
Night I say.
Bon nuit, Monsieur Jool.
OK I say.
There's a stranger in every corner in the dark where these lamps don't reach but the house is mine and we'll close the sunroom door. She's quiet when we fuck, but it's not my fault. All these lamps and golden circles on the floor and roof and the week's so swollen it's nine on a Friday night.

8:54.

Six more minutes and I'll let her in the gate.

Shoes.

Teeth.

Hair.

Piss.

Still some beef in the teeth.

Coat.

Fuck the gloves.

Fuck it's cold.

The driveway's long in winter.

RCMP.

Maybe she's here.

Hi.

Sir.

You must be cold standing here.

The heater in my booth's OK.

Nice. I have a friend coming.

Yes, sir.

I don't know what to say. I have nothing to say about that or them or anything.

That may be your friend, sir.

She's thin and shy in that coat and I can see her breath. That's her I say.

I wave.

She waves. She's smiling.

Hi.

Hi.

Thanks, man.

Sir. Ma'am.

Thanks.

I keep my distance.

Your teeth are perfect I'm saying. There's that tiny gap down low on the side, I want to kiss it.

You will.

We're walking apart.

Maybe it'll snow she says.

I love your smile.

I love yours.

We're smiling up to the house.

Mmm she says. It's warm in here.

Yeah. Here.

I take her cold coat and her neck's warm on my fingers.

I hang her cold coat.

She's gorgeous.

I look at her necklace.

We hug.

We kiss.

It's a soft one.

We're hugging.

I love her.

Hm she says.

Her eyes are closed and she licks her lips.

I turn off the light in the hall.

We're not strangers.

Do you want anything.

No thanks.

Marie-Claude's gone to bed.

Has she.

Everyone's gone.

I tell her that so she'll be comfortable.

I'm telling you that so you'll be comfortable.

I know.

We hug.

She smells so good.

I've been thinking about you she says.

Have you.

Mmh hmm.

What about.

Secret things.

I kiss her smile.

Her lips are tight. I'm thinking she doesn't want to kiss.

She opens her mouth.

She wants to kiss.

Her tongue's so soft and wet and hard and warm and cold. I kiss her lips and say Inside your mouth it's like everything good that can't be together.

Hm.

I kiss her lips.

We press our foreheads together and do the eye thing, hers are one and mine must be one so four becomes two and that's algebra.

I love your eyes she says.

I love yours I say. They're so beautiful. They're green for fuck's sakes I say and I pick her up and she's mine.

I put her down.

It's like you make me calm and excite me at the same time she says. That's what I was thinking about on the way here.

I'm thinking I like the way she thinks.

And it's our anniversary in, like, five weeks she says.

Yeah.

Yeah.

You sure you don't want anything.

I want a chocolate fondue she says.

There's a noise upstairs.

It's still early I say. Maybe not everyone's asleep yet. I can get Marie-Claude for your chocolate.

I'm kidding she says. I need the bathroom.

I watch her walk out.

I look at the wood panels.

There's gold and silver and wood and something purple in the middle of everything.

I should study tomorrow.

I can hear her piss.

I don't want to.

I'm humming.

Flush.

Maybe I should go too.

I'm holding out my arms for a hug.

Hi.

Hi.

Mmm.

We should go to the sunroom.

There's a noise upstairs.

OK.

It can get pretty cold in there.

That's OK she says.

We're walking through gold and past a flag and the sunroom's black and freezing.

Brr she says.

Leave the doors open, get some heat in here I say.

OK.

Just for a minute.

There's a noise in the house.

Look at the stars she says. It's beautiful.

Wait here.

I can't remember where I put the candles. Kitchen. I'm Julius getting the candles from the kitchen in this huge place which is mine and I'm calm and we're hanging out and I do not have a hard-on. We'll get a place of our own.

I'll light one and carry it.

Ouch.

Stupid.

Ouch that feels good.

Pretty she says.

I'm burning myself with the wax I say.

Are you OK.

I forgot candlesticks.

I saw some she says.

She goes. I love her. Wax feels good. Why do people wear leather and whip each other, they look stupid.

Here she says. They have eagles on them. So many eagles in this place she says.

She takes the other candles and pushes them into the sticks.

I'll light them.

I light them.

Phoo.

I love the smell of candles she says.

I'm putting the burned candle down and thinking it smells warm and it drips wax and that'll piss off one of the maids.

She hugs me from behind.

I like that.

She kisses my neck.

I like that.

It's not about sex tonight I'm thinking. In your own house, you get to know each other.

What was your favourite birthday I say.

Hm she says.

She lets go.

My favourite birthday. I think it'll be this year she says. I'll spend it with you.

She smiles.

We can change together she says.

Fuck I love her. I don't understand her.

I hold her hips and press.

I fuckin love her so much.

We do the eye thing.

There's a noise in the house.

Her eyes move after the noise and we don't say anything.

We walk right up to the windows. My arm's around her and we're looking at things we can't really see and when I change my eyes I'm seeing my face, I look good in this shirt, and I breathe in through my nose and smell the candle and cold.

She's pretty tall.

I see more of the river and black twigs of trees.

We're quiet and looking and loving. She's reaching over and she's rubbing the change in my pocket cause I think she thinks it's my cock. There. That's my cock. She's rubbing it in a calm way like she's never done and I pull her closer and I smell her hair and she hugs me with her other arm and keeps rubbing, I like it, and I feel like we could be the parents of the things outside the windows.

It's beautiful she says.

I like it I say.

She squeezes. We'll have lots of sex tonight, I've decided.

I'll close the door I say. You're not too cold I say.

Hug me she says.

There's a flame and us in every window.

It looks warm I say. Anyway.

She pushes her head into my neck.

I kiss the top of her head.

She's pushing her chest into me.

Her hips move away.

I'm thinking about boats.

She undoes her own belt. There's a look in her eyes like she's trying something new, and she's shy and I'm shy and I swear to god we'll have a lot of sex tonight.

I touch her panties with the back of my fingers and I'm looking in her eyes and someone turned off a lamp in there and now she's a warm dark eye in the bushes looking at something it loves to eat, Hoa god.

My hard-on's sucking the blood from my jaw. I'm gonna come already, those fingers under my waist, Hoa ho.

I kiss her.

We bang teeth and I'm not gonna come.

Sorry she says.

Tongues tell secret stories she told me.

That's my cock.

I hope she thinks it's big.

Hoa she says.

I want to hurt her and love her, o god how good does that feel I've gotta tell someone.

Her panties are red and Christmas is coming and wet red velvet all over the house, it's so SECRET and BEAUTIFUL how wet she is, I love that she's letting me touch her.

Hoa god.

Tongues.

How about that. How about that. Do you like that. Do I like that. I fuckin love that o god I'm gonna let go and let her touch me it's all about me for a minute.

I should kiss her more. How about that. She's so open tonight, how good does that feel, we're fighting and sliding down the warm dark hill: stop it feels so good, stop stop.

We do the eye thing. She smells good. Her eyes are smoked and dark and shy, my Fall.

She's going down.

She's standing up.

She's gone.

She blows out one candle.

She tries the other.

It burns.

She smiles.

She tucks her hair behind her ears and walks back sexy and shy and her belly looks big, no it doesn't, and I should grab her but she was in the middle of it I'll let her go down: she kisses me.

She's going down.

She pulls my jeans right down.

Boxers.

It springs and it's funny but serious.

There's a noise in the house.

There's a breeze on my balls.

I feel like a monkey.

I should be shy.

Her eyes are closed.

She's shy.

I feel like she's changing me.

I'm shy.

My mom must have dressed me some days.

Her hand feels so good, Hoa haaah.

Her little mouth.

She looks up.

O fuck.

I'm gonna come already that's so fuckin soft and warm and look.

. . .

. . .

Hoo.

Hya.

God.

. . .

HOOO.

HOOOAA.

Fuck.

I'm sorry.

It's OK.

There's come in her hair.

Fuck.

God.

Hoo.

I'm sorry.

I'm trying to pick her up.

It's OK.

I love her.

I love you.

I love you she says, so nicely.

She's standing.

I'm trying to get rid of the come in her hair and it smells like a swimming pool and I feel young and pantless but she's kissing me and I'm feeling older and I don't mind that I'm kissing her. I'm not a fag.

I'm still hard.

Hoa she says.

Her nipple's hard through her sweater, just that one.

There's the other one.

We do the eye thing.

We're hugging. I feel like we should go somewhere. I feel like everything could end but it won't if I move my fingers right and she's so HERE tonight I think she really loves me.

She walks over and blows hard on the last candle.

I take off my shirt and I'm here if you want and I don't care what anyone thinks I just want to be here if you want and I'll do anything if you come with me. And that's what your eyes look like tonight, o Fall.

I saw those raccoons come out chewing on a chicken bone near school and they shared it, those two raccoons sharing the bone they both wanted and their eyes all red and curious.

I undo her jeans and there's the river over her shoulder.

Fingers up her sweater feeling goosebumps up her back.

She's mine.

I kiss her.

I want to bite her.

Should I.

That wet Fall inside, it's warm as blood, she's my secret Fall on my fingers.

I'm moving to my jeans like it's not breaking the rhythm and I hate fuckin condoms.

Did she look at my ass when I bent over.

I have six condoms.

I walk back and slide her jeans down all the way and her belt hits the carpet like a belt.

I could taste her.

I want to.

Why would you kiss there she always says. I want to.

I look up at her.

Her eyes are closed.

I like the smell.

I love her smell I've decided.

I pull her panties down.

She holds my head to pull me up.

I stand up.

We do the eye thing.

She kisses me deep all tongue and she's ahead in the race and she pulls her feet out of her jeans and panties and there's her leg up around the back of my leg and I want to fuck her standing up but how do you do that.

No one else has this I say.

J.

We bang teeth it's my fault.

She's all new muscles tonight.

Her arms around my neck and she wants to be picked up and I pick her up and I could slide inside so easy like I feel its breath saying you have to come here, you have to.

Hoa.

I put her on the table where I eat with Dad, her ass instead of his grapefruit.

Condom.

Fuss fuck.

I love you she says.

I love you.

Fuss.

Her thumbs are on my hips.

I'm there.

Maybe she looks like she doesn't want to fall further but I'll push her, she does and so do I: push hard.

Ow.

Sorry.

It's OK.

Sorry.

Gyooo.

That's Fall she's melting the rubber hoa hee.

. . .
. . .
. . .

Are we close o my god she feels good. Are we close.

She's the prettiest girl in the school.

I talk to her in class.

. . .

We're fucking.

. . .

Hoo.

I want to be closer.

The table's hurting my elbows.

Dark furniture, ghost tours and places I want to go, who knows, Death Valley, you can drive as fast as a jet, I'm here.

I say Hoa.

Stop she says.

Are you OK.

Yeah.

She breathes.

It's OK she says.

Is it over.

She wants to stand and I'm helping her.

Let's go to the floor she says.

Heh.

We're walking to the windows. My condom's up in the air.

She lies down and I push back in and her eyes say it's good it's not painful and o my god it is good.

She's small I don't want to hurt her, she's moving. When she moves I want to come.

Haa.

She squirms out and says Turn over and puts her mouth on my mouth cause we're shy.

She's on top, we've never done this.

Hoa.

She's hugging me and I want to look at her. She's up there and I want to see her. I want her to take her sweater off. She's hugging me. I put my hands on her ass and she's grinding, ouch, she's really fuckin grinding, I like it. She's fast and goofy and doing her own thing and fuck I'm gonna come

Here.

Oh.

A.

Hya.

I'm sorry.

Shhh.

Hoh. I'm sorry.

Haa she says.

You're just so pretty I say.

Sh.

She's hugging me.

I didn't really come it just spilled out of me and the condom's full and on my belly and she's hugging and I'm embarrassed.

I want to make you come I say.

It's OK she says. Let me lie with you.

I move and my head presses the saucer under that big fuckin plant and it tips and I save it and I don't feel cool and the condom's cold and wet so I put it on the carpet.

She lies and puts her head on my chest.

That was nice she says.

Was it.

. . .

. . .

You have a beautiful cock she says.

. . .

She's so shy and quiet sometimes, and she just said that like it's our secret: like she never talks like that and only the two of us know it. It's the hottest thing I've ever heard and I'm also thinking Thanks.

She's pressing against my leg. Squirming.

God I love you, Julius.

I squeeze her.

There are stars up there and glass between us and the stars and I'm in my father's house. Those are the chair legs and the carpet's itchy. I feel calm and cold and itchy.

There's nothing else she says.

I don't need anything else I say.

I can smell the dirt in the plant.

She's quiet.

I wish I made her come.

I put her on her back and I'm beside her and I'm kissing her. I'm finding some new way to kiss her.

Like this.

We're walking through the family room, she's back in her sweater and jeans and her fingers are on the wood panels and I think girls' hands are for touching things, and when we first moved into this house Dad knocked on those panels like he was testing them and said Hm.

She's quiet and walking ahead and dragging her fingers over the panels and she's a girl in her sweater but she showed me her secrets. We're close and these are new seconds.

What's through here.

The dining room I say.

She flicks the light and it's thick white paint and gold.

It's the state dining room I say. I never eat here. Twice.

It's hilarious she says.

She's walking around the table touching the backs of chairs and she's pretty.

We should have our anniversary dinner here she says. It's hilarious.

My fingers are in the grooves of this column and I'm watching Fall and I knock on the column knock knock.

So huge she says.

She's walking around the long table like a kid and she's thinking. She touches the rope that calls the butler.

If you pull that it flushes all the toilets I say.

She keeps walking and says So many eagles.

She touches that piece of furniture over there and keeps walking.

I'm folding my arms.

She looks up to the ceiling and I'm thinking you could put ten more Falls on her shoulders and the one on top would touch the ceiling like she's touching that chair, those fingers were down my pants. We'd look really small to whoever's looking down from the ceiling.

What's through here she says.

How's she so far away.

That's the reception hall.

She goes through the door.

I walk to catch up. I feel like running but I'm walking.

She's found the rope for the chandelier and she's across the hall and my feet and my laugh just echoed. She's like a little girl.

Her fingers are touching the flag.

I want to hug her.

There's a smile in her eyes.

She's trying to get away but I'm coming in for the hug.

We're hugging.

She pushes away and she runs.

What's through here she says running.

I'm picturing her smile.

FALL WAS MISSING from school on the tenth of December, an anniversary I have since marked every year.

On my birthday when I turned nine my parents bought me a kitten, which I hadn't really wanted. Two years later I wanted a new bicycle for my birthday but received a month of swimming lessons, so I cut off the tail of the cat. It was upsetting for everyone – my first memorable experience of wanting to go back in time – and my subsequent birthdays became carefully moderated affairs.

I have focused thoughtfully on annual celebrations since. I believe in marking the passage of time, the humbling benefit of taking stock, recognising decline, acknowledging community. I choose to do it on the tenth of December.

I make an effort on the evening of the ninth to say tomorrow will be a day I must recognise as a day, and I don't wake up with the anticipation of benefit or the breathlessness of rue. At least, I try. From the first it was a day on which I didn't know what would happen next, and I try to maintain the spirit of that. Whatever happened on the evening of the ninth, the tenth would be the day of whatever was to come.

This year I awoke, went to work, accepted the usual invitation to the Commission's Christmas party. I went to the grocery store and saw a deaf couple, a man and a woman, speaking to each other in sign language, and felt moved by their passionate animation and silence. I wished I knew their code, wished that everyone could be so openly private. Inevitably emotions creep in.

Whenever I was overseas with my father as a boy, people would ask me where I was from. My accent always identified me as foreign. 'I'm from Canada,' I would say, and 'Ottawa' if they were any more curious. I remember telling an ignoramus in England that Ottawa was the capital of Hawaii and he said he thought he had a cousin there. I remember thinking that perhaps Ottawa was indeed in Hawaii, perhaps Ottawa was everywhere and nowhere, a place with a name but no identity. I yearned for many years to speak in a language or an accent that would plant my feet squarely in a place. An Englishman, a Texan, a Quebecer or a Scot. For people to know, without knowing me, that that is who I am.

But I've come to think of my city or nation as something I want to become – something definite, but up ahead. On December tenth I square my shoulders and go for walks and know I will belong. I know these buildings can't exist elsewhere.

On the ninth my fingers were sore and my shoes were wet from the river.

The room was dark when I returned but Julius was awake in bed.

'Have you seen Fall?' he said.

'No.'

'She hurt her ankle last night,' he said.

I had thought that I would be nervous when I saw him, that I would have to explain myself or apologise or simply cower as I waited for him to discover how I had behaved with Fall. But as the night passed an anger grew; it started as a defensive reaction and then settled as something like a conviction. No one owns beauty but the perceiver. What I thought of Fall was my own.

I never gave him her letter and he never saw her, and instead of confrontation that night he offered that one innocent question, 'Have you seen Fall?'

My feet were cold. I had been walking through the snow, around the parks and embassies of Sutton, wondering how to undo what's done.

I hated everyone on my walk, every huge house I looked into. I felt like such a fool to have revealed myself to her; I hated the look on her face.

I didn't think about how she actually was when I left her, I thought about how she would be when I saw her again.

On my way back to St Ebury I slipped near the front of the school and fell into a bush. It scratched my hands and face.

'Easy with the noise,' said Julius.

I was banging drawers shut in the dark as I undressed. I got into bed beneath him.

'People were looking for you,' he said.

'So.'

'I covered for you. I said you were sick at dinner and you were helping someone at Prep.'

'I've never missed dinner or Prep in my life,' I said.

We didn't say anything more to each other.

In the morning my hands and face looked worse than I had expected. One of the scratches was deep enough that I still have this faint scar, just here beside my ear.

'I fell into a bush,' I said. I was in the mirror, in front of him for a change. I could tell he was impatient and wanted to use the sink, but I swelled my back and spent a long time swishing the toothpaste and saliva in my mouth before I spat.

I kept to myself through the day. I skipped lunch. I went straight to the weight room after school and stayed there for hours. Julius came in at one point and asked if I had seen Fall. I said I hadn't.

'I wonder where she's limping to,' he said.

Whenever he tried to talk during Prep that night I would answer as tersely as possible. Christmas exams were approaching so I had a good excuse to be studying diligently. But I couldn't concentrate on words in books. Letters looked like snapped twigs, a fractured record of whatever life had dragged across them.

Julius left after Prep, I assumed to go for a smoke. He went looking for Fall. When he came back to the room he realised I had turned the lights out early. He turned them on.

'I went to Fall's room,' he said. 'Nobody's seen her.' It felt like he was confronting me but he was only slightly breathless as he undressed. He looked rather skinny to me. He hadn't lifted weights in a couple of weeks. 'Maybe she stayed home,' he said. 'Foot up on the couch.'

He sometimes fixed his hair before bed. I found it risibly vain.

'Turn the lights out,' I said.

★   ★   ★

Julius put his hands on my shoulders after breakfast the next morning. 'Let's have coffee,' he said. He wanted me to meet him in the room after school.

We had had coffee from his new pot a couple of times during his gating. Our routine was that I would boil the kettle I had bought him and he would put the coffee in the pot. I would pour the water, he would depress the plunger. I had suggested the routine.

I met him in the room and filled the kettle at the sink. I was expecting him to say something about Fall and again instead of being nervous I was angry.

Julius liked to put more coffee in each time to see how much we could abide without grimacing. I didn't enjoy it.

I wondered whether he would notice my sullenness, whether he would be looking for signs or changes in my behaviour, but as usual he was oblivious.

'I called Fall's mom's place but nobody answered. I keep looking for Sarah to see if she knows anything but I can't find her either. Every time I try to go over to the Girls' Flats some fuckin Master says, "Where are you going?" They think I'm still gated.'

'This coffee is disgusting,' I said.

'Another cup?'

'No.'

'But you haven't seen her for sure?'

'I don't think so.'

'I can't remember if her mom was going away. Maybe she was going to Cuba.'

I didn't want to stay sitting there with him. The taste of bad coffee always reminds me of that afternoon, that mixture of disquiet and bitter revulsion.

'I saw her,' said Ant.

'Did you?' said Julius. 'Where?'

'I saw her.'

'He has that dumb smile,' said Chuck. 'He's gonna tell a joke.'

'What's the joke?' said Julius.

'No joke,' said Ant. 'I have a dumb smile. Chuck has a fat gut. Noel here has a, uh, has a tight jacket. Chuck was stating the facts. Chuck was being a fat journalist.'

'Did you fuckin see her or not?'

'I don't remember. Maybe in the library.'

Julius left the room.

'What's so fuckin serious about not finding Fall?'

Chuck left the room.

'What's up with those two?' said Ant.

'I don't know what the fuck Ant was talking about. And I saw Sarah. She said none of Fall's stuff was gone. She didn't pack a bag. Don't you think if she went to her mom's place she would have packed a bag?'

'I don't know.'

'I need your help, man.'

'With what?'

'I don't know. I'm stuck. I've gotta vacuum another fuckin apartment tomorrow. They caught me smoking. Will you look for her?'

'Well,' I said. 'She's not in school. Why would I know where to look?'

'Maybe she'll show up tomorrow. Maybe I could give you one more note to give her.'

'You can give it to her yourself.'

'I've gotta clean a fuckin apartment.'

He looked so childish and querulous.

'Leave the note on my desk,' I said.

I read the note.

It was touching.

I threw it out.

I tried quite rigorously to keep my last sight of Fall from my mind. I have a habit of thinking of something I find cleansing whenever unpleasant memories arise. Swimming in Australia once I was caught in a cloud of sea nettles. I felt stings all over my body and face, but there was something benign in the pain. I was stung into a refreshed awareness of myself, of my body alone. I try to conjure that sensation whenever I don't want to be afraid.

Teachers began to ask questions about Fall in class. Has anybody seen her? Is she away? Some of them became urgent.

A few students had been known to be whisked away for family

trips at odd times of the year, a sort of *noblesse oblige* among parents which the school would silently indulge. In Algebra, Mr Staples said that he would try to contact her mother after she missed three classes.

Julius and I worked out once together that week. I spotted him on the bench press and I subtly resisted his press instead of helping him. When he couldn't push the bar any further I suddenly changed from push to pull and slammed the bar home on the rack. It was quite satisfying. I also pressed thirty per cent more weight than he had when it was my turn.

He enlisted Chuck's help because he had access to a car. I spent more time with Ant. Chuck had a brother in town whose car Chuck could borrow. He said they would drive out to Fall's mom's place, since Julius was never able to reach her mother by phone.

Ant stole a bottle of single malt from his aunt. He and I drank it on a Thursday night in the weight room and I vomited in a corner of the gym in the most dizzying beautiful darkness. I avoided my room; Ant and I went down to the weight room after midnight. We sat under the fluorescent lights, he on the flat bench, I a few feet away on the bench I used for sit-ups. It was a tiny space and we barely had to reach forward to pass the bottle to each other. We talked about anger and did not understand each other. I think now about adolescent conversations and how often connection was a matter of gesture. As in diplomacy there was no genuine understanding, just a body language that acknowledged we would respect each other broadly while we were close.

I think nonetheless of the intensity of those gestures: how the more we drank the closer we felt despite our minimal similarity. Close enough for Ant to declare that he had never expected to become my friend. Close enough for him to clasp my shoulder warmly, for him not to care if our shoes knocked together as we shifted.

My head started spinning after little more than an hour. Ant had heard how much I could push on the military press. I tried 215 pounds and could only do three repetitions. Ant said that when you work out drunk you always think you're stronger than you are.

I thought about strength. I thought about what happened with Fall and I tried to think of the sea nettles but it made me aware of my body in the wrong way and that is when my head started spinning.

I stood up often and Ant would put his arm around me saying, 'Are you all right, man?' Out in the unlit gym I threw up in the corner, shouting as I did so. Ant kept telling me to be quieter but I loved the opportunity to shout. It was so dark I could just make out the basketball hoop near where I threw up. I loved thinking that a room is defined by what one fills it with. In the day this is a gym; right now it's a toilet.

I had been loud coming back to the room so Julius was loud getting ready in the morning. He said I was going to miss Chapel and I said I didn't care. I slept through my first class and thought about signing myself into the Infirmary, but I realised that once the vomit was discovered my being in the nurse's care would amount to a confession. I wasn't ill, I was only tired. I wanted to hide. My dreams were lit by white.

The weekend was coming. Fall was called for in English class and several people knowingly said 'she's sick'.

I longed for Friday night, to spend as much time over the weekend as I could away from the room. I avoided Julius completely.

Friday was a warm day.

'Her eyeliner is totally sitting on the shelf. You know, the little shelf under the mirror? Maybe you guys don't have that?'

'Yeah.'

'She doesn't go anywhere without her eyeliner.'

'I didn't know that,' said Julius.

He and Sarah were talking on the porch below the latticed beams at the front of the school.

'Nothing's packed,' she said.

'It's weird,' he said.

'I bet her mom's taken her away. Cuba or something.'

'I don't know.'

'I'll look for her bathing suit. She has so many clothes though, right? She has doubles of everything at home. But not her bathing suit. I think. Does she?'

'I don't know.'

'You're supposed to be her boyfriend.'

'I don't swim with her.'

'If she's sick she probably wouldn't want her eyeliner. She cuddles up like a ball, like a little kitten. So cute. Her mom's weird anyway, right? I could see her taking Fall away and not telling anyone.'

'I don't know.'

'She's bossy,' Sarah said. 'She bosses Fall around. She plays emotional games with her. And when she comes into the room. Has Fall told you?'

'Maybe.'

'She'll come to pick up Fall or take us out to dinner or whatever and she'll totally play this game, like she's our boss but she's one of us. She's given me the creeps a couple of times. Has Fall told you?'

'I don't know.'

'She tells us to clean up the room, and this one time she picks up a pair of my, like, panties, and she doesn't sniff them exactly, but she kind of loves them in a weird way. Then she said, "My daughter went to New York when she was your age." And it gave me the creeps that night like I was supposed to be Fall's sister at dinner or something.'

'Right.'

'Anyways. And she's told Fall, "One day we might have to move and you'll have to say goodbye to everything."'

'Really?'

'She hasn't told you? You're her boyfriend. She says *don't get used to anything*.'

'Yeah, I've heard her . . .'

'So maybe they've moved.'

'No way.'

'I don't know,' she said. 'But I'm worried. She hasn't talked to either of us.'

I took a black sweater belonging to Julius and I went to Café Wim. I brought a notebook and pen along, and I wrote down the conversation between Julius and Sarah as I remembered it.

I thought about what Sarah had said about Fall's mother. Taking someone away in recognition of the fact that things can be taken away. I thought about evasion and avenues of escape.

Had I become myself by avoiding others? I thought of myself as detached, as bookish, as some sort of precociously wise fringe dweller who could be safe from the ugliness of the world through cunning and evasion. The most I ever wondered was whether that detachment was entirely voluntary. Perhaps I existed on the fringe because that's where others kept me; perhaps my past of having few friends had not been entirely my choice.

I must have cut a philosophical figure in the café, with my pen and black sweater. I saw a young man staring at me, I felt self-conscious and wanted to feel the bone in his nose give way. When I returned to school at 12:30 the Duty Master said, 'You should have been in bed at midnight.' I stared at him and said nothing as I walked towards my room.

They tried to make us men, I thought. We wore suits. We were old enough to vote. We were better educated than others our age in the city, had a sense of humanism that would have been unknown to most eighteen-year-olds. We knew creeds and notions of honour. There were quotes from Milton and Tennyson on the windows of our chapel. There was none of that bulletin-board inspiration one finds at other schools – the slogans pinned to felt, the wordplay nonsense from the Church of the Daily Platitude. When I revisit the written principles and traditions of our school there is little I disagree with, little I would not hold up as a model for all human beings to consider.

But all those rules. The schedules, the conventions, the not being allowed to walk through certain doors. We were childish to follow them and childish to break them. They were rules which we could do nothing with, hollow laws that left me so ill-prepared for the throb of blood or the animal choices that truly guided my life.

Now I follow rules endlessly. I describe them daily. Rules and guiding principles are created only after mistakes are made. I knew the rules of the school, and I was very much in the middle of my mistake.

When Fall did not appear for Chapel on Sunday her House Mistress got formally involved. It turned out that her mother was in fact unreachable. Messages were left and not returned. Julius and Chuck had driven out together to look at the house and it was dark and Julius remembered that her mother had planned to go to Cuba. No one was there, no sign of a car. It was assumed that Fall had joined her mother on the trip.

It was only a couple of weeks before the Christmas break. 'Strange timing,' everyone said.

William

I DRIVE LIKE a dream on a pillow. No matter what I'm driving.
I like to think that you could only do this job if you were wise or really stupid. I know I'm not stupid.

There's another old guy rides the shuttle on Thursday nights when there's the free buffet at the casino. Most times he gets off the bus saying what would life be if you got what you wanted.

If I could see myself now when I was young and full of juice I would have stood in front of a train and smiled. Run me down. Blow me backwards so I don't have to be what I am.

But here I am, fat behind the wheel in a parking lot, and I'm telling you, young William, I'm glad you did what you were about to do whenever it was you did it. Sometimes.

I get mad. I get so goddamn mad and confused. There's a skinny old William inside me who's waving a stick and he's still saying after all these years that there is a right way, there is a right way, and he's looking tired and ugly but he's waving his stick just as hard. I look out at all the kids with their headphones and think people just don't want to know people, they want music and things on screens, and the cranky old fart with his stick could not be more right: the whole thing's wrong, going wrong, gone wrong.

First letter I got from Julius was two years after I was fired. He remembered my address from when he stayed at my place and there were words I couldn't read because he writes like a drunk on a bus. He said sorry a couple of times and I thought, that really is a sweet kid, all he's been through.

And I was a little sorry for myself there, I'll admit that. It was a plum job. Maybe. I was drinking from the bigger flask those days though. Maybe I wasn't laughing and smiling all day, but like I say.

I was pretty goddamn angry.

I liked his father. Never called him more than Mr Ambassador, but if we were two naked guys in a jungle with no names we probably would have been buddies. Couple of the Ambassadors before him wanted me to call them Your Excellency.

They flew him in an F-18 when he travelled. I couldn't believe it when he told me that. If he was going on a trip to the north he'd fly in an F-18. You wouldn't believe the speed he said.

The only way is up and out I said.

I told him I'd driven a couple of stock cars. You could rent a Nascar Dodge in those days out there for an hour of racing up in the track in the Hills. He knew I liked speed. We agreed on that. Before my post is up, he said, I'm going to get you in that plane.

Nice man.

Never happened.

He used to go up on the roof of that big house and smoke cigars he said. He told me not to tell Julius. It was the only place he could be in peace. Security wouldn't follow him up there. He said I should come up there sometime and have a smoke. That never happened.

I truly liked going to all those embassy parties, though. Waiting outside with the other drivers. I remember there was a guy driving for the Spanish Ambassador who was always sent out at night for chocolate. Always bitching about how the maids, nobody else, ever had to buy chocolate. He always said, I took this job because I wanted some intrigue, international intrigue he said. Drive hoors to the back of the Russian Embassy at midnight. But all I'm doing is driving around a bagful of Dairy Milk.

I miss those conversations. Looking back at it, I figured meeting a guy who was driving around looking for chocolate for a Spanish guy who loved chocolate – that was as good as life could get. I mean the meeting of him.

The driver who replaced me, Tom. He was a good-looking guy if you like youth and hair and smiles. I always tell the ladies that my bald fat beauty is the kind that lasts. I bumped into Tom a while back and he says he picked up Julius one day from the hospital back then and there were bandages poking out from his shirt and he was limping. I didn't like to hear that. Tom says he didn't see much more of him before he left.

I got his first letter after a couple of years and I felt like someone turned the lights back on in some rooms I'd forgotten.

I was drinking in that wrong way. Sorry for myself for losing that plum. Taking the worst job because I thought I lost the best. You untie your rope and drift out into that lake of poison and you're alone. If you're lucky, someone hops into your boat out of nowhere – wakes you up – and you realise how much time has passed and that Time is crazier and crueller than your drunken mother's mother. Tick-tock is the biggest lie of them all, there's nothing regular about it. My mother's mother put lipstick on at the age of eighty-two and walked out naked down the street saying Tell the filthy iceman I had to go to school. The truth about Time is that we aren't where we are, and when we are where we are it's when Time stands still – which is always the time we remember.

So Julius's little letter hopped into my boat, Dear William. Nothing much to it, but I realised I had to write back. You can't write about yourself without thinking about yourself. That first one I wrote was short, but I've got into the thing and I'm writing letters now that he'll never have the time to read. And I figure I truly am wise.

You can't get surprised when bad things happen. You make up all these things to pretend life isn't what it is, and then you get surprised. The malls, the churches, the casinos. Or if you think about it a little, you think, well, if life is fuckin awful you might as well make something up like a God who makes it better or a jackpot that paints the dirt gold. If you believe in dirt in the first place, the surprises have to be sweeter.

What I myself try to settle for some days is a conversation, or the right night of beer, or one of those letters. Or, even better: a woman I'd never met who gets on the bus and says, in her country, on the first day of spring, they put an orange in a bowl of water and wait for it to spin while the earth rolls on to some-where new. I love a surprise from a stranger.

I remember talking to Julius's dad about countries. It's on my mind now because I think that woman was from Iran, if I remember, and I'm thinking there are probably thousands of guys like me, in the States or over there in Europe or wherever. Guys driving shuttle buses to casinos or something equally stupid. It doesn't look to me like something worth fighting for.

His father told me a story about some politician somewhere who was asked, do you love your country? And this politician didn't say yes or no or anything like that. All he said was, I love my wife.

I'm not completely down. Maybe there are some mornings I wouldn't mind a bit of company. Lie on my side a little, let's say, and someone could try to throw her arm around me. A few years back there was that nice lady, Rassy. Funny name. She held my tiny old joint from behind me one morning and said it's all gonna be OK.

That was nice.

Red hotel

THERE ARE BETTER things to do I say, but if he's gonna throw aerosol into the room every night, let's get him back.

We'll flood him I say.

Let's flood him says Noel.

I don't know why I'm excited.

Hee hee.

Giggle.

Two little mice.

Tickle splish. Splish splish. We're gonna fuckin soak him. These buckets weigh a ton.

Ho!

Hee!

Ya!

What the fu!

Bang!

Assholes!

Hee!

Shit.

Aren't you guys eighteen.

Yes, sir.

I'll talk to you in the morning.

* * *

Fuck me. Fuck's sakessss. Fuck. Three fuckin weeks, you're fuckin kidding. Cunt. Klunt. Fluck it. Fuckin idiot. I'm fuckin eighteen. I'm a fuckin idiot.

Kunt.

I read a book called pappiyon says Chuck where a guy's in prison. All kinds of prison. And the advice he gets is don't jack off. It wastes too much energy. If you're in prison for three weeks, J, my advice is to meditate. Think about the universal peace that exists in the soul of every object and don't count the days. Get to know yourself.

She blew out the candles and blew me.

She blew out the candles and blew me.

She blew out the candles and her tight little mouth.

Fur coat.

She's in a fur.

Gya.

Hn.

I'll sleep.

Dear J,

I miss you but it's fun writing you notes, and I'll see you by the tree at ten.

Can you smell my perfume?

Kiss,

F

Look, Mom. Have you noticed how good I'm getting at vacuuming. Did you ever vacuum this much.

Did you ever know a grown man who lived in a room like this, in a school. He says he has dates over sometimes, did you hear that. Would you date a guy like that.

Would you teach me the mysteries of women.

Would you vacuum under that couch.

Fuck that.

Well it's just an interesting experiment about weeks I'm saying. It's all in the head.

Good she says.

It's three weeks but if I close my eyes to time. Chuck taught me this. If I close my eyes to time, and focus on what's important.

Namely me she says.

Exactly. The time passes. Focus only on the important things is how I'm seeing it. I just close my eyes.

I see she says.

And I'm jacking off a really filthy amount but that's my little secret I'm thinking.

You're smart, J.

Am I.

Come here she says.

I miss you.

J ULIUS WAS UP early on the Saturday but he didn't seem to do much. I pretended to sleep and watched him carefully. He had a brown housecoat which he called 'the animal'. He wore it on the rare occasions that he needed comfort or warmth. He was wearing the animal and sitting at his desk. He looked at a book occasionally but I could tell he wasn't reading.

Ant and I went out. He let me sign out to his aunt's place and we ended up in Hull. I was so grateful to be taken away from school that Saturday. 'I don't know where Chuck and J are tonight,' he said.

We went to his aunt's place, a large apartment on the canal, and we drank and got ready to go out. His aunt was in Paris. She had a fully stocked bar and a vast array of Dresden ware which Ant ignorantly referred to as China. 'Don't go to China,' he said, meaning don't break the dishes. We drank tequila, which I had never had before. I was wearing a white shirt, which I had untucked, and a pair of jeans.

Ant said that I should borrow a shirt. We went into his bedroom and he tossed me a red T-shirt that he said would look good on me. We got changed together.

'I don't know what the big deal is with J's fuckin girlfriend not showing up at school. He's gated for weeks and now he doesn't even want to go out. And Chuckie. Fuckin Chuckie's like an old man suddenly.'

Tequila was a miserable thing, a bottled salt pool where every sad herb had drained as it died. It warmed us both with bitter intent. 'That shirt really looks good on you,' Ant said.

We took a cab to Hull, where I had never been. It attracted younger revellers across the river and was little more than a collection of nightclubs and bars. There was a cinema showing pornographic films.

We were early. Not many people were around. I let Ant be my guide and he took us to a bar. 'This place is full of losers,' he said. 'It's really funny.' He said he always came here first, usually with Chuck, and they sat and drank and laughed at everyone else. It was a Greek restaurant, in fact, but it had a long bar. There was one waitress, but otherwise only men, and not many. 'Not a lot of chicks here,' Ant observed, 'but there never is. Tank up and we'll hit the clubs.'

We drank beer, which enlivened the tequila in me. There was a group of slightly older guys wearing baseball caps, sitting at a table not far from us. One of them stared at me with a smile on his face. He was wearing a red cap. He said something to his friends, who turned to look at me and laughed. I looked across the bar and saw myself in the mirror. The red T-shirt which Ant had given me looked very tight.

'I don't even think Fall's that hot. Nobody at that fuckin school is truly hot. We'll go to Chez Henri soon.'

'I hope you realise I don't dance,' I said.

'You've gotta dance,' he said.

'Dancing is insitutionalised vanity,' I said. 'It's about individuals losing their individuality; pretending to be individual while following socially delimited moves. I find it laughable.'

'Whatever. We can stay here all night if you want.'

'I don't like those guys over there.'

We finished our beer.

It was still early. We walked a couple of blocks to Chez Henri, a nightclub with a bouncer at the door. His shoulders were no bigger than mine but he was tall. I felt instinctively polite towards him like I wanted him to be my friend, and then I quickly resented that feeling.

It was very dark and very loud in the nightclub and there were still not many people. Ant ordered some shots of peppermint schnapps. I found them a relief. He ordered more.

There was a group of single girls on the dance floor. Ant said they were all fuckin ugly. I was surprised that I wasn't feeling drunk. Ant ordered more schnapps and I wanted to bite the glass.

I hated the music. I hated the way everyone danced. I liked that it was too loud to converse.

The place filled up. I went to the bathroom, pushing past hundreds of people. I saw myself in the mirror and I looked unfamiliar.

When I stood at the urinal someone came out of a cubicle, brushed by me and said, 'Nice shirt, sweetie.' I looked over my shoulder and it was the guy in the red cap from the Greek restaurant. He left the bathroom before I could finish urinating.

I tried to make my way back towards Ant. I remember feeling suddenly like a stranger, that everyone belonged but me. I heard people laugh. A girl shouted 'whoo'. I heard a laugh again. I saw Red Cap who was standing with his friends. He had a beer in his hand.

I pushed my way through to him, not knowing what I was going to say. When I got close to him I felt a pain throb through me that ended in my throat and I realised he had kneed me in the groin.

While my mind was catching up to the pain someone bumped my shoulder and knocked me off balance. I couldn't see Red Cap and I felt like I wanted to be hugging my knees in bed.

I made my way back to Ant. He had ordered some beer. I stared at the now-full dance floor and thought about everyone hoping to love. 'I'm going to kill someone tonight,' I said. Ant didn't hear me. I drank the beer quickly and walked away with the glass in my hand. I heard Ant shouting 'where you going' behind me.

I found my way to Red Cap who had his back to me. I focused on his hat and tried to smash the glass on his head. The handle broke off but the glass didn't break. He was on the ground and his hat was knocked off.

My neck cracked and I was on the floor, holding my eye before knowing why. I felt a shoe. My nose popped and my throat was soaked in warmth. I felt fingers under the back of my collar and I was yanked up. I tasted more blood in my throat and through my tears I saw one of the other caps winding up. I ducked and tried to punch him in the stomach but I hit his belt buckle.

I saw Red Cap still lying face down on the floor. There were hands under my arms and my feet left the floor and I was spun around and thrust through the crowd. The bouncer was carrying me. I squirmed to try to get both feet on the floor but he was able to keep me up and was carrying me to the back of the club.

He lost his footing and I ran for the back door and out into the winter. I ran as fast as I could.

My nose felt like it was being permanently pressed against metal. I could only breathe through my mouth, but I ran without thinking of breathing. I ran away from all the bars, away from the lights, through the courtyard of an office block. I heard running and shouting behind me and felt like everything was catching up to me, a feeling that unless I ran I would have to be myself.

'Will you please fuckin wait?' Ant shouted.

I looked over my shoulder and saw him running. No one else was around. I leaned forward and my heart was sending pulses of pain to everything I had injured.

'Let's get a cab,' Ant said.

Neither of us had coats.

I awoke the next morning with a sheet stuck to the back of my hand. I made my way to the bathroom and saw blood on the sheet. I needed to get my head lower. I kneeled by the toilet and looked around at his aunt's luxurious bathroom. The sheet was stuck to my hand with dried blood. I pulled it back slowly and revealed a gash between my knuckles which I had opened when I punched the belt buckle. I pulled the sheet right off and vomited. My hand was bleeding without the bandage of the sheet. I slept or passed out.

Ant woke me and said, 'Are you OK, I need to piss.'

We looked at my hand and decided I needed stitches. Ant had to go to a lunch with a family friend that day. He loaned me a coat.

On the bus to the hospital everyone looked away from my face. I got thirteen stitches in my hand and they set and bandaged my nose.

'We're supposed to report this sort of thing,' the doctor said.

I COULD KISS YOU all night she says.
 She hugs me like I hugged that pole when I was a kid and I'm not telling anyone about that.

When I was a kid I'm saying, Maybe eight, I hugged a pole, really pressed myself into it, right there in the playground. I guess my body was waking up I say.

I said it.

That's so cute she says.

I think we should see a movie tomorrow.

I'll do anything you want she says.

I believe it. I can't believe I'm free I say.

It's midnight she says. I should go.

She's not moving because she's mine.

I guess so I'm saying.

I'm gonna see her tomorrow. It'll be Saturday and bright and I'll open every door like a present.

Today!

We're walking and I had too much popcorn.

Look at that guy I say.

I saw him she says.

Hilarious I say.

We're walking.

I had too much popcorn I say.

She doesn't like talking about movies so I'm not talking

about it but I want to say something otherwise the movie didn't exist.

Did you like it.

What.

The movie.

Yeah.

Me too.

She's holding my hand.

I need to fart. Which way's the wind blowing.

It was kind of violent she says.

Yeah.

She doesn't even like seeing someone get punched in the face.

I want a frozen yogurt she says. And a small piece of chocolate.

Slürp's over there I say.

Let's go to Slürp.

I'm farting.

Why the little smile she says.

Our anniversary's in a week I say.

I know she says. I wanna plan something she says.

I've got plans I say.

Do you.

An idea.

Yeah.

A red hotel I say.

Really.

Kind of.

William, as per the secret man's secret agreement, will be standing outside the servant's entrance, because William says he's my servant. I love the grey in his sideburns, and I'll have the same one day but I'm blond.

Hey, fellas, I'm just getting something from the house, OK. Hush-hush. And William's gonna drive me back to school, OK. Bum knee. Right. Hush-hush.

I love the wink. I love a winking marine. I love to be understood. I love cigarettes.

William's lit up over there like a spy movie. He's sucking the fire through his cigarette and I'm thinking about the grey in his burns and a crackle of age and sex and secrets, snap.

You look excited he says.

I am excited I say.

I saw a woman today he says, flick, get in the car, who was putting on lipstick.

Chunk.

I was down in the food court he says through the window and he's walking around and he's in.

Chunk.

And she was putting on lipstick with one of those contact, compact things, what's it called, and she was *loving* her lips he says. I could tell by the look on her she was loving her lips. The sight of herself. She was applying . . . caressing, with the lipstick, her beautiful lips. I found it very sexy.

You find everything sexy I say.

And it was nice. I liked how much she loved her lips. I remember getting my first sunburn when I was a kid and thinking, I like the look of that sunburn. I haven't liked myself since. I like how much she loved her lips.

I like lips I say and I know exactly what he's gonna say, *be careful* . . .

Be careful of lips. I've had two wives.

I know.

You know. Be careful of lips he says.

I'm gonna wait while he drinks some beer I'm thinking.

I love William.

You're nice to me, William.

Well, you tell your girl to be nice to you.

She is.

So tell her to be mean. Tell her to be something she's not. That's my advice.

Dad says you don't get wise you only get old.

Your father's wise he says.

We'll drive down to the Chateau Lafayette and William will take his hat off and put it on the seat just there and he'll be a bald chauffeur with salted burns going away to drink some beer I bought him. I'm the luckiest guy alive.

I'm thirsty he says.

I know.

No you don't. You don't know thirst.

No.

There's something . . . I don't know. One day on my boat when you're grown up . . .

Hair . . .

When you have hair on your balls, we'll talk over a beer about what life is really like. You're going to find out. And I mean that with all due respect. You're going to find out what life is really like.

Go have a beer, William. Please go have a beer. I have to be back by 10:30. How many beers in an hour and a half I say.

Fifteen minutes a pint. Enough to get the fat and muscles humming.

I can't wait to see you.

You're young. Look in the mirror and remember that.

William scratches his sideburns.

William makes noises like a fattish guy on a car seat.

William smells like a party.

I've had haemorrhoids on and off for a decade he says. I don't wish them on you, young Julius, it's a piece of your gut pinched out of your ass and when you're young that's a troubling idea.

Yes it is I say.

So keep your girl out of my bathroom cabinet there, the one above the sink, and otherwise the place is yours, you can use it as you like.

You're such a buddy, William.

Well he says. Maybe don't drink the whiskey either. Or the gin. Maybe none of the, uh, spirits there. Beer, sure. One each.

I won't drink your booze, man.

I wouldn't say no to a beer right now come to think of it.

You just had some.

True enough. And thanks for getting me off duty there for a spell.

You bet.

But I'll tell you. You have your father to thank. He always lets me off, most weekends, so if it wasn't for him I wouldn't be going fishing this weekend and my apartment wouldn't be empty for you and your beautiful romance. Keep your seed off my sheets by the way. Be decent about it.

Where do you fish in December I say.

I don't want to think about sleeping in his bed.

A place called Mullet Lake way up. It's tiny. Freezes early. We drink. We stop at the liquor store on the way up and buy SCOTCH. Big goddamn vat of it at the store with no name except SCOTCH. And my buddy and I we talk about life and how hard it is to find a woman to love and it's not because we're fat. I'm telling you, Julius, the older you get the pickier you get.

OK.

You know, people my age they're more willing to forgive the human things, the haemorrhoids and the mistakes, but somehow it's harder than ever to find that perfect match because we've got our habits and by now we really know what we don't like.

Right.

So we sit in the boat and once we saw a trout but we didn't know how to catch it. We never get drunk enough.

Anyways it's really nice of you.

It's nothing.

It's just one night I say.

It's nothing. And don't eat my food either.

We'll go out.

That's the way. Take her out to dinner. Lots of places around there.

William, man, have you noticed you give me a lot of advice. Instructions.

Well you've got your girlfriend and your looks and your whole life ahead of you. But I know better about everything.

I appreciate it.

And don't tell your father.

There's a noise of scratching, he's whiskers and fat.

Of course I'm not telling Dad.

And don't make too much noise. The neighbours are really nice. Don't wake them up.

OK.

And meet them. Meet the neighbours. Meet some people, Julius.

I just want some space I say.

Yeah, well he says.

I FELT HOMELESS. I think part of me actually wanted to go back to Ant's aunt's place. I felt like I could hide there amid her strangely frigid luxury and be absorbed by a new life. I thought about my parents in Australia and how distant we were. I never felt comfort from parents, though I know my mother loved me. Our culture, with its unquestioning belief in psychological consequence, in the ramifications of childhood, seems to have no room for the agency of a child. The onus is on parents to create the ideal life, and their inevitable failure is the cause of a child's maladjustment. There is little credit given to the possibility that a child might not love, that there can be unbridgeable distance, even ill will, that has nothing to do with how his parents treated him. I was born hungry, and no matter what my parents did to determine what I ate, my hunger was always my own. Distance was what I felt; distance was my choice.

I had thought I had a home with Julius, but I couldn't get Fall out of my mind. I got angry when I thought about her. I was so cold that Sunday, with black eyes, my nose in a bandage, my hand wrapped up, the internal pain spreading through my body.

I had read G.K. Chesterton's letters that term and had marked a passage: 'For children are innocent and love justice, while most of us are wicked and naturally prefer mercy.' I think I had underlined it because I no longer felt innocent. I wanted comfort that Sunday.

Naturally everyone was curious about my face. I told the Masters I had broken my nose playing basketball. Ant told everyone else about my fight. Julius asked all about it. I told him the details in the dark before we slept. It was the first time that we spoke in the old intimate way.

'There's nothing fun about fights,' he said. 'Every one I've been in has been . . . I don't know. There's that second when you step back and think *we're hurting each other.*'

He was trying to understand. The pain in my nose made my eyes water anyway, but I was crying. He was being so nice. I wanted to tell him that I liked the idea of hurting someone.

Her mother came to the school to drop something off, and the comforting idea that Fall had been with her all this time fell apart.

The nature of everything changed. Everyone realised that Fall was actually missing. The news spread through the school immediately and everyone's movements slowed to the pace of incredulity.

The police were called that day. I don't know whether they looked alien or whether their presence suddenly made the whole school seem so. In any case, it felt like they introduced a new reality or were putting an end to a game.

Police, with their sticks and guns and cuffs and radios, seekers of truth with preposterous tools. What could those tools do to me? What would that mustachioed man with the belly and grave propriety ever know about my life?

I went up to the Flats. Housemasters did random inspections of rooms to make sure no one was up on the Flats during the school day; I would have daytime naps on the floor of my closet, covering myself with blankets and shoes and whatever else belonged on the floor in case a Master popped his head in. I didn't think I would be able to sleep, but I slept.

Julius couldn't believe that she was missing. I realised he hadn't been worried about her before, he had simply been pining for her: wondering where his love was rather than thinking she was gone.

He slept at his father's house that night. I left the curtains open, watched the blue light shine on the papers on his desk.

'I'm scared,' he said the next night. 'I'm really scared.'

'Don't be scared,' I said. 'There's a simple explanation.'

In the dark I tried to work things out with him; certain words, guttural consonants, would loosen the back of my palate and blood from my healing nose would ease down my throat. I remember what it felt like to say 'she's not gone', the nasal difficulty of the 'not', the 'gone' making me taste my blood.

Naturally none of us was privy to all that was going on. I pieced some of it together later. Julius spent many hours helping the police. At some point his help elided into explanation and self-defence. The whole business moved more quickly than it normally might have; the people involved – Julius's father, Fall's mother – ensured that.

Christmas exams were approaching. I was expected to fly to Australia for the holiday. None of us knew how long this would go on.

I told Julius every night that there was a simple explanation. To me then it seemed simpler than it does now.

'Do you think she ran away?' he said. To him that was somehow saddest.

This is a date

THIS IS A neighbourhood I'm thinking.
He said it's apartment C I say.

C she says.

You first she says.

The light in the stairway's yellow. I guess C's on the third floor I say.

Someone's cooking onions she whispers.

I'm starving.

William says we should meet the neighbours I whisper.

Who are they she whispers.

I haven't met them I whisper.

C.

Click.

Shouldn't we knock.

He's fishing.

It's dark she says.

It smells.

Be nice.

Where's the light.

There.

I wonder if we'll fuck or eat first.

We're not allowed to drink, eat or have sex here I'm saying. And you're not allowed to go into the bathroom cause you'll see he has haemorrhoids.

Do you talk about sex with William.

No I say. Yes.

Do you tell him about me.

Are you hungry.

A little. Let's sit down for a second.

K.

You sit there in the big chair. That must be where William sits.

William I say.

William. He's so nice she says. I feel so weird being here, but he's so nice to let us.

It's so strange to see how someone lives she says. This is where he lives.

I'm sitting.

This is where he puts his body I'm thinking.

He thinks here she says.

He has a fuckin toy car I say. He has a little metal Nascar thing ho ho.

That's so cute.

William. So he sits here and drinks his drink. Should we go through his drawers.

No.

Come on.

No.

You look so pretty, Fall.

She's quiet.

Are you sad.

No.

What's in the head.

Nothing. I'm just thinking about William. I wonder how my dad lives sometimes.

Yeah.

Does he sit on a big chair like that. What does he think about.

Yeah.

Was William ever married she says.

Yeah. Twice.

Why are you standing.

I don't know.

You're so restless, J, sit down.

I'm sitting.

Does he have girlfriends.

I think so. Yeah. I don't know if he takes them back here. If they stay here.

They must she says. I wonder if they're comfortable.

Fuck no.

Why not.

I don't know. Look at it.

I like it she says. It's a man's place.

You like a man's place.

Yeah.

I guess it's nice I say. It is nice. It's small I say. I'm wondering why our parents' places are so fuckin big.

Why are you standing.

I wanna look around. I wanna find more toys. Come on.

There's the kitchen.

It's so small.

Maybe he can't cook I say. I can't cook.

Here's the bedroom she says.

I'm standing behind her. We're cuddling. I kiss the back of her head.

I guess William gets a cuddle too sometimes. A nice fat cuddle and a woman with arms like cold cheese. This place is great I'm thinking. You just need a quiet small box with love and breathing and a fridge and a candle and maybe a little toy car.

You know I say. Dad's got this place where you can fly a flock of eagles in the dining room and I bet William feels lucky he lives here.

Yeah she says.

I don't know though I say. It smells like an old suit.

We're not going to fuck right now and it's right.

William she says.

This is Chinatown and Little Italy's down the street she says.

Is it.

I've been here once with Mom.

We're holding hands through gloves.

I forget we're in a city I say. You know what I mean.

We don't get out she says.

This is a city.

Spare any change.

No.

Sorry.

Have a good night.

It's a city.

Let's do everything I'm saying. Let's have a perfect dinner. A big fuckin pasta or something small and pretty like you like and some beer or wine and dessert.

Let's have some food we've never had she says. It's our anniversary.

Yeah. But it has to be something delicious and gigantic. And small and pretty like you like.

Vietnamese.

Sure.

Indian.

OK.

Thai.

Why not.

Or Italian.

Who knows.

I should have worn black she says.

She flips her hair. I'm not sure I like it when girls flip their hair but fuck she's pretty and she's Fall.

She knows how many guys like her. I know she knows. I like how many guys like her. I don't love it I'm thinking, but I like it. This guy coming here with his girlfriend he's gonna look at Fall for a second.

Yep.

And his girlfriend's pretty but she's not as BEAUtiful as Fall, uh uh.

She's mine.

You're mine I say.

Am I.

What's this place it's packed.

Oh I think I heard about it she says.

It's packed.

Wanna try it.

Maybe.

I feel like I don't even know how to walk into that place she says.

Let's keep walking I say and maybe there's another place, or we could come back.

OK.

Spare any change, folks.

Sorry.

Sorry.

Have a nice night.

Thanks she says.

How about this place.

It's cute she says.

Yeah.

I don't know.

No.

Let's keep walking.

I squeeze her hand.

I look at her.

She's smiling but not looking at me.

It's cold on my face and warm in my coat and the world's behind glass and we'll open the door.

I've never had Korean food I say.

Neither have I she says.

That place was Korean.

Yeah.

Wanna look.

Sure.

It's crowded.

It's bright.

Could be good.

They're cooking their own.

Mm.

They're cooking their own food. Look. They've got, like, barbecues on the tables. Fun she says.

I can't cook.

Let's try she says.

Can I have a steak.

Come on, J, let's try.

Let's do it.

Ling-a-ling.

Fuck me it's hot.

Hello good evening.

Hello.

Two.

Please.

Follow me.

She's pretty.

I've gotta take my coat off. It's hot I say.

Please. Enjoy.

She's pretty.

I'll take Fall's coat because I'm a gentleman.

Where do we put these I say.

I saw a rack near the door she says.

She looks young.

I'm walking back to the front. Everyone's staring at me but they're not, they're eating, I don't know how to cook, I guess I just hang the coats here. Plastic. Noel says a coat loses its shape unless it's hung on a wooden coat hanger.

She's pretty.

Will I fuck an older woman one day.

I love chopsticks and they make me nervous. People eat with different things.

My Fall.

Hi.

So what do we eat.

Are you OK sitting there she says.

Yeah it's great.

We can change if you want I say.

Let's change halfway through she says, I'm happy just looking at you. I just wanna see everyone cooking it's so fun in here. You can order, like, beef or chicken and then she says, See, I was watching those people over there, and he sort of picked a bunch of meat from a bowl and he's cooking it.

She stops. She's cute and excited and she stops. It's great I say. Where's the waitress.

There's no rush she says.

She smiles.

I'm smiling.

I'm excited.

I'm young.

Kimchi.

Dak-gui.

Gimbap.

Japchae.

I have no fuckin . . . What do you feel like I say.

I feel like number 148, cheonggukjang-jjigae she says.

Just kidding she says.

There's chicken I say. And beef.

And salads she says.

Maybe we should ask.

Maybe I should be cooler for a minute.

There's a hot fuckin barbecue in the middle of the table.

Hi.

Hello. Ready to order.

Maybe.

You be here before.

No.

OK. So. You order what you want from here. 1, 2, 3, like you want. Meat. Fish. But, say number 1, you cook, 2, you cook, 6, all cook. I bring chicken, you cook here.

OK. Do you cook anything.

Chef she says.

Pardon.

I cook nothing. Ha ha. I come back.

That couple's not talking, they're staring at us. He's staring at Fall. I'm staring at him. Fall's staring at the menu.

Fun she says.

Let's get drunk I say.

OK.

Beer.

No. I want a cocktail or something. Or wine.

Do they have wine. I'll try wine.

There's a wine list she says. You order.

I don't know what to choose. What's the most expensive.

A hundred and ninety-five.

Get that.

No.

That guy was staring at you I whisper.

I know she whispers.

Some couples don't talk I'm whispering. They don't have sex and they don't talk.

We won't be like that she whispers.

We can whisper instead of talking sometimes I whisper.

We can whisper when we have sex she whispers.

I'm starting a hard-on.

. . .

There.

Could we order drinks I say. My wife would like a glass of white wine. And I'll take a beer.

What kind.

Um.

You try OB. Korean beer.

OK.

Let's order, my stomach's eating the bottom of my tongue I swear.

You should order that beef thing, number 5 she says. You cook it. And I'll have a mango salad. And let's try that combo thing, the kimchi and everything. I think I've heard of that. I think that's what those people got she whispers.

I liked calling you my wife, it made me feel sort of smart and fat.

Good.

Happy anniversary, Fall.

Happy anniversary, J.

I'm so fuckin hungry.

Now his wife or whatever is staring at me. I'm pretty sure she's staring.

I'm getting good at cooking. I'm gonna become a Korean chef I say.

You are a Korean chef she says.

This beef is so fff . . . It's so good.

This is all so good she says.

That woman's staring for sure I'm thinking. Should I say hi to her.

I'll smile at her.

She's smiling.

That's nice.

Have you kids been here before she says.

No we say.

We like it a lot she says.

We do too says Fall.

There's the waitress. Could we get more drinks.

Our kids aren't as adventurous as you guys she says.

Huh I'm saying to my mind. Huh. A little phoney laugh. Why did I smile at that woman. Huh. Do we have to talk to them all night.

Do you kids live near here.

Just down the street I say. I drive cars for a living I say. Kind of a car jockey.

Her husband's smiling. He's wearing all black. I'm gonna ask him if he's a thief. Are you a gay thief I'm thinking and smiling at him.

Well enjoy the rest of your meal she says.

Thank you we say and I feel like moving.

Hm says Fall.

The beer.

What's that wine like I say.

It's OK.

She's my home. She's my safe place after weird strangers. They're talking like phoney. They can't hear us any more.

I'm not crazy about these pickles I'm saying.

They're OK she says. I've had something like them at a Japanese restaurant. Mom has a friend who eats nothing but stuff like this and I have to stand far away from her or her breath will, like, gas me. It's true. She's Mom's best friend but they're so fake with each other sometimes. I love your Lexus, I miss the older models. You know.

Yeah.

But there's like a weird connection. Mom has thousands of friends, but she's her only real friend.

OK.

It's like you look at them and you can tell maybe that they've been hurt the same way or something.

Look at her. I think she's really smart. I don't really understand.

I don't know she says.

This is our anniversary I'm thinking. She's smart over there and talking and thinking her thoughts and maybe life's not smarter or bigger than this.

I don't know she says. I kind of love her. She's mom's best friend. But her breath smells like pickles.

I'm reaching over the barbecue and holding her hand and my forearm's gonna melt and we'll eat it with hot wine. I've had two beers and I need to piss.

I'm coming back I say.

The couple's gone.

They've left.

Thank god she says.

Why don't we change seats.

Please she says. I wish we changed before.

Sorry.

That guy was a creep.

Was he.

Totally. He was staring.

I know.

No, but more than staring. When you were in the bathroom.

What.

His wife's looking down, paying the bill, and I look over at them, right. And I caught his eye for a second and he's looking at me and he's going like this: You're Hot.

What.

Not saying it out loud, but moving his lips. You're Hot.

What!

While his wife's right there she says.

That fuckin middle-aged guy!

Yes! You're Hot. I didn't know where to look. I think I was staring at him, you know. Wondering if he was really saying that.

I'm gonna kick his ass.

You should.

Is he gone.

I think so.

She's laughing.

What's funny.

When they were leaving he dropped this in my lap. His card.

No!

Yeah.

No way!

His phone number.

No! Didn't she say they had kids our age. You could be his kid.

It's not like I wanted it.

What a slimy fucker. Let's call him.

No.

Yes I say. Call him and tell him He's Hot.

There's a payphone near the bathroom.

Don't, J.

Come on.

After dinner. Let's do it after dinner.

OK.

There's more meat.

She's good with chopsticks. Look at those fingers.

What does it say on his card.

Just his name she says. Here.

Sean McAdams 515-849-5929.

I think you should talk to him I say.

No way, J. You're my husband. You have to call and be, like, outraged. But eat. I want dessert. I want green-tea ice cream.

I wonder if there's a way I'm saying to stop the meat sticking to the grill like this. Maybe you could rub it with Vaseline or something.

I can't eat any more she says.

She's puffing out her face.

She's funny.

For a pretty girl you do funny faces.

Pretty girls can do all kinds of things she says. We can, like, hold up numbers in boxing. Between rounds.

Bikini.

I think we've talked mostly about food tonight she says.

I wanna call that guy I say.

Will you be outraged.

I think you should talk I say.

Should I tell him I can't stop thinking about him.

Tell him you wanna back into him. You wanna pull down your jeans and back into him.

Straight to the point she says.

I'll talk to him I say. I wanna talk to him.

I'm definitely not talking to him she says.

Let's go to the payphone. He won't know.

Calm down for a second. We have to pay.

She calls for the waitress like a woman with long fingers.

It's an answering machine.

Hang up she says. What were you gonna say anyway.

I don't know. I was gonna see what he said.

If it's an answering machine I'll call she says. Give me the credit card.

Really.

I was scared of talking to him.

What'll you say.

That I love him.

Make him cry.

No. I'll be honest she says.

She's smiling.

She's dialling.

She breathes in deep through her nose and I feel like giggling and squeezing my little boy's cock like I'm playing hide-and-seek.

Hi she says. I hope I've reached Sean McAdams. You left me your card earlier tonight and . . . I don't know . . . I wanted to talk to you as soon as I was alone.

Hee.

She's getting sexy.

I can't leave you my number in case my boyfriend answers so maybe I'll try again later.

She hangs up.

Hee I say. Do it again.

Should I.

Fuck yeah.

What if he answers.

You can hang up.

Hee we say.

She's dialling.

Hi, Sean. It's Fallon, from before. I . . . uh . . . I just wanted to see if you were around yet. It's just me here. Maybe you'll pick up. It's just me here with my . . . um . . . cat. Julius. He's purring.

She hangs up.

Hoo.

Do it again.

No way! He'll pick up.

So hang up. Here. I wanna call.

I'll do it she says. I wanna do it, it's me he was hitting on.

She's dialling.

Hoo I'm thinking. What's funny what's funny what's funny.

Hi, Sean. It's Fallon again. I guess you're still out. Was that your wife you were with at dinner. I wish I could talk to you . . .

She's quiet for a while what's . . .

You looked really interesting she says.

She hangs up and I say Ooo, that was convincing. Spooky convincing. Do it again.

No.

Tell him you're wearing nothing but lips.

No.

Come on.

We're standing next to the bathroom she says.

I take his card from the top of the phone.

This is a date.

This is a date she says. I want to sit somewhere quiet with you.

Like a bar.

Not smoky.

Like a lounge.

Yeah. Like on a couch.

Nice.

I should have worn black she says.

I'm thinking there's a hole in my sock.

Sometimes I wanna eat you, Fall, I swear. Sometimes I just wanna know everything about you. You tell me every minute of every day since you were born. You tell me every minute that made your skin into what it is, OK, and those eyes into that shape, then I'll know where you came from and it'll be the same as eating you.

She's quiet.

I love you I say.

I'm so in love with you, Julius.

In the middle of my brain there's a tiny red pool and a thousand long toes of chicks in bikinis are warming and kicking and stirring, plish plip.

How fuckin hip and warm is this bathroom, I'm gonna sit here for a while.

She just said something and I'm smiling but I couldn't hear and I'm wondering if I should say what.

I'm smiling.

She's smiling.

I guess that smiling's enough.

I left you a note under your door at school she says.

Cool I say. This is a cool place.

I love it she says.

I feel like getting high. We should sit on the same couch I'm thinking but I like looking at her over there on her own on that big couch she's in the middle of the world's open hand.

I feel like getting high I say.

She's laughing.

There's a question in her eye and she's drinking. This place isn't as quiet as it looks outside.

You look cute over there on that couch she says. You look like a little boy or something she shouts. Sitting inya . . .

I can't hear.

I'll move closer in a second. I should come here with Chuckie.

I'm moving.

I can't hear I say. I think you said something like I can't believe how smart you are, you're the guy with the yard-long cock.

That's right she says. Sit back over there.

I'm kissing her head and her hair smells like hair.

She's touching my arm and it tickles.

I'm thinking about telling her that she's quiet but she gets mad when I tell her she's quiet.

You're quiet I say.

No I'm not.

What's in the head.

I don't know. I'm just having a good time.

She's mad. No she's not.

Me too I say. I'm gonna buy some shots.

OK.

Who knows what's gonna happen tonight.

That bartender is beautiful, oof.

Some tits are like a home and an adventure at the same time.

I'm gonna write that down.

Can I have two shots of tequila.

Sure.

She's looking like she wants to card me but they carded me at the door, she knows that.

Something's bothering me.

She's so fuckin hot.

What was. Something's bothering me.

That fuckin guy at the restaurant. You can't just say to some-body's girlfriend You're Hot. What did Fall do, anyway, what was she like when he said that. Did she smile. I don't know what she's like when I'm not around. Maybe she fuckin smiled. She should have told me right away. Maybe she said something to him. She's mine. He didn't respect that. I respected his wife. I did. He's a skinny black-wearing faggot I should have barbecued him.

Here you go.

Oh, nice. Thanks.

What a smile.

I don't know how to carry the lemon and everything. I'll come back.

I'm spilling it.

Where am I. These couches are so cool. I'm never gonna sit in a living room I'm gonna come to places like this. I'm gonna live with William, except he'll be Fall.

Hey, shots!

It's tequila. I've gotta get the lemon and salt.

I'll wait she says.

What else happens when I'm not near her.

Am I jealous. What would I do if some other guy gave her his card like that and she didn't tell me. I have his card. I'm gonna call him later.

What if she has a closet full of cards of bald gay thieves who want to steal her. What if some of them are beefy and hot and hung and ripped and cut. Does anyone like tequila.

That was fast she says.

I have to keep my eye on you I say.

Do you.

Let's have some tequila she says.

You're beautiful I say.

You're beautiful she says.

I like being alone with you.

Me too. I was thinking about Sarah and Chuck and some of those guys she says, and I was thinking how nice it is that it's just the two of us. Right. We can have fun like there's lots of us, but it's just us two.

OK.

Cheers.

Cheers.

Lick.

Shake.

Drink.

Suck.

Hoo that's disgusting.

Let's get two more.

We're getting the next round together I say. I'm watching you all night I say.

How will the missing react to being found? Will there be relief in being brought back in to the arms of the world or will we find new places to hide?

A search party was organised by the community and the police. It was assumed that if Fall had been abducted there might be local clues, an earring resting on the snow by the road. Or if she had been despondent she might have gone to a familiar place to end her life. They say that suicides are contemplated from high points, with views of the land we want to leave.

The search took place on a weekday. I, along with most of the rest of the school, took part. Many residents of Sutton were also involved. We rallied at the front of the school, near the Girls' Flats, and were given instructions by the police on how to search and how to alert each other if something significant was found. I had a few glimpses of Fall's mother.

We weren't told to join hands but many people did as they walked. People took it very seriously or with a contained giddiness of purpose. I saw strangers at a distance.

I felt ill.

The search was to culminate by the river. It took almost two hours to get there as we slowly fined through the parks of Sutton. Riversides are where questions are asked or silenced. The police took a more careful role as we approached the slopes near the water.

It's a quiet memory, despite what was going through my mind at the time. Our feet in the snow, the delicate conversations of people wanting to discover, not wanting to discover. I kept looking up and seeing everyone moving forward with the same silent backs. I found it impossible to imagine myself doing anything but joining them; how wrong it would be to see one lone figure darting, or even walking, away in a different direction.

It seems like the beginning of my days. The minor distractions on the ground, the slow united march towards an artificial purpose. As I commute to work I look up sometimes and can't believe that we are all doing it together. I can't believe how necessary it has been for me.

As I stood by the river some memories came back and I swallowed my vomit so I wouldn't draw attention.

I remember leaning on a tree, looking around and wondering whether everyone was looking for myself or for her. The logic of the search began to make sense – it made sense that I was a part of it.

I saw Fall's mother looking as completely remote as a stranger could look. She was elegant and small and I couldn't imagine what was going through her mind. I saw her talking to Julius once.

It was best to look at those dark wet willows, the hats and jackets, to look around and be part of the mumbled momentum; hope to be able to hide in it; silence the part of myself that wanted to boast how I was somehow the cause of all this.

There was despair and suspense when the day came to an end. Where should we all look next? We went back to our houses and rooms.

The closet was the only place I could find any rest. I slept there after school a couple of times, even when I didn't need to hide. I piled things on top of myself – ostensibly so I couldn't be detected, but really because it was comforting to be part of a gathering of objects. During one spare period a Master came around to inspect the room. He opened the door of the closet and I lay perfectly still. I felt like giggling, expecting to be caught, and all the more so when I knew he hadn't noticed a human being under all those coats and cleats.

The police had appeared a few times in school. I tried to avoid them, but we were called in once or twice in small groups and asked when we had last seen Fall. My memory is of drifting rather than fear.

There was such a series of liminal moments in those weeks that I find it difficult to articulate the movement of my thoughts or the change to the mood of the school's small space. I've said that I became aware of the transition in Julius from one who was pining to one who was afraid. I suppose I myself changed from one who was afraid to one who was pining.

I had so irrationally focused on the look on Fall's face when I declared myself to her. I was obsessed with trying to determine what I meant when I said that I owned her, how I must have looked to her. My mind presented such a fevered kaleidoscope of imaginary problems. I was afraid of what she might say to Julius. I was afraid of her not understanding and therefore not loving me. If I allowed myself truly to ponder her disappearance it was only to feel some sort of relief that embarrassment and disappointment might be postponed. I can see now that I was too proud to acknowledge how much the perception of others meant. Anger was my defence.

I slowly stopped thinking of Fall as someone who could hurt me. And it remained inconceivable, at least imponderable, that she couldn't return at least some of my love; that she couldn't see my adoration, my perfect appreciation, and at least nod back at me, at least smile slightly and say 'there's promise'. A person can't lie in the sun and not grow warm.

I was too involved to note the changes that took place to every corner of the room, every room in the school, all the minds that drifted past each other between classes. Some people talked about her. Hysterical groups would form for a time like birds for a nightly feed. If I walked through the downstairs common room and saw the sniffling red faces of Jess and Sarah and some random sensitive boy, I would know that there had been discussion of Fall. Where *is* she? Always the same emphasis.

There's nothing more oppressive or repellent than collective mourning. People don't want to admit that they don't know how to confront something incomprehensible. It's easiest to copy a neighbour. That random sensitive boy knew nothing about Fall but he sniffled like everyone else. The greater truth was that few people properly cared. The schedule of school went on, the walls didn't move, exams went forward.

The common remark was that someone so popular, someone so beautiful, would never run away. 'She just wouldn't,' everyone said. But I knew her. I had a sense that her not needing to be loved might prompt a fugitive impulse if she felt too much love from others. Julius's notes to her, certainly, seemed constrainingly fulsome to me. And who knew what went on with her at home? Perhaps between Julius and her mother she felt she had no space for herself. She had to get away.

This was the sort of thing I had wanted to say to her. I understand you, Fall. I knew that you were so much more than a beautiful, popular girl; that a beautiful, popular girl could still possess an aching, solitary soul. As much as I knew that Julius loved you, and knew certain sides of you, I also knew from scores of night-time conversations that there were things he didn't see. That low note in your voice which to him meant nothing but sex, to me meant a momentary perception of the gravity of life. Of course you were beautiful, but your beauty came from subtle appreciation of the tissue beneath the skin, the rich red world of cells and salt that drives our bodies to unpredictable and inevitable sadness.

In the closet, in my nest of human cloth, I dreamt of skinless people, a world of living meat, clinched in a wounded hug and finally understanding. We would truly feel the cold, we would truly know each other.

And when I climbed out, to go to class, to go to dinner, I felt a new sort of want. I wanted you to take me away from that world of pretence and progress, of people claiming to know each other, lining up for exams mumbling formulas to themselves. Giving, gathering, manipulating answers in order to get ahead, elbowing each other while pretending to care: where *is* she.

I pined. Julius kept me informed. Julius's previously endearing hyperactivity turned into something more worrying. His searching eyes were suddenly afraid of what they would find; and there is something about that shift from curiosity to fear that drives other people away unless they share your fear.

'I think they think I did something to her,' he said.

The lead-up to exams before the Christmas holidays was always a paradoxical time. Quiet was required and quiet wasn't possible. Many were nervous about exams, but on the other side of exams was the first chance of the year for most to go home. The real world of parents, old friends, familiar weather and comfort, which had all become a dream over the past several months, was suddenly growing more visible.

Prep was extended by an hour and Masters were more strict about certain rules, but there was universal restlessness. The drama of Fall's absence made our little room unendurable.

I found ways out. People were often permitted to study together and Seniors were usually left alone. Ant and I pretended to work in the library, but we occupied ourselves elsewhere. Sometimes we sparred with each other. Ant liked to provoke me by taking 'mock' roundhouse kicks whose wind had a kick of its own. My nose was still very tender, so I lost patience quickly and I generally had him on the ground. 'Fuck you're strong,' he would say in the manner of the politely injured. He had such a stupid red face.

I suppose I was growing belatedly mischievous. That term had awakened things in me that I had concealed according to the custom of the quiet and the loud. Sometimes character only emerges when it is publicly acknowledged that one can have character. Until that recognition it exists as a constant germination, some sort of dark, relentless involution.

Beware the silent ones, my father used to say. He had that knack of making clichés seem like weighty and original truths. I've often thought that quiet people are the most interesting, not because they can have thoughtful responses but because the louder world has generally suppressed them into some sort of perversion. All that time under the earth, they're bound to present something unusually shaped when they emerge. I know so well the anger that builds in silence.

I had such a hunger for aggravation. That pre-exam atmosphere of anticipation and urgency was a nursery of irrationality; and somehow Fall's disappearance seemed like an opening rather than the looming black wall that it seemed to Julius. There was some part of me that felt she had gone out into the world, she had found a path of her own, there were unknown places which she went to discover and I would somehow follow her to them.

People would have late-night showers to relax themselves. Ant and I would throw pails of cold water on them. We regularly doused people in their sleep. Sometimes Ant or I would let go of the pail so it hit their heads after the water.

I found myself with a particular loathing for a few of the younger students. Edward, primarily, but there was a kid named Carlos, one year below me, who came from Barcelona and had a laugh like a burst of insults. He always showered with what appeared to be half an erection, and he had one of those obscene uncircumcised penises whose smegmaed eye constantly leer through their hood with an oozy wink. It made me think of Bavaria and how little good can emerge from a meat-loving culture.

I went into his room during one of my spare periods, while he and his room-mates were in class. I closed the door behind me. I wasn't particularly nervous. Other people's rooms can feel so full of possibility. All those strange objects so familiar to their owners. The posters of Barcelona, buildings with a fleshy dimension that Carlos could never communicate to his room-mates. Whose photo is that? Whose books are those?

The possibility of strangers' rooms increases, though, when you cease trying to learn about their occupants and wonder what you can *do* to them. The memories invoked by that poster would acquire a new poignancy if I tore it.

I looked around. I tried to determine what belonged to Carlos. There were three toothbrushes at the sink. One was sitting in a mug that read *Catalunya Ràdio*. I took that toothbrush and went back to my room.

I thought about lines, what makes one person from head to toe more beautiful than another. I thought about the bodies I'd seen on beaches in Sydney, tanning, heated like encaustics on the surface of my mind. I summoned them. I summoned perfection. This head like my father's box full of slides, the lines and colours, bent and warmed, bodies on the beach and the tension of a scrum.

I ejaculated on the toothbrush and brought it back to Carlos's room, dropping it back in the mug.

There wasn't much time before my first exam, and when I fetched my books I felt that lifelong nervousness. Algebra, particularly, was a worry.

I'M GONNA FIGURE it out. If everything in this dark street with the lights is life and the wind on my eyes cold and gentle. If her tight little hand through leather and wool and the side of her face are my friends. If her own secret street looks like mine, but, like, lower cause she's shorter. I'm gonna figure it out.

I'll figure out this second but it's gone. I'll figure out the second after this second it'll settle into my eyes. I'm gonna keep my eyes open for the wind and cold surprises and she'll look at me and laugh.

There's beer and gas–pump tequila and a flower in my throat. There's the stem of a flower on the top of my heart and my secrets blow out with my breath and when they're out I don't know what they are. I don't know what I want. I'm feeling it all and I don't know what it is.

Where we going she says.

Who knows.

Maybe she likes my smile. Maybe she's thinking about my smile. Maybe I shouldn't be thinking about my smile it's vain. Maybe she's undressing that guy from his coat, no way I'm buff and delicious.

That's pretty she says.

The dress I say.

The top she says.

There we are in the window and I'm looking like my dad

and my mom who's gone and in me. The store looks warm and golden.

I want a top like that for the winter she says.

It is winter.

Yeah.

I think I had a shirt, same brand as that I'm saying.

You did she says. Dark blue.

She knows my shirts.

Clothes don't last I'm thinking.

You were cute in it.

I love her.

I'm gonna buy her that whole store on this day in ten years because I'll have a job. Happy anniversary I'll say.

We're quiet.

I forgot to buy you a present I say. I'll buy you one every year. Later.

I bought you one she says. Maybe you'll get it tomorrow.

Nice I'm thinking.

We're walking and her arm's in mine.

I've never been older or happier I'm thinking. I like the warm in this jacket. I like that crunchy salt under my shoes, there's a guy who sprays it all over the street and I never want to be him.

Lay down your future now Dad says. You'll be surprised how much of your future you can determine at your age.

I'm laying it down, crunch crunch.

I'm gonna figure it out.

It's nice just walking she says.

She's wearing more perfume and I'm not sure I like it but she's a woman tonight and I'll make myself love it.

It's really nice just walking I'm thinking and I said it. It's so fuckin nice this calm right now. I've never felt older. I'm not gonna tell her I've never felt happier.

There's one perfect thing I wanna eat and drink and fuck. I'll keep my eyes wide open.

I love how it warms up before it snows she says.

It's warm in my jacket I say.

Maybe I should come in she says.

We're stopping.

We're hugging.

My tongue's on the bed of her tongue.

I wanna go to William's and fuck her with years on every side like she's a woman in perfume but I'm not saying anything. My tongue's on the bed of her tongue.

Mmm she says.

We're walking.

I'm holding my cock through my pocket and everyone can see it but nobody's around right now. My cock is my thigh's warm friend, squeeze hi.

The wind's in my eyes and I'm gonna figure it out. Tears on my cheeks and my cock in my pocket and I'm gonna figure it out. These are all new lights and corners. I can feel it. It's all new but it was there before. I'm almost there I can feel it. There's a middle of everything and I'm gonna figure it out.

There's an eye. There's a green eye of Fall. There's a city in the middle of nowhere.

There's a country in the middle of nowhere.

There are lights like these and colours like these and all the colours brighter when you're closer to the middle of night. And night right in the middle.

There's Fall's green eye. And colours of blue and yellow and brown and jungle animals all inside the green, and right in the middle is the deep blue-black looking back and taking in. Fall's pupil's up ahead, in the middle of that street. I'm so fuckin close.

You're walking too fast.

I'll run and I'll be in the middle.

You're walking too fast she says, Jumping Bunny. Take it easy.

I wanna go somewhere I'm saying.

Slow down she says. It's early.

I want a hot dog I'm saying. Something with meat and bread and mustard.

Sounds like a hot dog she says.

Where do you wanna go I say.

Stop she says.

Stop.

Open your mouth she says. Wider.

She puts her lips inside mine.

I love you she says inside my mouth and she blows it down to my belly.

It's only nine o'clock she says.

Teeth

MY LOWEST MARK was an A minus that term. I was destined to ease into university like a train into a station.

In all honesty I cannot remember exactly how Julius performed in his exams. Not very well, I think. And there were no final results for that whole year for either of us because neither of us made it through.

Christmas exams ended earlier at St Ebury than they did for other schools in the city, allowing most of us to fly away to our distant homes. Fall had been missing for little more than a week when I left for Sydney.

It was customary to have a Christmas party for the boarders near the end of exams before we all departed. We drew names from a toque at the end of chapel one morning as we all filed out, and were obliged to buy a present for the person whose name we drew.

It was my lot to buy a gift for Carlos. We weren't expected to spend much. The party was meant to be a warm celebration of our odd little community, the usual Christmas pretence that through the exchange of gewgaws we could claim to care for others. I tried to think of something for Carlos that would adequately reflect the silent oppugnance I felt for all he represented and I settled on a fish.

Ant came up to me after he drew from the toque and showed me Fall's name typed on his little slip of paper. 'Looks like I don't have to buy a present,' he said.

I asked Julius if he would like to go shopping with me.

We hadn't been off school grounds together for many weeks. 'No,' he said.

There is a type of 'no' that carries with it a heroic and unshakeable self-knowledge, an implication that to be considerate of others is somehow to be craven and dishonest.

I took a bus downtown and went to the fish market. I felt a mischievous glee at the prospect of Carlos unwrapping his present in front of everyone and discovering not something benign or merely gestural, but something wet and offensive. I sought out the largest, cheapest fish available, wrapped in wax and newspaper, I bought red paper and a pretty bow and I wandered through town delaying my return to school, my mind feeling relieved by the subsidence of study and the reminder that the world was larger than St Ebury. A warm day in December when the clouds were bloated with snow.

I was eating as much as I could, despite being nervous most of the time. I wanted to stay strong. I remember treating myself to a hot chocolate after I bought the fish.

I was wearing a pair of Julius's trousers – simple grey flannels – and a pair of his shoes as well. The shoes never felt like my own because of the imprint of his toes, but I always felt like his trousers could be his and mine together. I continue to believe that there can be an intimacy between two people that is simpler and subtler than the social mind or words like love or friendship can ever adequately encompass. It is there in the feeling of flannel on thigh, and even to describe it as intimacy is to summon it from the dictionary where all good feelings have died.

When my drink was ready, the girl behind the counter shouted 'Hot chocolate for Julius!' and I smiled and took my cup.

'The cops wanted to know what happened to your face,' Julius said. 'They saw your bandages.'

The lights were out.

'What did you tell them?'

'I said you were playing basketball.'

It was a loyal thing to say.

'They're asking about everybody,' he said. 'I'm supposed to answer about everybody.'

'What are they asking about me?'

'It's an investigation,' he said, as though he couldn't believe it.

I was still in my energised state and was worried about what I would say to Julius, whether I would say something offensive or not appropriately comforting.

'They found hair,' he said.

'Don't worry,' I said.

'In her room. Right? I thought, yeah, you found hair in her room. There's hair in my room. My bald uncle has hair in his room, right: it doesn't mean he's dead.'

'No one's talking about dead, Julius.'

'No,' he said.

'No.'

'Everyone's thinking it,' he said. 'It's hair with roots. A clump of Fall's hair with roots.'

We lay quiet for a long time. He wasn't crying.

I discovered later that they asked Sarah whether she could offer any explanation for Fall's hair in the room. Sarah had turned to pulling her own hair out. Anxiety drove her to maim herself in various ways over the coming months, and I wonder now about the memories inside her, the half-dead woman in the convenience store. All the lively limber bodies in the world, bending and smiling at experience. All the swollen barrels of grief and guilt standing upright in our middle age.

I think it was the intrusion of an outside reality that made everyone nervous. Julius was not directly declared a suspect for legal reasons, primarily because of diplomatic immunity. Here was a grand legal concept appearing in our little world. As the son of a US diplomat he could not be charged with any crime in Canada. Of course, this was not just a concept: the close relations between the two countries, the fact that his father was not just an ordinary diplomat but the Ambassador – the more compelling reality, no doubt, was simple fear of controversy. Julius's father and the Embassy had lawyers watching everything closely from the beginning.

And, of course, there was nothing yet linking Julius with Fall's disappearance.

'I saw her that morning and that was it. Her mom saw her after I did.'

'I could tell them,' I said. 'When will they ask me what happened?'

'Who knows.'

I didn't want to talk, but I said, 'I can tell them everything.' Never again was I willing to tell them, to help you. I still wanted to be your friend so badly. I can see us, like I never could, our stature, our hairless vulnerability. I can see us today like we were and we weren't.

'I don't know where I am.'

'Don't worry.'

'I can't catch up.'

'Don't worry. There's a simple explanation.'

You stood in your boxers and only one sock and I genuinely felt sorry.

How can one capture the romantic vicissitudes and mysterious infuriations that occur between two people? Day after day. There is never a moment when two bodies are even. I know that couples sometimes hope for stasis in the wave tank that contains them, but something outside always shifts the container. I wasn't mature enough to recognise what was in action that year, how one moment Julius seemed like he dominated the room, and the next he was quiet and feckless. How, in the subsequent truncated and ugly term, I felt completely impotent, the tank always tipping against me.

We all gathered in the common room downstairs. It was a space that students filed through daily, a combination of classroom, lounge, hall and cafeteria. All the boarders sat on the floor and gave the space a gaudy dimension. MERRY CHRISTMAS in banners around the walls.

Juilus had left before the party, head down in the room with his duffel bag on his shoulders. His sadness is clearer to me now.

I sat with Ant and Chuck and watched students of every age unwrap presents in front of each other. The Housemaster presided as Santa Claus.

'It has been a difficult term,' he said. 'A difficult thing has happened at a difficult time and we have all been affected in different ways. But the staff and I have every confidence that there will be a happy resolution and we will finish the school year, indeed start the new year, with our number as it was before.

For now, I want to congratulate you,' and so on. He intoned an ecumenical prayer.

Somebody bought me a keyring.

When Carlos unwrapped his fish there was a brief silence. Ant's laughter prompted everyone to laugh, including Carlos himself – who looked at me quizzically towards the end of his always sneering smile. I hoped that my face would make him uneasy.

I flew to Sydney the next day with a cold feeling in my stomach. A cab to the airport in the dark early morning.

I looked at myself in the bathroom mirror on the plane, feeling contemplative in the way that solitary travel encourages. My black eyes were gone, my bad eye settled into its regular deformity.

Chuck and I had both been waiting for cabs outside the front of the school to take us to different flights. I had said good morning to him and he had said nothing. It was customary for people to shake hands before Christmas. He gripped mine very hard when his cab came. 'I hope you liked the keyring,' he said. 'I didn't know what to buy a guy like you.'

I sat on the plane, Sydney ahead, being rushed to the brutal sun. I learned early in life that contemplation on an airplane is doomed to be flawed. The mind may be full, but it is only bewildered at watching the body being thrown so far ahead of it. The true coldness of my departure would land in my body weeks later.

My mother would meet me. She would hug me and say 'welcome home'.

IT'S A FEAST!
 It's a hot dog.
 It's a feast!
 There's mustard on your chin she says.
 You sure you don't want a bite.
 Positive.
 Myum myam myum I say.
 There's mustard on your chin she says.
 I'm wiping it.
 Hey, Julius. There's mustard on the back of your hand she says.

I wanna go to Italy she says. Florence.
 OK.
 Look at paintings.
 OK.
 I have favourites.
 What.
 Paintings.
 OK.
 I wanna see them. In person she says. It's so different. I saw the *Mona Lisa* when I was fourteen and it was so different. You have to think about it.
 I'm thinking about it.
 I don't know what she means.
 You're staring at it with all these other people, so you have to wonder why you're staring at it.

Right.

And it's, you know. It's emotional. Emotionally moving she says and she's biting my hand.

Hungry I say.

And Rome she says.

She's excited.

I think I don't like Italians I'm saying.

Why.

I don't know.

Why she says.

They'll pinch your ass and whistle and they never pass the ball.

I won't be playing soccer with them.

Don't.

I won't. Your great-great-grandfather was Italian she says. And your name's Julius.

It's true I say.

And you'll be with me to fight them when they whistle me. Pinch.

I don't want to fight I say.

Let's look at paintings in Florence she says.

OK.

I'm thinking I don't know what to think about paintings.

No, there's nothing.

Let's do things, Julius she says.

Fuck I remember sitting in the park by the parkway with Chuckie just like this I say.

Like this she says.

No not like this I guess, but I remember. Sitting there with a little bottle of vodka and dreaming.

Mmm she says.

Every year you feel so different I'm saying.

Yeah.

Don't you.

Yeah. If you're thinking about next year she says. Don't.

I'm not. I'm thinking about vodka.

OK.

And Chuckie.

I love Chuck she says. I could tickle his belly.

Her fingers.

He's all fat and funny.

He's not fat.

So we're sitting in a park when we're seventeen and now Chuck's got hair on his belly and I'm here with you.

Yeah. I never knew about this park she says.

She's rubbing her legs through her coat.

My ass is cold I say.

It's quiet.

Are we both thinking about my ass.

What's in the head I say.

Nothing.

It's funny right. Me and Chuck and the vodka. Even drinking. I'm not liking the drinking so much any more. Shit-faced with the boys. I like drinking and talking. You know.

Mmm she says.

Joint.

Sure she says.

I light it.

Sweet burn noseflesh.

Eat my nose.

Hoo! I shout.

Hoo! shouts the Fall.

Hyoo! shouts J.

Fraa says the girl.

Fraa I'm thinking. It's fuckin hilarious.

              H   H

H

                                  H

    H

    H!

Christ I can't stop

                H!

                              H

    H

I'm drooling.

That's the funniest fuckin

Hoo.

That's the funniest thing I ever heard.

What is she says.

H

                    H

H

H.

Fraa I say.

Hih.

That's Fall.

That's my girlfriend.

That's my Fall in her little red coat blowing trumpet on the road cone.

The grass is dark.

That's my funny Fall.

Joooolius she says.

Fall.

Hphweem she says. I'm an elephant.

I don't wanna go home she says.

William's I say.

I know she says. Let's not go yet.

Fuckin A. Let's stay out.

We can sleep in she says.

All day.

That's so nice. That's so nice she says.

It's opening.

The lights and the dark.

Driving into the opening.

Where in Hull says the back of his head.

Chez Henri I say.

I'm looking at her.

Smells like a cab in here I say.

It looks like one she says.

My hand's between her legs.

I can put my hand between her legs I'm thinking. I'm allowed.

I'll pay you if you dance with me I say.

I'll pay you not to dance she says.

Nice I say.

I'll film you one day. Show you what you look like she says.

I thought you liked my dancing.

I love your dancing, my J. I'm kidding.

Squeeze.

I'll pay you if you dance with me I say. Again.

I'll pay you she says.

It's opening.

I'm pretty fuckin high.

I should have worn black she says.

We're crossing the bridge.

It's pretty she says. The lights.

On the water I say.

So pretty.

Halfway over the bridge and there's steel and light and I don't want to barf tonight.

So pretty she says.

Breathe in through the nose. Sit up straight. I'm a man. I will make a serious comment.

I guess there's a border somewhere on this bridge I say.

She laughs.

I laugh.

What are you laughing at I say.

I don't know she says.

You're laughing at me cause I said whatever I said. What did I say. There's a border.

Pfff she says.

What.

She can't stop laughing.

I think it's notionally in the middle says the cab driver.

What.

The river itself is the border between Ontario and Quebec but the actual dividing line, I think, is notionally in the middle of the river.

I see I say. What the fuck.

King george the third determined that the river would be the border in seventeen ninety-one.

I'm so fuckin confused.
Interesting Fall says.

Night tastes wetter than day on that bag in the back of the throat.
What were you laughing at in the cab I say.
I don't know she says. Honestly.
We're hugging.
It's hard to explain.
You were laughing at me.
I wasn't. Not exactly she says.
Not exactly.
I think I was kind of laughing about how much I love you.
Hm I say.
I don't know she says. I love you a lot, J.
We're hugging.
This is a long fuckin line I say.
We're here right at eleven. Everyone gets here at eleven.
I'm high.
I'm laughing.
She's laughing.
Who knows.

She's hot.
She's cute.
She's not.
He's big.
She's cute.
She's old.
Old's good.
No it's not.
That guy just bumped my shoulder and I'm not gonna turn around.
Let's get a table she shouts!
It's packed I shout!
We'll probably ha to air!
I couldn't hear that. OK I shout!
I'm spilling my beer.
I feel like shouting but I don't know what.
There's some seats she shouts!

There's four people I shout!
There's room she shouts!
OK I shout!
Two guys. Two girls laughing.
Can we sit here shouts Fall!
Sure shouts a guy!
Me and Fall and girls and guys, check check check check check check, we're all OK, check check.
I know you shouts a guy!
Me I shout!
Yeah he shouts!
Where I shout!
We played you he shouts!
I'm sitting.
I'm at Glebe he shouts! Left wing!
OK I shout! You guys beat us I shout!
You scored a beautiful goal he shouts!
We like each other.

I was just in the bathroom she shouts!
I know!
And these girls were putting eyeliner on some of their teeth! Blacking them out!
Why!
To make their teeth look ugly! I asked them! They said we want to make ourselves look ugly! When guys hit on them! When they ask them to dance, they smile and say Sure and their teeth look rotten!
That's hilarious!
And the guys go away!
That's hilarious!
I want you to ask them to dance she shouts!
That's hilarious!
Wait she shouts!
She's coming over.
She's got her eyeliner.
Smile!
I'm smiling.
She's blacking out my tooth.

Try not to taste it!
I taste it.
Tastes like sand!
OK!
I'm smiling.
She's laughing.
Where are they!
The blonde in the green over there!
Nice!
With the blonde in the black! Red purse!
Nice!
I'm not gonna dance with you if you can't get them to dance!
You're gonna dance! I'm gonna dance like a fuckin idiot!
We'll see!
I'm walking.
I'm dancing.
I'm walking.
I'm trying not to smile.
Hey!
Hi!
I was over there! I saw you guys from over there! I like your purse!
Thanks! She flashes the teeth. Can't smile yet. Can't smile yet.
They're both smiling.
It's FUCKIN hilarious.
I'm smiling.
They see the tooth.
        H
               H
  H
H
  H!
You stole our trick!
  H!
        H!
  H.
My girlfriend won't dance with me if I don't get you two to
dance!
Let's dance says Green!

★   ★   ★

Hoo!

Never dance seriously.

Hoo!

Never.

Ever.

Dance.

Seriously.

Hoo!

They're laughing and their teeth look so fuckin funny.

You've got three girls shouts Fall! You've got a rotten front tooth and three pretty girls!

Those two aren't pretty! Look at their teeth!

Hoo!

My girlfriend and I are gonna hang out on the fire escape shouts Green!

It's hot I shout!

I know!

Fall! Let's hang out on the fire escape!

OK!

We're walking.

I'm sweating.

I'm dancing.

I'm walking.

It's so fuckin crowded in here.

Green's kind of flirty.

Green has a nice ass.

Black has a nice ass.

Fall's ass is perfect I've seen it. Hey, everyone. All you guys with your beer and no girls: I've seen that girl's ass and it's perfect.

Outside!

Whoo it's cold says Black.

Green puts her arms around her.

We're all standing close and other people are standing close and there's a shoe in the door so we can all get back to the noise.

It's quiet out here I say.

They're laughing. Black and Green with their arms around each other and rotten-tooth laughs and they're pretty.

I can't take any of you seriously says Fall.

You should do it too says Green.

No way says Fall. I want guys to pick me up. I'm looking for a guy with nice teeth tonight.

I'm thinking about braces and the time I drooled on the dentist's assistant and now I'm thinking about a nurse's hand on my balls, cough cough, and red candy. I don't want a hard-on.

We met a dental hygiene girl in line tonight I say.

That's true says Fall.

She could clean us up.

That's true.

That's the job we should have says Black. No one could hit on us because they'd always have drills and . . . things in their mouth.

The dentist could hit on you I say.

We're travel agents says Black.

She ignored me.

And everyone's hitting on us all day. Guys come in and want to fly to New York and next thing you know they're inviting us down to Barbados.

I'm kind of smiling.

Fall's kind of smiling.

I think we don't like Black. I think I don't like girls who always talk about getting hit on.

I like Green's eyes she's looking at me.

Does Fall see her looking at me.

I'm thinking why do girls who don't want to get hit on come to Chez Henri in pretty dresses and legs. Throats.

Smoke I say.

I hand them out.

I pass the lighter around because I do not light people's cigarettes.

Music's through the door and I'm dancing.

Julius likes dancing.

I'm smiling my tooth.

Green has a nice laugh.

She's looking at me.

Is that a shooting star or an airplane says Black.

Black's not so pretty she looks mean.

It has red lights on it says Fall.

Black looks at Fall.

I think they don't like each other.

My name's Julius I say.

Parvannie says Black.

Pardon.

P-A-R-V-A-N-E-H she says. It's Persian. It means butterfly.
Butterfly.

Pretty says Fall.

I'm Julie says Green. It means girl from Southern Ontario.

Pretty I say.

I'm thinking whatshername does not look like a butterfly.

I'm dancing a little like I wanna go back in. I'm showing the
tooth.

I KNOW I didn't hit her.
    I know my feet were wet so hers were deeper in the river.
I know she kept backing away from me, but I couldn't believe it.
    I told her that there was no time left and she had to be herself.
She kept lunging for her crutches and I felt they were a distrac-
tion from the issue. Lovers fight over objects that have nothing
to do with love.
    She said 'let me go', but I know I wasn't holding her.
    I felt logic and reason bursting through me like gusts of pepper.
It makes no sense that you're not with me.
    'I don't like you,' was all she could say.
    I know she was alive when I left her and ran up the hill, and
I never saw the scene as grave.
    Life never walked through my door and smiled, never said there
was so much more outside. I know there are many like me.
    Someone went down there and helped her. Someone found
her and that life we can never know was known.

My father took an interest when I said someone was missing from
St Ebury. 'The son of the US Ambassador is involved?'
    There was something caricaturish about my father. All the
manners of the Canadian Ambassador class: the Anglophilia, the
learned unflappability, the nose for rank and status. He pretended
not to be surprised by anything, to be familiar with every conceiv-
able outcome of all human behaviour; but he had the prurience
of a common journalist and could feed on gossip like a kitchen

maid. He wanted every detail of Fall's disappearance and naturally I told him little.

He hosted a small party which I was forced to attend that Christmas. Everything in Australia was casual, which my father embraced with characteristic mendacity. I have met few more formal men in my life, but during those years in Australia my father, in certain company, was a back-slapping, glad-handing, shorts-wearing lover of mateship and Rugby League. We sat around the living room, I, my father, a handful of colleagues and acquaintances, and my father forced me to recount some of the drama of that term. He pronounced 'drama' with a soupçon of local flavour.

I responded with sullen adolescent brevity and we really didn't discuss the matter much more. What I recall most vividly from that party was watching him listen to the story of one of his guests; he had a drink on his bare knee and was leaning back on the couch. I watched him silently nodding, smiling and so on, and I noticed that half of his scrotum was protruding through the leg of his shorts. I found it quite funny and was waiting for other people to see it, but my father noticed it himself during an inattentive nod. I watched the shock and embarrassment flash over his face, the hope that no one had seen. I watched him continue to pretend that he was listening to the story, and I could see so clearly how ashamed he was to reveal himself, how thoroughly he believed that a man so dignified couldn't possibly possess that absurd, vulnerable walnut.

How much further from himself did my little father travel when he adjusted the leg of his shorts?

I took up boxing at the gym in Sydney. The heavy bag was my favourite: shifting weight with my fists, the slow dance, the leather's dumb embrace. I didn't fight anyone until I returned to St Ebury, and that hardly qualified as boxing, but hitting the bag for those couple of weeks was the perfect antidote to reasoned meditation.

I ate a lot, avoided my parents, went to the beach. I read widely. My father had a good library.

And what is the role of books? What good did it do me to learn these words, to travel the ruts of other minds?

It allowed me to be perceived as calm and bookish. It meant my father felt certain of my future, that there would be these rooms in my later life.

And where do bullies come from?

The books give us truth and remedies, saying the bullies are the bullied, the bygone victims of what they are inflicting. We can root them out. Bullies were once downtrodden, they address insecurites through instilling them in others. We can cure them. They come from bully fathers. Women are rarely bullies. There is a solution in words.

Religion, Psychology, Philosophy, Fiction: charlatan words pretending to capture a moment, to know the future, to exist beyond death. The more we weave patterns, the more we think we cover the body of life. Whenever holes appear we adjust the weave, add more words, pretend that our days are not doomed to unpredictability.

I want to believe in patterns.

Where do bullies come from? They come from the burn of blood in monkey hearts. They are flashes of teeth under hungry primordial moons. Bullies are older than words, and anger is more enduring. The things I did could not have been stopped, and words could never erase them.

Show me the perfect way to deal with life's surprises. Show me how desire and hunger could possibly be ethical. Show me a library, and I'll show you what concealed but couldn't hold me.

THE MUSIC'S IN my ribs and the table's under my elbows.
That guy's dancing like his joints need oiling.
Is he doing that on purpose I shout!
I think so shouts Fall!
Her smile's getting blurry.
The table's all ours.
Her smile's not blurry if I focus.
I'm kind of fucked I shout!
Me too she shouts!
Wanna dance!
Not yet!
We're watching.

It's called a banquette she shouts!
We're sitting on it.
She's close and my hand's on her hip and I feel like I own the place.
She's looking at me.
I'm looking at that guy, that guy, that girl, that drink, that girl, that ass, that laugh, that arm, it's big, those tits, that coaster.
I haven't seen anyone we know she shouts!
No!
It's so crowded!
I know!
Look at that guy!

The fat guy!
Yeah!
He's pretty fat!
Does he remind you of anybody!
No!
No!
Who!
Your room-mate!
Him!
Noel!
But he's fat I shout!
I can totally see Noel looking like that in, like, twenty years!
No!
Thirty years!
No!
If he got fat!
Maybe!
Totally!
So what does he do! Fat Noel!
I don't know she shouts! Dental hygiene!
Funny!
He owns something she shouts! Controls something!
Maybe!
Totally!
So what's he doing in a nightclub!
He's looking for his daughter she shouts!
Not a girlfriend!
No!
And who's his daughter!
She's smiling.
I am!
Ha!
Weird!
Spooky!
Bizarre!
Totally!
I'm fucked!
Me too!
I'm going to the bathroom!

We kiss.
Wash your tooth she shouts!

Aah fresh air. Mmmjulius, I love this air. Julius Julius Julius she says.
Fresh air's good I say.
Sgood. The fire escape's good she says.
Yeah.
Alone she says. Parvaneh. She looked at a plane with red flashing lights and she said is that a shooting star. Sha.
Pff I say.
Hmm. I'm having such a good night she says.
Me too. I'm drunk. I'm thinking this: wewz.
I love watching your hand when you smoke she says. Beautiful stories in your fingers.
Syrup on a pancake. My Fall.
So many things I wanna do with you she says.
There's an inch of water on your eyes I say.
I'm thinking she says. I just like watching you sometimes. There's so much . . .
Let me hold her let me hold her let me hold her.
That's nice she says. It's cold out here.
We should dance.
I wanna stay.
K.
It's nice.
She's probably thinking I'm strong. She's probably liking my muscles.
I hope you never feel like there's no one looking after you she says.
Whaddaya mean.
I don't know. You're young. We're young. I want you to know. Look at me. I want you to know you're loved. That I love you.
Don't cry.
It's not. I'm not sad. It's. I don't know what's gonna happen. What you'll want. I love it so much when you tell me stories when you were a little boy. I can see you so clearly. You're just a little boy.
I'm a big strong man.
You're just a little boy she says. With beautiful fingers. And everything's going to be fun.

Fuckin A.

I want to see you as a man. Some wrinkles here and here.

Hm.

I am a man I say.

I'm buying a beer I don't need.

The lights are full of water.

Everyone's pretty.

We're friends.

Except that guy.

And that guy.

Where's Fall.

That's not our table.

Where's Fall.

The fat guy has his mouth on her ear.

What the fuck.

Who was that guy!

I don't know!

What was he doing!

I don't know!

What'd he say!

Nothing! He's gross! Give me a sip!

She's drinking.

She's chugging.

Let's dance she shouts!

What's going on!

Let's dance!

OK!

She's leading me.

I'm looking around for that guy.

I think I'm mad.

I think I'm gonna make myself mad.

We're dancing.

Fall's dancing.

I've stopped.

She's doing the hips and the hair and the hands above the head thing.

She's drunk.

I'm fucked.
She's jumping.
I'm trying to jump.
I can't remember why I'm mad oh yeah.
She's jumping.
I want my beer.
She fell.

They're jumping around my girlfriend.
She's laughing.
She's limping.
I'm dancing.
She's smiling.
No she's not.
She's sitting on the floor.
She's gonna get crushed.
What's wrong!
I can't stand up!
Here!
Ow! My ankle!
Do you wanna barf!
It's my ankle!
Put your arm around me!
I want these fuckin jumping people out of the way.
Watch it!
Fuck off! She's hurt!
You fuck off!
There's a seat over there!
My purse!
Can you make it back to the table! I can see your purse!
Stop for a second!
Which ankle is it!
The one I'm holding up!
Right! Come on and sit down!
Is that creep gone!
I guess so! There's your purse!
Ow!
There! You OK!
Yeah! I don't know! I really can't stand on it!

Give it a minute!

I'm thinking I should have some water or something. Or she should.

Want some water!

No! Thanks! Yes! Don't go! Maybe a waitress!

Just give it a minute! Let me see it!

Boot.

I feel like a dad.

I'm fucked.

I forget what I'm doing.

Sock.

Is this serious.

It looks OK I shout!

Does it!

I can't really tell! Let me see the other one!

That's OK! Let's just wait!

Is it throbbing!

Yeah!

Keep it on my lap!

Her heel's on my thigh.

The butterfly's dancing with a bald guy in black.

J ANUARY, THE TWO-FACED month.

'Why don't you call us more this term?' asked my mother. 'Or write. You know I love your letters.'

It will always be the month of questions, often ones I'm afraid to answer. What happened and what will come.

Do you miss her?

And the feeling in the lungs of Canada's midwinter. Shallow intake of the coldest conviction. Every January my lids lie lower while I try not to believe that my heart still beats in this bleakness.

There were signs that Julius had moved back into the room. I saw other people, but I felt like I could pass right through them.

Do you miss her?

And I truly wanted to find Julius. My confidant. My friend. I was realising that something had been lost. How can you sleep so close to someone and be so far away?

You say you were friends. Do you miss her?

On the first day of school a new voice entered my life in the shape of Sergeant Richard D'Arcy of the RCMP.

I was called to the office of the Admissions Counsellor, the teacher whose days were devoted to helping us Seniors find places in universities. For a while his office became a place where Sergeant D'Arcy asked questions of various people.

The RCMP were investigating because of the involvement of a foreign diplomat's son, whom they were theoretically meant to protect. He was part of the Protective Policing Unit, so I thought at first that he wasn't formally investigating things; he was simply helping.

I was assured by the Admissions Counsellor that these were interviews conducted with scores of students, that I wasn't being singled out, and that there was no need to feel uncomfortable. He kept a tape recorder on the desk. He otherwise sat mutely in the corner while the interview progressed.

Where did you get the tan?

Sydney.

I'll bet that was a nice escape.

It was.

Furthest I've been is Sydney Nova Scotia. Is it your parents?

Yes.

Lucky you. But you must miss them when you're here.

Not really.

So you like it here?

More or less.

Is that why you came back?

I have a term to finish.

I was just wondering. Some of the students I've interviewed thought about not coming back. They're upset. Scared that a student could go missing.

I wouldn't say I'm not upset. But I am in the middle of my final year.

And you like it here.

I like it well enough.

Do you like your fellow students?

Yes.

All of them?

I don't mind.

You don't mind? I know what you mean. I can't say I like all of my colleagues, but I don't mind them. I keep to myself. Is that what you do, would you say? Keep to yourself?

I suppose. I have friends.

I'm sure you do. Was Fallon DeStindt your friend?

Was?

Is. What I mean is before she went missing, was she your friend?

Yes.

Were you close friends?

263

I think so.

You hung out.

We went shopping together. Went to cafés. She's my room-mate's girlfriend.

Of course. So you know a lot about her.

I suppose.

Where do you think she might be? I'm trying to get as many opinions on this as I can. I'm getting a surprising range.

I don't know.

You haven't thought about it?

I often think about it.

Do you? Could you tell me your thoughts?

Well. She probably ran away, didn't she? That's what makes sense to me.

Does it?

Yes. Compared to the alternatives. It makes more sense to me that she would run away than, let's say, being taken or whatever.

Taken?

Isn't that what some people think? She was taken from her room.

Do they?

There would have been noises or screams. Some sort of a struggle. How would someone get into her room to take her? How could her room-mate not notice? It doesn't make sense to me.

She may not have been taken from her room. She may have been walking outside. Does that make sense to you?

I suppose. It just seems unlikely. School grounds. Who would come onto school grounds and abduct her? I've read about a phenomenon called the Availability Heuristic. It is in our nature, let's say, when we are alone in a park at night to imagine being attacked. Our minds instinctively try to discover the worst possible thing that can happen, but the likelihood of anything happening is extremely low.

The Availa . . . ?

Availability Heuristic. From the Greek, to discover or find.

I'm struck by the intelligence of you guys. I've gotta say. The minds. The vocabulary. So you think it makes sense that Fallon ran away?

Yes.

Any idea what she would run away from? Anything your room-mate told you, for example?

I don't know. Not really.

Would you protect your room-mate from anything?

I don't know. I wouldn't lie.

Did he ever tell you that Fall was unhappy?

No. Maybe. He said she could get sad sometimes. He said her mother . . . I think she may have felt claustrophobic.

Is that what he said?

Maybe.

And what do you think he meant?

I don't know. Too much pressure, maybe. She is very popular. Very . . . She's attractive and people like her. I could imagine that she could sometimes feel too much, let's say, love, or something of the sort. Perhaps she felt that she received too much attention.

Do you feel claustrophobic?

Here?

Anywhere.

It is hard not to feel it here sometimes. It's a small world. That's what I'm trying to say. And if you can't feel comfortable at home and Julius is . . . If you feel like there's nowhere to escape to. It's easy to feel like there's nowhere to go.

So she ran away?

I suppose so. It doesn't seem so incredible to me.

You seem to be very reasonable. Did she ever tell you that she was thinking of running away?

No. Not really. She told me about family life a little. She never said, 'I'm going to run away.' I don't think one would do that. Running away is running away. You run.

People usually leave clues. People plan. In my experience, there are usually signs.

I think she was sad.

Was she sad the last time you talked to her?

I think there was always some sort of sadness in her.

When was the last time you saw her?

I think it was that night. The night before she went.

Really?

December ninth. She wasn't in school on the tenth. I remember.

You have a good memory. I hope you don't mind if I ask you more questions later. Do you?

Not at all.

Thank you.

It was interesting.

It was interesting. I remember feeling slightly excited that I had spent so much time talking to a genuine officer of the RCMP. I remember doing some research, and learning, for example, that they originally wore buff trousers, but through sharing clothes with American counterparts they began to wear blue ones.

Julius appeared noticeably older and less healthy. The sun and exercise had done me good, and when I caught glimpses of both of us in the mirror I found the contrast quite striking.

He didn't have much to say to me. Short responses about his holiday revealed that he had 'done some investigating', which I understood to mean he had helped with the investigation.

Gradually he spoke more, occasionally after Lights Out. He said the Duty Mistress of the Girls' Flats had attracted some criticism for her lack of vigilance. People had been able to come and go through her front door, as I had experienced, with ease. Julius wanted her fired.

He wanted many people fired, in fact. His father and his lawyers were turning the tables somewhat, focusing on the poor security of the school, suggesting proper inquiries into how students came and went and how they ought to be monitored. I found this a bit rich, that calls to monitor the students should originate from Julius.

Generally speaking, he seemed rather angry.

No one wanted to believe that Fall ran away. I began to realise the role of a pretty girl in our society. No one attracts our solicitation as much as a pretty girl. She is a vessel of our hopes, we suggest her future, instinctively give her guidance, love to watch her, expect to watch her move through extraordinary spaces. And if something goes wrong, we instinctively imagine her as the victim, a passive player in a beautiful tragedy, a flower which was never meant to survive in our bitter soil. But what we hate to acknowledge is her volition. That a pretty girl should have agency or choice. It's repugnant to think she could choose to do wrong.

I expatiated upon this with Julius. He was incapable of seeing her as anything but the victim of someone else's misdeeds.

He believed that she was missing but not lost. This was natural.

Fall had a sister in New York. She was older and, according to Julius, had left home quite young because she did not get along with their mother. She had opted for a boarding school far away, had left before graduating and had made a life for herself in New York.

Julius believed that if Fall went anywhere it was to be with her sister. They had made a pact that if things were ever difficult they would be together.

Over Christmas the police, Julius and Fall's mother made an effort to contact Fall's sister. She had made a point of being incommunicado with their mother, but a search of Fall's things at home revealed her number and address.

All parties tried to get in touch with her, with no success. Julius wanted to go down to New York, but his father believed that he should not return to the US while the investigation was at this stage.

At that point in early January it seemed that Fall's sister was missing as well.

There was the fact that Fall had packed no bag. She had such a vast quantity of clothing at home and at school that it was impossible to know whether anything was missing. But there were no obvious signs that she had taken anything.

Julius didn't want to think about it. This was natural.

This change in Julius. Our room felt completely different. There was a slightly chilly politeness now, a respect of each other's space that hadn't existed before.

My jet lag from Australia always took weeks to wear off. I found myself wide awake in the middle of the night. The whole school felt quieter, colder.

Ant had been in Paris with his aunt. He brought back a new haircut. We were both slightly surprised, I think, to find how pleased we were to see each other. He for his own reasons, I for having someone to spar with.

'I've heard of places where you can go and fight other guys,' he said. 'You just show up and fist fight. Just strip down. It's a cool idea. But I was thinking when I was away in Paris. I was out one night, kind of in Pigalle, and I saw this guy, all on his own, walk up to a bunch of guys and he just started beating on one of them. I have no idea what it was about. And the other guys started laying into him and soon he was fighting all of them and getting the shit kicked out of himself. It kind of reminded me of you at Chez Henri. But I was thinking, you know, whether you have a reason or not, the best fight is a fight like that.'

It was true. I admit, in fact, that I found it compelling. Boxing, or any organised type of combat, removed some of the thrill of fighting. Most of the thrill is in the fear. A spontaneous fight is a rare opportunity to experience genuine chaos. Why put gentle-manly limits and conventions around that? How often are we truly able to test our strength in our organised lives?

What Ant proposed was not ganging up on or surprising a solitary victim. It was walking into a dangerous situation where fairness would simply not play a role. We imagined various scenarios and talked about the matter quite often.

I watched Julius with Chuck and with other people. I remember looking out the window and seeing him in an earnest-looking conversation with the Head Boy. I had somehow forgotten that Julius had many friends. I couldn't overhear their conversation. The window was very hard to open discreetly in the winter because ice would freeze it shut.

He often looked earnest, though, and busy. Never busy with schoolwork, but busy with finding his girlfriend, with trying to set right everything he felt was wrong. He believed that he had played by the rules, that when he was gated he obeyed the Masters, got his sheet signed. How could they have focused on that sort of thing but shown absolutely no diligence in protecting students, in keeping danger away. Simple security.

When he was angry I felt strangely silenced, perhaps even acquiescent. I let him have his way sometimes with little things.

I didn't want to do anything that might offend him. He rarely directed anger at me, but I could tell he was watching me, evaluating me, always ready to take offence – and, initially, I was careful not to give it.

When he succumbed to petulance, he began to annoy me. I understood that concentrating on schoolwork was difficult for him – it was difficult for all of us. But he often whined the same refrain: 'How can they expect me to *con*centrate?' At first I offered to do some of his work for him – I would write things for him, do his Algebra homework, etc. But his whining continued and I lost energy in doing my own work, never mind his.

I had thought my helping him would be a way for us to reconnect, a form of washing each other's back. I hoped it would provide opportunities for trust and confession.

Was he a suspect? Was his focus on security and her supposed abduction a means of turning attention away from himself? I don't remember making a reasoned decision to make suspicion fall on him.

He had regular interviews with Sergeant D'Arcy. In his case there were also representatives from the US Embassy – a lawyer and occasionally an imposing American known as the Regional Security Officer. Their presence in the hallways sometimes caused excitement.

Julius told me about the interviews but rarely told me their content. 'I'm not supposed to talk about it,' he would say. I pictured him sitting in that small room, beleaguered by these figures of authority, wondering why it all had to be thus.

It was not an accurate picture.

'Have you been fucking with my toothbrush?'

'No.'

'It's older looking.'

'I haven't touched your toothbrush,' I said.

'I'm not gonna brush my teeth. Why do I need to brush my teeth? At this fuckin sink. You over my shoulder. Do you realise how fuckin weird this is? This whole thing?'

'Well. Yes,' I said.

I brushed my teeth while he got undressed. I noticed that he was more shy about undressing somehow. He turned off the light before I had finished at the sink and he got up onto the top bunk.

I got ready and got into my own bed. 'Don't turn off the light while I'm still brushing my teeth,' I said.

In the moments when he was calm, when the light and warmth in that room achieved their seldom alchemy, we softened into friends.

'I just want to get out of here,' he said. 'I want to get out of this country.'

I wondered sometimes whether he missed Fall any more. Grief seems to lengthen with age. He was only eighteen.

I didn't want to ask him.

Sometimes when I stood with Ant in the hall or any of the common rooms, I was aware of how people noticed us. We were big, and I was quite handsome with my tan. I thought of how I had watched Julius talking to his friends, and was certain that people were watching me in the same way. Sometimes I laughed in a way that I thought was quite warm.

I wanted to find some way of pleasing Chuck, some way to establish another version of the original triumvirate. I decided to give him the lighter which I had been carrying in my pocket for months. It was an attractive steel and lacquer affair, probably not immediately identifiable as Julius's; and since Chuck was such a passionate smoker I thought he would appreciate it. I wrapped it up and was ready to present it to him, but something stopped me. I think I simply liked having it in my pocket.

In the weeks before Fallon disappeared you saw a lot of her?

A certain amount.

Where's Fall?

Sorry?

Where's Fall? A few students have mentioned that you were asking that question often. Have you seen Fall?

Really?

I'm trying to get a clear picture of as much as I can. In the lead-up

*to your friend running away. That's why I'm conducting these interviews.
Time is very important with missing persons. Over a month has elapsed
now, you see, Noel. Much too long. But at this point I consider it necessary to get every detail I can. Even things people consider . . . what's
the word you might choose . . . insignificant.*

I was passing notes.

When?

Julius was gated. He wasn't able to move around outside the
main building. So he asked me to pass Fall notes. That's why I
was asking that question.

*I see. I thought it was kind of strange. You at every corner saying
'Where's Fall?'*

I wouldn't describe it that way. I don't know who told you
that.

*It's your eye for detail that I want, Noel. Tell me about Julius being
punished. Gated?*

It's when one cannot pass certain perimeters. One has to have
a sheet signed every hour.

And why was he gated?

For dousing. It seems very immature. We were involved in late-
night foolishness with a friend. We poured Coke on a friend.
Coke and water. On Antony. In retaliation. It's a long story which
would seem rather fatuous to you, I think.

So you were involved?

Yes. But Julius was caught. He didn't implicate me, which was
very nice of him.

He didn't do anything violent? Didn't hurt anyone?

No. Absolutely not.

No one was hurt?

Ant was hurt, but I did that. He was fine. It was very minor.
We're friends.

Just rough-housing?

Exactly.

So Julius was gated and you passed notes to Fall.

Yes. And notes from Fall to him.

Did they not see each other all this time?

They did. In class and so on. But their other time. They were
very limited in terms of seeing each other. So I helped whenever I could.

You liked them as a couple?

What do you mean?

Were they good together? Were the three of you close? Your impressions.

We were close. Julius told me a lot.

You've said that.

And I think they were, are, good together. I wouldn't say they will be together forever, necessarily. Fall is a very intelligent girl.

And Julius isn't intelligent?

I don't mean that. I don't know. I simply think that he probably doesn't see as much of her, let's say, her true self, as others might.

She is a very beautiful girl.

Yes. But there is so much more to her.

Did many people love her?

Love?

I guess that's a big word. I've heard you use it. Did you know many guys who . . . you know. You guys must talk up there, late at night.

Sure. I talk with Julius. I generally don't indulge in scandal. I think people were interested in her, to answer your question. Yes.

You've been here a while, right, Noel?

Since grade 8.

That's a long time. I was looking at your school record. I'm looking at everyone's. It says you actually came here halfway through grade 8.

That's right. My parents went away. They went to London first, where my father was number two at the High Commission, and then to Sydney where he is Consul. The warmth appealed to them.

I hear that. My car wouldn't start today.

Ha.

But those are nice places. Why didn't they take you with them?

They wanted stability for me. My schooling.

Of course. And your behavioural problems?

Pardon?

On your file. I don't mean to make you uncomfortable. Christ knows I had problems. They don't stop. But on your file. I've seen this on other students' files too. It says next to your admission details: Behaviour. Also a biting incident in grade 9.

I don't know, really. At my other school. At the beginning of grade 8. I didn't really get along. I'm surprised that's on the record.

I just wasn't fitting into that school, I suppose. Nothing happened. It sounds immodest, but the consensus, this isn't my opinion. The consensus among my teachers and parents was that I was too intelligent for that school. So they sent me to a better school.

This is a great school. I have no doubt it was a better fit. Do you feel that?

I think so.

Until December I guess. This has been disruptive for everyone.

Yes.

I should let you go. You say you were close friends. Do you miss her?

'I feel antsy,' I said.

'I hate fuckin January,' Ant said. 'You know, you shouldn't let this bullshit weigh on you. The thing we've gotta do is get out. Let's go out.'

I had never deliberately missed classes in the past, but Ant and I began to do it regularly. I was beginning to consolidate my sense of teachers as inferior members of society, their days of petty discipline and cookie-cutter curiosity. It's true, as Sergeant D'Arcy said, that St Ebury was superior to many, but I was moving beyond wanting to please my teachers and certainly beyond expecting to learn anything from them.

There was another high school halfway between St Ebury and the market, where we stopped for a while. It was near lunch hour and we waited by a fence around their yard until students began to come out. Since it was January, I didn't expect a crowd. Ant wanted to look at them. 'If a really big guy comes out, or like a group of them, you should go over and swing. See what happens.'

'Thanks,' I said.

I wasn't going to do anything of the kind, of course, but the idea amused us both. Three girls came out and promptly went back inside.

'It's fuckin freezing,' Ant said.

We walked towards the market.

'I feel like you're the only one who understands,' Ant said. 'Next year we're all maybe going to different places. We'll probably never have friendships like this again. You can't trust a lot of people.'

We went to a military outfitter where they sold knives.

Ant reminded me that years earlier, under a different Housemaster, there had been frequent room inspections and it had been next to impossible to hide things. Cigarettes, pornographic magazines, alcohol were regularly confiscated. 'You could never own a knife.' But things had become relaxed over the past couple of years. Until now.

I didn't want to return to school. We went to the Earl of Sussex and hoped we would be served. Ant took out his new knife near the end of our first beer.

'What do you think about all this Fall shit?'

'I don't know,' I said.

'I had to talk to that cop, too, you know. I never really thought it was serious before.' He put his knife away. 'He asked me where I was that night and I have no memory.'

'We're living in a boarding school,' I said. 'It's not like we need an alibi. We were in our rooms, in class . . .'

'I've got nothing to hide,' he said. 'Obviously. Chuck says we're not taking it seriously enough. He thinks she's dead.'

'No way,' I said. 'She ran away.'

'Or she was taken. She's in a basement somewhere and half a suburb's fucking her ass.'

We really had very little in common.

'Could be suicide, too,' he said. 'I guess Jules is taking it hard. That's why Chuck's all serious. What would you do if you found out Chuck was gay?'

'I don't know. Nothing.'

'Really?'

We took a bus back to school.

'It'd be easy though, wouldn't it?' he said. 'I could have taken one of my other knives, gone into her room, told her to shut the fuck up.'

What are you reading?

Hobbes.

Interesting?

He worries about rhetoric. About words. People get tricky with their words and it undermines society. He says the ability to argue both sides of a case can lead to harm. Damage the truth.

That is interesting.

That's what you do, isn't it?

What?

You're tricky with words for a living. You claim to want to see both sides.

Yes.

But there's only one real side for you. You work with right on one side and wrong on the other, and it's all about making right. You ask tricky questions.

Don't you think there is a right and a wrong?

There's a building called the truth. People live in it. The people are all right and wrong.

I'm going to destroy it.

I'm dreaming.

At an assembly for the entire school it was announced that security was going to be increased. Anyone who propped open a fire escape would be punished. Day students had to be off school property by 6 p.m. unless they had special permission.

Boarders were called to a separate assembly. New locks were installed on all outside doors, which would now be closed from 6 p.m. We were given a key to the one main door, which would be monitored, they said. We had to sign out whenever we left school grounds during the week, not only if we were going away on weekends. It was all for our own protection.

Somehow Julius managed to get out for a smoke some nights. I heard him sneaking out of bed, fishing for his cigarettes, coming back an hour later. Ant said Chuck did the same thing.

'I can't believe you, of all people, wanted all this security,' I said to Julius.

He shrugged. 'I think it'll get to the truth,' he said. I didn't know what he meant.

I thought about trying to follow him and Chuck but I couldn't see how it was possible. The school was so quiet now at night. Footsteps were easily heard. I knew that building, every hiding place, better than anyone. I couldn't imagine where, under this new regime, they would be able to smoke undetected.

★   ★   ★

I was told that you broke your nose last term. What happened?

I was playing basketball.

That's not what I heard. That was the official story, I know that. But it's not what I heard.

No?

I heard you were in a fight. Why didn't you tell me that?

I don't know. I'm not comfortable telling a policeman that I was in a fight, I suppose.

What do I care?

I don't know.

I've been in lots of fights. What happened to the other guy?

I don't know. I ran away. I had to.

Were you scared?

Of course. I didn't want to fight.

Is that when your eye was damaged?

My eye's not damaged. It's a lazy eye that I've had since birth.

You don't look like the kind of guy who would get into fights. I mean, you look like you could handle yourself. But you don't seem like a fighter. I've seen lots of fighters.

Yeah.

So the way I heard the story was, you were out in Hull with your friend Antony. You got into this fight and he looked after you.

Is that what he said?

I've been talking to several different people.

I stayed at his aunt's house that night and went to the hospital the next day.

And Antony wasn't involved in the fight? See, he looks to me like a fighter. You don't, but he does.

I don't know.

I could imagine him starting a fight and you stepping in to break it up. Do you know him well?

Ant? Reasonably well.

I'm trying to get a sense of relationships here, I guess. Would you say that Ant is your closest friend at school?

No. I don't think so.

Who is your closest friend?

. . .

Someone you would confide in?

. . .

Your room-mate?
Yes.

I have no illusions about being alone. I have known people who want to have children solely for the purpose of being cared for by them in their old age. For company. I suppose it is as good a reason as any. But I have no illusions.

I think about our hunger for oil. The planet warms, the seas grow. We worry that the planet will drown. We take our ships to melting seas. We fight for the oil underneath the ice. We drown.

I had a memory of being in the downstairs common room after dinner. Fall and Julius had their arms around each other. The three of us were talking. I was eating wine gums. The three of us were happy. Julius was still gated, which is why they were hanging around the common room instead of sneaking off somewhere.

Fall liked wine gums but Julius didn't. I held the bag while she fished out her favourite colour (orange) and if I moved my fingers slightly I could feel hers through the bag. But I didn't.

Julius had a pimple on his forehead. Fall was making fun of it and I joined in. She laughed with me. Julius was good-natured.

When Lights Out approached I gave her the wine gums, excused myself and left them alone. I went upstairs to my room while the fluorescent lights went out above them, the colours under the ice.

What were people saying about me? Had Ant misrepresented my fight for some reason? Who else was talking about me?

'What did you say to Sergeant D'Arcy?'

'I don't know,' said Ant. 'Not much.'

'Did you talk about my fight in Hull?'

'No fuckin way. He just asked me about Fall. What I knew about her. I don't know anything about her. He asked me who would want to hurt her?'

'He asked that?'

'Something like that.'

'Did he ask about me?'

'No.'

'You didn't say anything about me?'

'Nothing. We talked for like ten minutes. He's pretty ugly.'
'I haven't noticed.'

I've seen a lot, Noel.
Yes.
On my better days I like this job. I stand back from it and I think: This is life. How could I get a better view of life than from this job? And by better I mean — what do I mean? Complete? Not even that. I think on the days that I think about things, it's the days when I'm surprised. Something's happened that I never could have imagined. So it's not complete, exactly, because it's when I realise I haven't seen it all that I get this feeling. There are patterns, sure. Predictable things. I like to think sometimes that I can see them better than the next guy.
Yes.
Do you?
What?
See things better than the next guy?
I don't know.
Depends on who the next guy is, eh? I think you do. I get a good feeling from you, Noel. Intelligent. I don't mean to sound patronising. But I do feel surprised by some of the things some of the other students are saying about you. Destroying rooms . . . Intimidating . . . Like I said, you don't look like a fighter to me.
I can fight.
So you like fighting?
I don't know what exactly you are hearing, but I do nothing, I have done nothing that nobody else does. I . . . I haven't done anything out of the norm is what I mean.
Upstairs.
Yes, upstairs. Anywhere. It's all . . . it's the norm. Occasional rough-housing. Foolishness. I assure you that over the years people have done far worse, more hurtful things than I've done. I've barely got started.
What do you mean?
I mean I would look like an amateur . . . I do nothing that hasn't been done by others, often worse. You should hear stories.
From the past. I understand the dynamic. You can't house so many young guys together and not have fighting and weird things. I understand that.

And you grow up and get appointed to the Senate. I understand the general pattern. I'm just talking about you, Noel.

But why? Why is everyone talking about me? I thought we were looking for Fall.

We are. We are. I think you think I'm about to discipline you or something. Like you don't even want to be noticed. I'm not going to punish you for fooling around upstairs. That's for your Counsellor here or whoever. If you'll pardon me, I don't actually give two shits what a bunch of boys are doing to each other in their bedrooms, whether they're future Senators or not. I'm investigating the disappearance of a young woman, who seems to have had no reason to disappear. You can put it together, I think, Noel.

Do you suspect me?

I, personally, don't. No. I don't. Tell me why you began sleeping in your closet after Fallon disappeared.

Who told you that? Julius?

Why the closet?

He's the only one who would know. I slept in the closet because I was tired. It's a quiet place. You have no idea how hard it is to get away in this, in this life. You don't know what it's like. Doing *everything* in the same space. The closet's peaceful.

But why immediately after Fall went missing?

I don't . . . I don't think you have received accurate information. I've slept in closets for years. Julius has only been my room-mate this year.

You slept for hours each day after December tenth in your closet.

I missed her. I thought about her.

Yes, you said. You were close friends. You missed her right away, before people knew she was missing?

I can't believe where these questions are heading.

Calm down, Noel. I've told you. I just want the whole picture.

Never question the quiet ones. That should be the truth to spread, as much as the warning not to trust us. Never question a quiet person's sense of his own perfection. Distance has allowed me that wisdom.

We're quiet because we suspect we are imperfect. Grotesquely imperfect. But that suspicion must never be acknowledged; that suspicion is the quietest part of our soft-spoken souls.

Perfection is what we want. We will *never* admit that we can't find it. He should never have questioned my livid heart.

'Let's go downtown,' I said.
    'I'll get my coat,' Ant said.
    'Don't wear your uniform,' I said.

I've been thinking about things, Sergeant D'Arcy.
    Yeah?
Some moments last term. All this new security around the school has been making me think. About Julius especially. I don't know whether you've asked him, but he used to go on excursions. With Fall. He would go in his father's limousine. Has he told you?
    I don't believe he has.
I don't know everywhere he went. He just used to tell me what he would do to Fall in the car. But I don't know where he went. Maybe he could give you some leads. I know he was somehow in cahoots with his father's chauffeur. If he hasn't told you about it, it might be nothing. Maybe there were places they went.
    Thank you, Noel.

It was dark but I didn't want to hide.
    'Let's go to the mall,' I said.

Most nights he went out. I don't really know where he went.
    He never told you?
Not often. He usually smoked drugs with his friend Chuck. Sometimes they were near school. They still do it. Sometimes they went far away.
    And you weren't invited?
That's not why I'm telling you.

'Shouldn't we get drunk first?' said Ant.
    'No. I want to remember.'

Scaring a young fella named Edward. He seemed harmless to me.
    You don't know the whole story. He had a way of looking

at me. A way of looking at the world. There's a weakness in some people. It's just as destructive, as poisonous to a community, as aggression. You haven't asked him the right questions.

Would you like me to interview him here with you now?

I just didn't always . . . I wasn't comfortable with the way Julius talked about Fall.

What do you mean?

As though she were expendable somehow. As though she were just another girl.

He said that?

Yes. All the time.

I guess he is only eighteen. I suspect there will be more girls in his life. Are there girls in your life, Noel?

Of course.

And the mall was America.

I saw every one of your failures; your puffy absurdities; your swollen ignorance and hunger for things you knew would never be enough.

Huge.

Vain.

Chatty.

Shuffling.

Dreaming.

You troupes of baboons my age.

You siffling middle-aged complainers pouring colas and distraction into your cramped despicable bellies.

And I wanted to tell you to stop telling me what I should want.

I found a couple of guys in their twenties. Taller than I was, unlikely to be brought down. They both had coats slung over their arms and coffees in their hands.

I went up to one and pushed him. His coffee spilled on his sweater.

'I don't like the fuckin look of you,' I said. His shock was so predictable and funny. I punched his mouth from the side and felt a fang give way. He cowered and I hurt my knee on his forehead.

His friend swung at me and I ducked. I jumped on him and bent him forwards in a headlock. He tried to lift me up and I held him tighter. I wanted to tear his head off.

Because I've heard you had scratches.
I fell into a bush.
And you weren't at dinner. Or your study time. What do you call it?
Prep.
And you came back late. Next morning you're covered in scratches.
I don't know why he would tell you these things. I really don't. I fell into a bush. There was snow around that night and my shoes have leather soles. It's no more complicated than that. He's trying to distract you. Getting attention away from himself for once. Where was he that night? There's so much about that guy that you don't know. He's my friend.

Ant was laughing behind me all the way as we ran. On the bus back to school I remember smiling. 'I'm so unsatisfied,' I said.

I DON'T KNOW what to do.
  Get a cab.
Should I get an ambulance.
No way, J. I just can't walk on it.
Are you OK.
I just can't put any weight on it.
She's smiling like she wants to smile.
I'm scared.
It hurts but it's nothing, J. I promise.
I think we should go home.
Do you want to.
I'm sober I say.
No you're not.
I'm not.
I'm gonna be sick if I drink any more she says.
Let's go home I say.
I don't want to ruin the night.
You're not.
Am I lying.
It's a fuckin great night.
Happy anniversary, J.
Happy anniversary. I don't want you to hurt I say.
Let's get a cab.
I'll get the coats. Limp with me to the door gimpy limpy.
I'm holding her ass.

That's inappropriate she says.

I squeeze.

I'm walking to the coats cause I'm responsible. I'm walking to the coats because there are things you do when you're a dad and there's a thing of a serious nature going on and you prop your girl like a floppy smiling puppet near the door and she says I need to pee. You take her to the bathroom and all the smiles and shy eyes, in out, and Fall's in there peeing and nobody knows these things. Fall's sweet secrets for her and me, and back by the door, so close and I love her leaning on me.

What do you call this.

We're gonna fill these coats.

That's the fat guy. Goddamn I wanna go home now. That's the fat creep staring at me.

What the fuck, buddy. You want my coat.

What.

What the fuck are you looking at.

Go home, pretty boy.

Fuck you.

Don't ever feel like nobody's watching you, pretty boy.

What.

Someone's always lookin.

He's bigger than I thought.

Look at all the people who want cabs she says.

Fuck.

But look at all the cabs she says.

Oh yeah.

Everything looks like a light I say.

What.

What.

Do your whistle she says.

swhEE!

I love that. Do it again.

swhEE!

Here comes one. See. You called one.

I'm fucked.

Me too.

It's OK here's a cab.

I know.

It's OK. Are you OK.

Yeah.

I'm pretty fuckin hammered.

I'm putting her in like she's an old lady and I burp and I'm responsible.

Goodnight Saturday.

It smells like a cab in here.

Hi.

Hi.

Hi.

St Ebury please. In Sutton.

Ooo we're driving underwater really fast.

Ooo.

J.

Yeah.

J.

Yeah.

We're going the wrong way.

Are we.

We're going the wrong way.

Where.

We're going to school.

Yeah. Oh shit.

Yeah.

Driver she says. We're going the wrong way.

Sutton.

We're staying at William's she says.

Pardon.

William's I say. Murray Street.

Not Sutton.

No we're staying at William's tonight I say.

Is it a hotel.

It's an address. Wait.

Where's that fuckin paper.

Can this cab drive away from the smell of itself.

Pardon.

Here it is. C. G. Is that a C or a G.

I can't see it she says.

C.

114 Murray Street, apartment C. We'll. If you take us to 114 we'll take ourselves to the C upstairs.

I think I want a bed.

William's she says.

I can't remember what tomorrow's supposed to be.

114 Murray Street he says. In the market.

That's the place I say.

How could you forget William's she says.

Fff. Funny. I'm tired.

Me too.

Her head's on my shoulder.

I feel like I'm falling.

William

E VERYBODY'S LOOKING.
Signs are everywhere, they say.

Before and after whatever happens happens, everybody's looking for signs.

My second wife was short and cute. Lisette. We almost had a baby but he was born without breath. That was so sad. I remember feeling so sad for little Lisette. No light in her smile after that and no more hope in my head.

I remember thinking Lisette was what I wanted. That name's pretty. Lisette. Makes me think of pie and country curtains. I liked it anyway. She was so quiet after Sharon. Nice and cute and warm. Sharon had a pair of hips — I could tell you stories, boy — but she was a fang-toothed maniac with a brain for nothing but biting. Lisette was a home and a hug and a cup of hot chocolate.

Lisette.

She was what I wanted.

And then she wasn't.

And when you split up you start looking for signs. What went wrong? And she starts looking for signs, hm boy. Why don't you love that cute and beautiful Lisette, why don't you love me after all we've been through, boy. There was that time, she said, when you got drunk and never came home. I should have known then that you would leave, she said. And the truth is, that time I got drunk and didn't come home was the time I really wanted to drink and not go home. Sometimes there's nothing more to it. Not that time.

I never wanted to hurt anyone, I'll tell you that much, but it seems to me that the hurt would be quieter if everyone stopped thinking that love was the only thing in the world that wasn't going to change. In nature. Eh. Weeping and screaming when a hair turns grey or a fish can't do the finning.

Anyways, when it comes to signs there's none that really helps except WRONG WAY.

That split with Lisette. Jesus.

What I learned from that marriage was how much you can make someone up. You spend years with her, and when you split you look hard and see the person you loved was never there, she was the skin around what you wanted.

I know that's not the whole of it, that's not the whole of Lisette, but the other thing I learned about love is there is no whole of it, no. I've always been a kid in the carnival and whenever I'm seeing the truth, someone moves the mirrors. It changes every day.

Lisette went from warm to crueller than Sharon, like that. The truth about anyone is what they're like on their own. I believe that. What are you like when somebody's left you. What are you thinking about people and yourself when you're alone in your apartment. When you sit there on your own and you start looking back, and you say, yeah, maybe I should have seen that coming, maybe I could have changed, maybe I shouldn't have been surprised, maybe I wanted something different all along. You start looking for signs.

You're looking back and you forget that's not how you went through your days. Things came at you and you reacted. Sometimes it worked out and sometimes it didn't but putting a story on it later is not telling the truth about life. And looking for signs in other people. Come on.

Personally, I enjoy a drink.

There are lots of people, sure, who go through their days seeing the signs. A lot of them get on this bus. The guys who bet on sports are the funniest. They always think they see it coming. They'll say whatshisname has sprained his ankle so his team's gonna lose by ten, or they've got a new trainer so they'll make it to the play-offs. These guys have a bit more information so they think they know what's coming.

What's coming is me. I drive them back to the parking lot with nothing but a sigh in their wallet.

So I enjoy a drink. I sit there and say, I'm enjoying this. There's nothing more I can know.

Mr Ambassador, there. He said one day, William, there's one thing you can say about Canada: everybody's decent. I thought that was funny. The more I did that job, the more I thought what a goddamn joke this country business is. I've got a cousin who stole a million bucks from a charity for kids with cancer. He's Canadian. I'm a fat ugly drunk and I got angry at Sharon and hit her. I'm Canadian. There's Lisette. A year after I left her she stabbed my arm with a steak knife. She's Canadian. French-Canadian, but still.

I'd drive him from his big house to another big house with a different flag on it. And he was speaking for his country and the other guy was speaking for the other country. What a world of bullshit.

I get goofy old couples with running shoes and baseball caps getting on the bus looking hilariously American. And the man starts talking first all the time, and the woman smiling, and they're from Des Moines or Minneapolis or one of these places we know too much about because of fuckin television. And I'll say to myself, here come the Americans, or, there go the Americans, like that's going to box it all up. Underneath those baseball caps are the miscarriages, the daughters who don't talk, the smiles on pillows, the funny secrets and memories that no one else saw. Midnight chuckles and the crying. Calling them American's got nothing to do with it. But even they think it sums them up.

What are they like alone?

Julius said in one of his letters that they called the guy who maimed him a SOCIOPATH. He said that was some sort of comfort to his dad there, and himself for a while. And then he says later it wasn't. He knew that word sociopath wasn't the whole of it.

I think the guy was Canadian.

Now, of course, I'd be the first to admit that a lot of Italian women give me a happy feeling under my folds. I'm not saying countries aren't something to learn about. But I remember starting to think back then how stupid it all was. I know we're a bunch of families who don't like the smell of some of the other families. I myself am afraid of bicycle couriers. If there was a country full of bicycle couriers I might want it to fly a flag and keep its distance.

But I remember thinking, in this day and age, haven't we noticed that everyone's naked under their clothes. I said that to Julius's dad, there. He said everyone's decent in Canada and I said everyone's naked under their clothes. I'm not sure he got me right away. I saw him in the rear-view mirror.

I had a laugh with little Julius about that. I told your dad that everyone's naked under their clothes I said.

I wondered what losing his girl would do to him. What a thing.

Couple of years ago he was seeing a girl who drew pictures. Animation. My girlfriend's gonna draw a picture of me, he said, and there at the end of the letter was a picture of my young friend there, sure enough. Bit of age or a scar or something on his chin but not so different from when I knew him. I told him she should come up and draw a picture of me because she obviously made people look better than they do. I can't remember exactly how I said it.

Anyways, they broke up.

I just shrug, I told him.

I think I can tell from his letters that he knows better than I do.

You can't see any of it coming.

This is me

I POLISHED MY shoes during Prep. I got up from my desk when I had finished and took a pair of Julius's shoes back to my chair.

'What are you doing?'

'I'm polishing your shoes.'

'Why are you polishing my shoes?'

'They needed it.'

'Did I ask you to polish my shoes?'

'Of course not.'

'Do you think I want my shoes to be as shiny and perfect as yours?'

'I was bored.'

'What makes a guy pick up another guy's shoes and polish them? Do you want a tip?'

'Drop it. I was bored.'

'Put my shoes back,' he said.

He stared at me and I couldn't stare back.

Did you go out with them?

Not really. Mostly I heard about their nights out from Julius.

What did he say?

It sounded like they had . . . I suppose it sounds priggish if I say some of their nights sounded sordid.

Sordid?

I don't know. Places I've never been. And it's not because they didn't invite me. You keep implying that I was left out or jealous or something of the sort. I truly wasn't. Frankly, it's a relief when your room-mate goes away for the weekend. I think what I've been trying to say is that Julius has a tremendous force of personality. It's very hard to resist whatever he wants to do. And I feel like Fall really had trouble resisting.

So you think they went places against her will.

Yes.

Did she ever talk to you about these things or places?

Like I've said. She was uncomfortable. We had a long talk at a café once. I don't think Julius knows about this. And she told me, essentially, that she felt a sense of oppression. I remember at the time that it conjured stories I had heard from Julius. Stories about keeping her in his father's limousine, drugs, etc. I feel like I'm telling on him, but I'm not. I know you think I might be some sort of square, jealous guy. I just know that sometimes theirs was a world I didn't know and when she talked to me there was some slight fear.

Fear eh.

Not fear of me.

No no.

'I know you've got problems with my sweaty clothes and stuff. But I've gotta say. After your constant fuckin workouts you smell like a pair of balls. A really wet and dirty pair of balls.'

'I'm sorry.'

'And your books over there. Your little house of books.'

'I'll have a shower.'

'Have a long one.'

Do you trust him?

I don't know.

You say he's your best friend.

Yes.

Do you think he would confide in you? If he did something wrong? Do you think you could get him to be honest?

I don't know.

I hadn't thought about trust in any abstract way. I either liked someone or I didn't, and trust was some sort of concomitant.

I am writing all of this down because I wish to be more than a lonely collection of other people's perceptions. Trust has something to do with that. It's a product of perception; it isn't something fixed or solid, it floats in the cloudland of assumption. When trust is removed, when there is some sort of betrayal, it feels like something permanent has been dislodged, but it is only the pain of a shift in perception. Suddenly the world is not as you assumed it to be, and trust is among the casualties of that shift.

Did I trust Julius? Did Julius trust me? We were no longer the people we had assumed each other to be. The pain of betrayal had nothing to do with an abstract concept of trust. It was the result of realising I might have been wrong. I might have assumed he had perceived me in a way he never had.

'You hang around. You're always around. I don't just mean in the room. You're always right fuckin there, whenever I turn around.'

I thought of all the times I'd stood behind him at the sink, all the silent assumptions I'd made. It hurt so much to think that I'd been wrong to put myself so near.

I sometimes thought that I could simply tie him down in the bed. Lean over him and tell him to rest while I filled his shoes for a while. Make him contemplate things as I had done while I stepped out to greet the world. Make him aware of me so he could be more aware of himself, or perhaps more aware of himself so he could be more aware of me – the outcome would be the same.

I see people when I walk at night. Whoever you are, in your living room, your middle age, the space you call your own. I'm the thing you didn't look at. I am everything you've chosen to ignore. The lump on your leg. The frown in the window behind you when you leave. Everything you can't believe you uttered. I'm the rime at the edges of your belief that the person you love will never be able to hurt you.

I asked Julius if he ever remembered the occasion one year earlier when we played soccer together in gym class and I passed him the ball to score the winning goal. He couldn't recall.

But in gym class that January we wrestled. And I felt so much larger than he was. The rest of the class gathered around the mat.

Most of them cheered for him because I was never great at the sport. I was known for 'fleeing the hold', because my instinct when attacked is not to commit. Julius had me on the mat, and I remember feeling a strange intimidation despite knowing that I was stronger. I was not in my body as I thought I might be. I gave him a good fight, certainly, and he struggled, but he was behind me, on top of me, and I went quite limp. This can be a good strategy, but somehow it wasn't an act of will. When he rolled me over for the pin I saw his face, his smile. He was winking at me, intentionally mocking my eye. The rest of the class was laughing.

As the questions gathered that January, I wondered who I was. I didn't know whether I was lying to Sergeant D'Arcy or not. Daily demands seemed to keep my eyes forward.

I know now that I was only comfortable when I was with Ant. So comfortable with him and so uncomfortable with Julius that we occasionally talked about switching rooms. He talked about trying to convince Chuck to move in with Julius. The school had a policy of not allowing room changes except in extraordinary circumstances. We were to learn to get along with our room-mates, to see our way through discomfort and disputes.

But circumstances were extraordinary. By now the change to the school was universal. Everyone was afraid. Everyone was quiet. Not once in my years at that school had it ever been so quiet – not even the week that forty boarders were quarantined with the flu. I think about my state of mind at the beginning of that year, my quiet first weekend alone, my dragging my fist along the walls of empty hallways. Anticipation, fear, solipsism and anger; the school as a whole had now become my earlier self. I had propagated, bloomed; it was me.

Every door was locked at six. Everyone was vigilant. No wrong could get in as long as cracks were sealed with lies.

'Let's liven this place up,' said Ant, and we did.

We broke into the linens room and there were later complaints of stains and smells on the week's clean sheets.

Every building is me. Its breath is mine. Swell my shoulders and the room is mine.

We stole bags of road salt from the utilities shed, snuck into the gym at night and spread the salt over the middle of the floor. We ran at it and skidded in our shoes, destroying the varnish and scarring the wood. 'I want to shred his fuckin legs,' I said. Ant thought I blamed Julius for the atmosphere of the school.

I didn't know what Sergeant D'Arcy was doing with the information I was giving him, aside from playing us against each other and trying to make me feel guilty. But information escaped the school.

As I've noted, it was unsettling to find the outside world intruding – all the police, Embassy officials, lawyers – but it was inconceivable nonetheless that even more would take notice. Inconceivable that there would be any publicity about what was happening. But on January 23 an article appeared on the front page of the newspaper, a story that then appeared nationally. I have the article at home in a drawer with old coins and some mints I love – an English brand, now defunct so I am loath to eat them.

The article seemed strangely amusing at first. It focused equally on Fall's disappearance and the link with the US Embassy. Girl missing from prestigious school, son of the US Ambassador, etc. What I found amusing was the portrayal of our school. Adjectives like 'leafy' and 'exclusive' and a list of famous alumni; the more these words accumulated the more I realised they were simply not describing our school. There was a photo of the main building from an angle I could not work out.

I read the article more hungrily than I had ever read anything. I felt, in a way, like people were taking notice of me, personally, even though I was not named (as Julius and others were). All the surface details producing an idea of the school rather than the school itself. I suppose there was nothing amusing about it.

I might have felt that I wasn't really there, except I read that the Ambassador's chauffeur had been fired for irregular use of the limousine. The article said no more about it, but I recalled my conversations with Sergeant D'Arcy. I imagined that my mentioning the chauffeur had caused the Sergeant to question Julius, and probably to involve his father. I expect I was right to imagine that, and at the time it made me feel powerful.

I twitched some nights, dreaming of boxing.

★   ★   ★

Once the outside world became involved to that extent, the school sealed its doors even tighter. We were instructed at assembly, for the good of our school, the good of the community, for the privacy of families involved, not to talk to anyone beyond the doors about these matters. Indeed, we were encouraged, among ourselves, to find other things to talk about.

All of this because a girl was gone. I knew she had meant so much.

Ant had decided he wanted to go to a male-only university. There were a few choices in the US and one small college within a university in Canada. He spoke about the purity of it. Girls poison friendships, he said.

With the school sealed tight and the air so manured with suspicion, it was inevitable that the Masters organised a room raid.

I had never witnessed an inspection so complete. During Prep one night, when they could be certain that everyone was in his room, they interrupted the quiet and called us all out. We were told to stand in the hallway and to wait. When we emerged from our room I was surprised to see more than one Master involved. Normally room inspections were silent, individual affairs conducted while we were in class. Things would be confiscated; occasionally there would be punishment, rarely severe. Once the inspection was under way I looked down the perpendicular hallway and saw the same going on there, where there were actually daytime teachers involved. I learned later that the Head Master himself was there.

It was a painstaking business that went on beyond Lights Out. One Master would search each room, filling individual garbage bags with forbidden or questionable objects and he would staple each bag and a piece of paper to it, marking the room number. There was cynicism and nervous laughter among all of us in the hall, a curious quiet when a student was called back into his room to answer questions with his door shut.

Julius and I didn't look at each other. I had vaguely expected something like this inspection for a while, so I had taken one of Julius's little bags of marijuana out of his hiding place and put it on top of his books (which I knew he never shifted).

A building of boys whose secrets would be exposed. Upstairs

Edward's gargantuan collection of pornography was reportedly marvelled at more than anything. The youngest boy on the Flats was discovered to own rubber sheets and have a bed-wetting problem which he had hitherto been able to conceal.

Ant's knives were found and he was gated. The police took the knives for tests.

In the room which Julius and I shared, two Masters went to work, spending more than half an hour making a mess of everything, saying 'whose is this, whose is this' to every drawer and surface. Somehow they didn't find Julius's marijuana. Among my possessions, at the back of my desk drawer, they found Fall's last letter to Julius, which I had never given to him. I had focused on incriminating him and had forgotten about that note. I don't even know why I had kept it, except perhaps as something to look at later when I wanted to understand people.

114C.
   141C.
   I think I'm gonna show you that hot dog again.
   Don't.
   I can't remember where the bedroom is.
   I'll just have a nap with my coat on she says.
   Un.
   Un un I ss

T HERE WAS LITTLE doubt that the room raid was organised by the police. None was present from where I could see, but it seemed a neat solution where everyone could be searched under the rubric of school policy. The investigation would benefit.

Even from this distance I continue to believe that Julius had known the raid would happen. Not even a cigarette of his was found.

I didn't sleep very well that night. Julius had decamped to his father's house. Somehow, despite our soured relations, despite my fear of what he must be thinking about having kept Fall's note, I missed his presence in the bunk above.

Sergeant D'Arcy questioned me the next morning. I was kept back from class.

That's quite a note they found in your desk.

Yes.

Pretty personal.

Yes.

So why did you have it?

I don't know.

You've had a night to think about how you would explain this, and that's the best you can do?

Yes. I really don't know. I can't remember what I was thinking.

You remember every hour in the day, Noel. Every book here on your Counsellor's desk. But you don't remember why you have that note?

I remember several reasons, I just don't know which one is pivotal.

Let's find out.

Have you spoken with Julius?

Why?

I don't know. I just wanted to know what he thought.

Whether he suspects something?

What's to suspect?

I guess he could think you were hiding other things. Is that what you're worried about?

I'm not hiding anything. I just wonder what he thinks about my having the note. Did you let him read it? I'm sorry I never let him read it.

You're sorry? Tell me why you had the note.

I was taking letters back and forth between Fall and Julius. I told you. And I guess it was starting to annoy me. I don't think I saw it clearly last term, but maybe I felt like they were just using me. Maybe it kind of annoyed me so I figured I would keep it, or throw it out or something.

And there were no more notes after that because Fall went missing.

I guess I thought about giving it to him. A few times. I wanted payment of some sort. Thanks, or something.

Recognition.

I don't know.

We have all the notes that Julius wrote to Fall. They were in her desk. Did you read those as well?

No. How could I get into her room?

You didn't read any other notes?

I only read that last one.

They're pretty simple notes. Meet me here, meet me there. Some goofy stuff. Not worth keeping. The one you kept of hers – that was interesting. I can see why you kept it. They were supposed to meet that night, remember? Fall says 'by the tree at 5'. But Julius says he never knew.

I don't know why I kept it.

This brought me back to when I was a kid, you know. I remember my cousin Naomi was looking after me when I was eleven or so. She wasn't a lot older. Eighteen. I kind of had a crush on her. And I overheard her talking to her boyfriend that afternoon on the phone. In a way I'd never heard her talk. Kind of sexy, right, Noel? Disappointing somehow. And I was angry. Is that how you felt?

I'm not eleven.

I can still remember everything my cousin said. There must be things in that letter you remember.

I suppose.

'I love you so much. I can't wait to remember things.'

I didn't read it closely.

But you were their little servant.

Yes.

And you decide to read it and it says all that really private stuff. One thing I remember about overhearing my cousin was that I was never mentioned. That bothered me. When you're a kid, you want to be in people's conversations. Especially when they're being all private like that. It was all about her boyfriend.

I'm not a kid, Sergeant D'Arcy.

No. You're right. Were you aroused?

Certainly not.

So why did you keep it, Noel?

I don't know.

Julius says you behave oddly sometimes. Look at him in strange ways while he gets dressed sometimes.

What's that supposed to mean?

Do you love him?

No.

It's nothing to be ashamed of. He's a handsome guy.

I'm not a homosexual.

He says you spent a maximum of two hours alone with Fall in her life. He says she barely knew you. You went to a café with her once.

Julius doesn't know everything.

He says Fall thought you were a creep. She said you made her really uncomfortable at the café.

No she didn't.

Is that why you guys have knives?

I don't.

Those knives we found of Antony's. You like making people feel uncomfortable.

I don't own a knife.

You know she's dead, don't you?

What?

You know.

No.

You know. This has been a murder investigation for a long time, Noel. She didn't run away, like you always say. She could barely walk. She didn't pack a bag. Didn't leave a note. Hasn't contacted a single person. Her sister in New York. We found her, and she hasn't heard a thing. There are some pretty sad people around all this, Noel. Why are you crying?

She's not dead.

You know that?

She'll come back.

From where?

She's not. She's here.

In your head? What's that supposed to mean?

. . .

Quit crying and tell me why you kept her last note to Julius.

How could I have done anything to her? I don't like you.

Tell me.

I cared about her.

Did you?

Yes.

She barely knew you. You didn't know each other.

We were friends.

She was pretty.

So pretty.

So you and Antony took her somewhere. Things got out of hand. We're testing his knives. You're full of frustration because this is a weird little place and you took her somewhere.

Someone else took her. I don't know. Why wasn't she kidnapped? You read it all . . . People take young people.

You got annoyed. You read the note. In your anger you told her you loved her.

I never told her that.

You didn't go far. Her mother said she had crutches.

No.

People say you're always in some pointless corner of the school. You know all the cracks, and you and Antony took her to one of them. I can't even find the front office in this place.

You're not funny.

Some perfect little hiding place. You were a little worked up. Maybe Ant wasn't with you. Did you get her to lean on you? Everyone was at dinner. You had to get something off your chest. You told her she was gorgeous. She didn't react well, you had a little tussle. All accidental.

I did not.

You hurt her.

Where?

We've been looking for her body. We'll find her body. We've been through all your clothes. Your teachers have been through everything you own while you go to class and play your games. We'll find something. You're really blubbering there, Noel. Do you want to tell me what happened? Where you put her pretty body? It can be a relief. Let the tears go. Let the truth out. You're a young healthy guy and you wanted to have sex with a beautiful girl. You realised she didn't want to. Because it's clear, isn't it? In that note. That girl really loved Julius. Maybe not your kind of love. You wanted to tell her and she didn't want to hear it. You hurt her. Tell me why you're crying.

Dishonesty is the death of everything; and the beginning of the world. Every house, street and story is a lie. If we were as honest as hyenas our cities would be smaller. That job you do. I wish I could slough this fat. I wish I could be honest. I wish I could bite the meat off everyone I hate.

I haven't been honest with myself.

It's a depressing realisation at the age of thirty. I feel like so much has calcified already.

The responsibility of being honest with oneself should, naturally, be borne by oneself alone, but I am happy to blame others. Despite everything I did in those days, my odd attempts to find my nature, I was trapped in these four walls which most of us are trapped in. The belief that effort will improve things, that we can be perfected, always stronger, always smarter, always better to each other. No matter how our standards vary, or what experience teaches us, it is what we are told to do.

I have tried my best to be alone. Even at the large institution I was sent to later, where everything was communal, where we were constantly made to behave kindly to each other, I endeavoured to stay alone. I have believed that as long as there are other people there will be expectations. As long as there are expectations there is a need for definition, a hope for perfection; and as long as there is that hope, no one will be honest.

What should I call what I am?

I have read stories about love and love gone wrong. I read about a man who had everything, who had found abiding and unconditional love. He was happy, but the wheels of want kept spinning. He found love elsewhere and learned that his abiding and unconditional love was neither. 'Try to understand,' he said, but she wouldn't. All he could say to explain himself was 'with blood like this . . .'

I think I understood. And I have thought the solution would be solitude. I could be true to myself if there was no one to expect things from me. I could cause no pain if no one was near me.

Perhaps I was responsible for her death. I put it in motion. All she could say was I don't like you.

I know that with blood like this I walked upstairs that day, away from D'Arcy's infuriating questions, to my room where Julius was waiting. And when I came in he arose and pinned me against the wall by the door. 'You ugly fuckin prick,' he said.

I saw his punch coming and chose not to flinch. He held me by the throat and I remember a clarity in his eye. 'You've been saying you know her. You've been saying you know me. They told me to be nice. You're telling fuckin stories.'

I felt all the fear and hatred that I had perversely been yearning for. So much easier than honesty.

And I wanted to tell him that I wished I had given him that letter. I wanted to tell him that there was so much we could have talked about. To say that I loved them both and I didn't understand it.

If we could get into our bunks right now. If he is still alive, spry enough to get up top. We could turn off the light and try again, old enough to know that perfect isn't possible.

He spat in my face and left the room.

The article I recently read about oil in the north said: 'The US and Canada, among several other countries, continue to compete for the rights to whatever is under the ice in the Arctic.'

Underwater land that was once so unlikely, a richness of oil unparalleled, of minerals unimaginable. It talks of men in a distant room listening to foreign submarines. Trying to determine from their noises where they are from and whether they belong.

The oil, the minerals, we know will never be the answer. We acknowledge that the cure we seek is the cause of our greatest illness.

I think about the submarines surveying that land. What does it mean to be honest with oneself? Perhaps it's a matter of taking each wrong path to the very end, not by accident but by choice. To discover error with elaborate ceremony and make our discoveries known. The captains of those submarines, donning trousers and caps, searching through water that doesn't belong to them for treasure that might not be theirs. They should declare at every moment that there is violence ahead. Drills, disappointment and the hot black melt.

We will look in all the wrong places. With blood like this, we have no choice. We'll move our lips in a language we can't resist and across some sea might be someone who understands our foolish and intimate ping. All other words are liars.

I walked outside with a swelling lip.

For what I did to Julius I was almost charged and made to face an adult court. Many things conspired in that cloistered world to keep me from that future. I was expelled from St Ebury, though not before the school set up a tribunal at the request of my father. He met with Julius's father and I managed to show contrition, and somehow with all the attention being paid to the school and Julius's family, it was decided that formal charges would not be brought, that a suitable punishment could be privately determined. I was sent to a quasi-reformatory school for just over a year, where I read an awful lot. In a way I can't believe my luck.

Sergeant D'Arcy's suspicion of me, heightened by what I did later that day, eventually came to nothing. Fall never returned. D'Arcy visited me often but I was never able to tell him what happened that night.

Julius left the school. His father took him back to the US and resigned his post as Ambassador.

I burned the skin off his chest and belly and genitals. At the tribunal his chin was bandaged as well.

He sat in a room with strangers and authorities, made declarations about who he thought I was, who everyone thought

I was. I knew they were talking about me, but I still don't know who I am. I was only eighteen.

Everyone wondered how I could have done such a thing to someone who lost his girlfriend. I had no explanation.

At the tribunal we were both afraid of each other.

I wonder sometimes whether his neck has thickened, eyes retreated. Whether we would enjoy a moment as strangers. He might forgive me for his scars. He might be able to tell me about children or coaching or a corner of the world I never could have imagined.

I think I'm still afraid.

I walked outside with a swelling lip and his spit on my face which I left as a lingering insult. The air, this school, these trees are mine as much as yours. The spit dried in the cold, and the conviction grew in my heels that anger was my right. I walked and let it rise.

When I went back inside I didn't know precisely what I would do. I wasn't even sure that I would find him right away.

In the hallway, I passed the bathroom and heard a shower running. When I opened the door to our room I saw Julius's clothes in a pile on the chair.

I filled the kettle, waited for it to boil, and poured the water quickly into the Bodum. I walked down the hall and into the bathroom and threw the boiling water at him just as he turned off the shower.

As I was walking nervously back from the bathroom his noises kept surprising me. The cries of a little boy who learns that the world won't be what it was.

I'M JERKING LIKE a bunny.
  Lurky jerky.
I've got bunny legs, leap leap.
I'm jumping with my soft little bunny cock, feel how soft it is.
Feel it.
It's so soft.
I've gotta catch the witch, he's bald and he's riding the butterfly.
They're dragging Fall on the rope and if I bounce, leap leap, I'll
save her. Twitch. Look how fuckin fast I am on my long lean
bunny legs, twitch twitch.
Feel my cock on the back of your hand.
So soft.
It is so soft.
They're flying. They're flying away. The air's hot and it stinks
because the witch and the butterfly farted.
Poor Fall.
I've gotta catch her.
Twitch.
I've gotta save her.
Faster.
Twitch twitch.
What the fuck.
Where the fuck am I.

William's.
I'm naked on William's bed.

Fall's in her little red coat.

Her scarf is on my cock.

I'm gonna wake her up.

I'm gonna figure out exactly who and where I am.

I am Julius.

This is my naked ass on William's bed.

My cock is very hard and pretty big, in fact, and I'm gonna show it to Fall.

It's weird being on your bed, William, and I'm sorry and I'm not gonna think about it.

Fall is fully dressed and very cute and I don't know why I'm naked.

Is she alive.

Her nose is really cute.

I've never seen it like that.

Hey.

Hey.

Wake up, little girl.

Wake up.

Your scarf is really soft.

Wake up.

Kiss cheek.

M she says.

Hey soft soft.

Ooo she says.

I know I say.

Why are you naked she says.

Why are you in your coat I say.

Put some clothes on it's rude.

Take some off.

Put some of mine on.

Your scarf is really soft.

I'm gonna have to wash that she says.

Her breath stinks but I'm kissing her.

Please take some clothes off. I feel like a, like a pervert, but I also feel like you've got, you know; you're not being fair.

Let me look at you she says.

I'm shy.

Let me see.

I'm shy.

Move your hand.

Take your coat off.

Let me look at you. I wish I had a camera she says. I want a picture for William.

Take your clothes off.

I need to pee she says. I feel pretty gross she says.

Take your coat off.

Ow she says. My ankle.

What.

Ow ow ow.

She's crawling on all fours to the bathroom.

It's funny.

It's worrying.

It's sexy.

I'll get some ice I say.

Men walk naked in their homes I'm thinking.

You don't need clothes if you have a home.

William's little kitchen.

Peas are better than ice I'm thinking. Coach said Put frozen peas on your ankle when you get home and I said I don't have a home or peas so he gave me an ice pack.

That's chilly on the balls.

Why am I naked.

Peas.

William.

I'm gonna ask him if he cooks for himself.

Maybe he reads books.

Maybe he plays with his car.

Are you OK I shout!

Yeah she shouts!

Do you feel sick!

Kind of!

I feel good I shout! I'm surprised!

I'm coming out!

I have peas for you!

I'm not hungry she says and she's on her hands and knees in bra and panties and she's like a movie about Hot, but she's crippled.

You're beautiful I say. Are you OK.

She's laughing.

You're naked she says.

I have peas for your ankle.

Let's get under the covers.

Mm.

Phoo.

Ooo.

Aah.

Mm.

Sss.

Pha.

Sh.

Ga.

Ga.

Gah.

Sss.

Listen to the noises I'm making her make.

Sh.

Ss.

Ga.

God.

God.

J.

Oh!

Listen to that.

Mgod she says.

Yeah.

Homgod she says.

Mm.

That was the most amazing . . . she says.

I'm proud. I might have to tell people about that one I'm thinking.

Julius.

Yeah.
I love you.

I'm resting frozen peas on her ankle.
    I'm hungry.
    That feels good she says.
    What are we gonna do for breakfast I say.
    You eat a lot she says.
    Your peas are making me hungry.
    You can't eat my peas.
    How does it feel.
    It . . . I don't know. It hurts. Does it look bad to you.
    It's pretty swollen.
    I wish we had a car she says.
    Do you want to get it looked at.
    I don't know. Should I.
    My dad would know I'm thinking.
    Maybe I say.
    Maybe the peas will work she says.
    Ice is good.
    Brr she says. Come back under the covers.

Carrots.
    There's a carrot in her fish.
    She smells like fish.
    Guh I say. We fell asleep again.
    Yeah. What time is it.
    I don't know.
    I dreamt she says.
    Me too.
    I dreamt we were on a beach.
    Nice I say. I think I dreamt about fish.
    It was so nice she says. It was so. Everything was gold and like a blanket. My ankle was in the water. You had freckles on your nose she says.
    It still hasn't hit me that we're at William's.
    I know.
    Are you shy.
    No.

Shy about what we just did in William's bed.

Don't. Now you've made me shy.

Let's do it again.

Now I'm thinking about William she says.

This is where he takes his ladies. His ladyfriends.

Oo. Hey, J, my dream made me think about beaches. I think we should go somewhere warm together. I think my mom's gonna surprise me with a ski trip at Christmas, but how about I tell her to take me and you somewhere warm.

Nice.

Hot.

Nice.

I'll get a bikini.

Hot.

What colour.

Skin.

Skin colour. You're a classy guy.

Fuckin A.

Where should we go. Where's warm.

Noel'll be going to Australia.

That's too far. I don't want to go somewhere where we know someone.

I can't go anywhere anyway. Unless my dad comes. And he won't.

Yeah. Mom's going to Cuba tomorrow anyway. Let's pretend she says. It's cold in here.

It's the peas.

Let's go to Barbados.

OK.

OK.

Now what.

I don't know.

Let me look at your ankle.

Fuck she's beautiful.

That was such a fun anniversary she says.

I'm touching her leg. It's gorgeous and a little fat at the top because that's what real people look like. I am wise. It was great I say.

I don't remember coming home she says. Up the stairs.

I remember. You said you were gonna have a nap in your coat.
And then I don't remember. I don't know why I was naked.

You must have been excited.

Lalalalalololalolalalalalalolll
   double u double u
   lolanglanglo
   My mouth's between her legs.
   langlang
   What should I do loolululu.
   This.
   Liplipliplip.
   This.
   Latlatlatlatlat.
   Ooo.
   Yeah.
   That.
   Latlatlat.

That was so nice I say.

I feel shy she says.

I love her.

I'm standing. I'm wearing my boxers. Fall bought them, they have
monkeys on them. I'm cold.

I wish I had the Animal.

You don't need the Animal she says. You have me.

She's holding me from behind and I'm chilly and warm and
I'm loved, fuckin: mmm!

I want to live here I say.

Me too she says.

I want to get this fuckin year over, get out of school, get my
own place.

Maybe we'll live together.

Yeah.

I hope so she says.

Sad spills hot water on the heart.

I'd love to live with you she says.

Let's live here.

OK.

William lives in the car anyway.

We're skinny in our underwear.

Don't be sad.

No she says.

Don't be sad.

No.

She's wearing William's brown robe it's hilarious.

I'm wearing his pyjama bottoms and there's room for another Julius and a Fall and a village and an elephant. I need a belt I say.

There's eggs she says. I can make an omelette.

Can you.

You bet.

What else can you make.

Here.

Anywhere.

Lots of things.

Can you.

Sure.

Make me a steak.

There's no meat.

Make me a hamburger.

There's no meat.

What is there.

Not much. I think maybe William doesn't eat much.

He eats beer.

There's beer.

He said don't eat the beer. He warned me. I need a belt. I'm gonna get one.

It smells like suits in here I'm thinking. It smells like wisdom and whiskers and I really love my dad.

I need a belt.

What's in those boxes. Secrets I'm thinking.

There's a belt.

Wait. His belt's gonna be too big. I'll wear my belt. I'll take a box and go through William's personal secrets and problems and I'll get my belt.

My pyjamas fell.

What's that.

It's a box of pictures I say.

William's.

I found them in his closet.

You can't go through those.

Sure I can.

I feel bad about eating his food she says. I found a tomato and an onion but he has eggs, tomato, an onion and some beer. That's it. And something I can't tell, maybe beef jerky or salami.

I think that's a penis. I had a dog with a penis just like that.

So we shouldn't eat it.

Please make me an omelette. Please. Not with the dog's penis, but the other stuff. I'm so fuckin hungry. We'll replace his stuff. We'll shop, or I'll leave some money. I was gonna leave money.

You can't leave money. And you can't go through his pictures.

Why not.

They're private.

William would go through my stuff. If he stayed at my place.

No he wouldn't.

He would. He'd go through your stuff. He'd have your panties on his head.

Don't say that.

We'll have an omelette first.

OK.

Can I watch.

Sure.

I'm standing back.

We could live here I'm thinking.

She's cracking an egg like she knows what she's doing.

You look like my grandmother in that robe.

Thanks she says.

You're cute.

I'm warm. You look like you're in a circus.

Thanks.

You look like a Russian dancer she says. That's what it is.
She hoplimps to the stove.
Can I watch.
Sure.

A girl's never made me an omelette before.
I've never made one for a boy she says.
Smells so good.

Box of photos on the floor.
She's in her robe and we'll sit on the floor and go through
old times with William.
I want to eat on the floor I say.
There's no table she says.
Exactly.
We've got to wash everything and leave it exactly like it was
she says. And we've got to buy a new tomato and onion. And
eggs.
OK. That looks exactly like an omelette.
That's what it is.
That's so cool. You made a real omelette.
I hope it's good.
It looks so fuckin great.
Get some knives and forks and carry me she says.

Fall made me an omelette.

Look at Willliam with the neat hair. Look look look. Rolled-up
jeans.
So cute she says.
How old do you think he is.
I don't know.
There's a letter.
Don't read it.
Why not.
I'll be really mad if you read that letter.
It looks really old. Maybe it's a love letter.
Put it away. Let me see some pictures.
Look at him with his buddies here.

Cute.

How come people get so fat.

These are such great pictures she says.

Everything's kind of yellow and pale and there's some in black
and white and I don't know what colour things were before my
eyes were born.

Your omelette was delicious I say and I'm kind of lying but
only because omelettes are boring, I've learned.

I'd love a blow job.

That Korean food was so good last night she says. So fun.

That reminds me.

What.

Nothing.

What.

I wanna make a phone call.

To who.

It's a secret.

I don't feel so great she says.

Your ankle.

Maybe.

Korean food.

I think it's a hangover.

You were drunk.

You were drunk.

I was fucked.

I was fucked.

Hm.

Ha.

We're looking at each other.

She's on the couch.

She's reading a book.

She's chewing her nails.

We live here.

514–849–5929

Hi. This is a message for Sean McAdams. You're bald and you
look like a fag and my girlfriend's way too young for you.

★　　★　　★

Can you carry me to the shower she says.

You bet.

She's heavy in her robe.

You're heavy in your robe.

So take it off.

Godgod.

I can't stop smiling.

She can't stop smiling.

Hee I say.

She turns to the water and fills her mouth and spits it warm at my face.

Hee.

I'm gonna do that when she doesn't expect it.

Aah she says. This is, like, the best shower I've ever had.

I really love my girlfriend. She's standing on one leg.

She fits.

She's tall but she fits.

Her ass against my hips.

Clean clothes and hair on my nose all fresh from the shower and nobody owns us or knows. I'm holding my Fall and that's what I'm thinking.

J she says.

Yeah.

Scratch my back.

We're on our backs on William's bed and our eyes are closed and we're not asleep, maybe both of us thinking what's next.

It's dark blue in my head. And there's a Nascar car and a nice guy with sideburns and a room down there with a brown couch and chair and a Sunday light. And we'll have to go out to the grey and the cold.

We had a shower together.

We did things nobody's done, maybe.

It's really hurting she says.

Maybe you should go to the hospital.

Do you think.

We could take a cab.

I've gotta see my mom later anyway. Maybe she could take me.

Do you wanna call her.

Maybe.

I'll get the phone.

I'm worried about her but I've sprained my ankle before. It's no big deal.

I can clean everything up I say.

Really.

Totally.

You'll do it right.

Yeah.

You have to be respectful, Julius.

I am.

I want to help.

Just relax until your mom gets here. I'll clean after you leave.

You'll buy the food.

Yep. Onion, eggs, tomato.

You promise.

I promise.

What are you gonna tell your mom.

I've told her William's a friend from school.

OK. And what about the fact that he lives in a shithole.

She won't come up. We'll meet her outside and I'll tell her William's parents own the building.

OK. You make it up and tell me later.

OK she says. I wish we could stay she says.

Me too.

Promise to clean up properly.

I'll go straight to the store when I get you in the car.

Promise.

Promise.

Come here she says. The day's not over. I've got plans she says.

There's a smile in her eyes and a joke I don't get and I love her.

★　★　★

Away in her gold car, and it's not so cold.

I like the grey.

I don't know how to choose an onion and I don't know how to choose a tomato and I don't know where the store is.

I feel tall. Or lighter.

Nobody in this store had a night or morning as fun or dirty as I did.

Did they.

Everyone's quiet.

Everyone's plucking oranges and meat for houses full of bellies.

Can anyone see what Fall and I did this morning. Can anyone smell how much I've lived.

Excuse me, what's the difference between the big onions and the small ones.

Size.

I see.

I'll get William a big one.

I'm picking an onion for William.

I am in this store.

I am on my own.

Fall's far away.

School's far away.

Dad's far away.

William's on a highway.

I'm on my own.

I love it.

I'm gonna look this old guy in the eye.

Hi.

Hello.

How nice was that. A light went on in him, flick.

I'll buy a big tomato.

William lives in his car because he has too many stairs.

His neighbour's playing the piano.

I'm gonna open this door and Fall's not gonna be there.

So here it is.

It smells like an onion and William and things I know and don't.

I can hear the neighbour's piano.

So here I am.

I'm feeling something.

I've got some cleaning to do.

Maybe people wash the sheets.

He didn't tell me to. She didn't tell me to.

There's one of her hairs.

She was here and we were naked.

I feel sore in my chest and so much closer now she's far away.

I don't remember that plant.

William's coins and his tie clip.

Those are my feet getting hugged by the rug.

I don't think we made that stain.

I'm touching the counter and looking at this room.

Something happened here.

I can't hear the neighbour.

This is me alone.

I will never eat a breakfast that I have to clean up.

I will never wash another frying pan.

I will eat glue before I eat another egg.

I will never touch steel wool.

I'm not gonna smoke so much.

It's cleaner than it was.

I'm gonna leave the eggs and the onion and tomato on the counter to show him I bought them and I'm generous. That's a huge fuckin onion.

I should write him a note.

Something happened here.

William, I can't tell you.

William, I can't tell anyone.

The flower in my throat.

It's mine.

I'll go like a ghost.

I'll go like a ghost leaving eggs, onion, tomato.

I'll go back to school and I won't need to tell anyone about any of it.

Fall is with her mom.

She'll tell me what she wants.

My feet are on this rug.

Coat.

Bag.

Smokes.

I'm gonna catch the bus.

I'm gonna see it at the end of that street.

I'll run beside the cars.

I'll run beside myself and say Go faster, I'll race you, I'll win.

I'm running.

Acknowledgements

Thank you Alex Bowler, Robin Robertson and others at Cape.

www.vintage-books.co.uk